Luke —

I can't believe we're finally graduating. We've known eachother for so long — it'll be weird not seeing you next year. I'll definitely miss your jokes and sarcasm, but I know you'll do great no matter where you end up.

Ashlyn Myers

Burnout Stars

Ashlyn Myers

BURNOUT STARS

ISBN: 978-0-9831825-0-4

Printed in the United States of America
Cover design by Anna Iovine and Stéfany Péloquin
Cover photography by Noora Aljabi

First Printing

I dedicate this book to my parents, Jessica, and Walt Disney.*

* Note correct serial comma usage, Mr. Z.

BURNOUT STARS

He met her in a bar on the shady side of town on a rainy Tuesday evening. The second she had entered the smoke-filled establishment, time seemed to slow down. He had watched in astonishment as she took careful, measured steps toward the bar, the sound of the heels of her boots against the creaking wood echoing in his ears. The balls on the pool table began to roll slower across the smooth surface. Smoke that escaped from a middle-aged man's parted lips hung in the air for an extra second before rising to the ceiling to join its counterparts.

She had an aura like a black hole, seeming to suck the universe towards her. She pulled everyone and everything in until there was nothing left but herself, shining faintly in the dim room.

Once she sat down on the stool beside him, the world started spinning again. The mixed sounds of laughter and arguments grew louder until they were at their original pitch, and he could suddenly feel his heart beating steadily again, not lurching and hanging for seconds at a time like it had been. He released a sigh of relief and watched the drops of condensation slide down the sides of his beer.

After he worked up the courage, he glimpsed at her out of the corner of his eye. Her hair was wet and matted, falling over her face in a vain attempt to make her less noticeable.

He was struck with a sudden sense of familiarity while observing her appearance. The slumped posture, the quiet demeanor, the blinking sign that read, "Don't notice me! Look away!"—he recognized the look from his own reflection in the mirror.

So he obeyed the sign's words. For awhile, that was.

He couldn't put his finger on it, but there was something else familiar about her: something reminiscent of

5

home and a peculiar connection to someone that was on his mind. He caught himself staring at the way her hair cascaded down her back, and quickly looked away. He reminded himself that staring was rude.

His mind wandered into the fantasy world inside his head, where everything was perfect and how it should have been.

They're eating Thai food on the couch. He's pretending to pay attention to the movie—*Breakfast at Tiffany's*, obviously her choice—but is really using it as an excuse to sit close enough to her to smell her perfume. She always smelled like a combination of lilies, cotton candy, and dryer sheets. It completely baffled him. He would spend hours marveling at her scent. During one of their escapades to escape the community Easter egg hunt, she had left one of her sweaters in his car. It was pink and soft, and she scolded him every time he called it a sweater, always correcting him with "cardigan, Jess, cardigan." Later that night, he noticed the forgotten article of clothing when the ghost of her scent followed him home. He had returned it to her the next day, purposely leaving it overnight in his closet in a failed attempt to bring some of her smell with him in whatever outfit he wore.

He remembered tentatively approaching the circle of people surrounding her in the school hallways, staring at her smooth legs revealed by the floral skirt she had on that day, noticing where her fiery red hair hit her shoulders. She had thanked him, calling him "Jessie" even though she knew he hated it. She would always say the nickname in a teasing way, and he always expected her to ruffle his hair afterwards. She didn't though, thankfully.

He drifted out of his memories and back into his perfect dream world. He's cracking jokes at the movie, and she giggles softly. Her eyelids have been threatening to fall closed for three scenes now. When her head finally lands on his shoulder, he thanks God repeatedly in his head as he takes in the peaceful look on her sleeping face.

The dream world shattered the moment he opened his eyes. He casually glanced over at the girl to his left. He took note of the dark blue jacket she was wearing, noticing that she was shaking, just slightly. It wasn't enough to be seen from across the room, but it was noticeable under some scrutiny.

He wondered if he ever shook involuntarily these days.

His mouth opened once, twice, three times, but no sound escaped. He shook his head, trying to ignore the buzzing headache he has had for days. Beneath the surface of denial he had built up in his head, he knew that it was caused by his frequent trips to the bar. Inside his perfect dream world, the headache was caused by the thoughts that dwelled a second too long on hints of her.

Finally, he asked the girl if he could buy her a drink.

She turned her head, ever so slightly, toward him until he could see brown eyes, reflecting the same hollow look as his. He wondered if she felt like she was holding onto the cracks in her fragile shell, wondering how much longer she could hold on before she shattered to pieces.

The girl smiled, bringing life into her face, and said, "No, thank you."

Another ten to thirty minutes passed while he thought about what could have been.

He thought of a New Years Eve in the infinitely distant future in this very bar. Snow is covering the ground outside, but the inside of the building is warm and toasty. She makes a stunning entrance into the room wearing a velvet, blue jacket. The second she steps foot in the bar, time slows down around the party goers. The sound of the heels of her shoes echo in his ears as—

He shook his head a few times. Once he was back in reality, he found himself staring at the girl's blue jacket. He turned his head away trying not to be so obvious.

"What is it then?" she asked, her voice shaking him out of his thoughts like an earthquake. She must have read the confused expression on his face, because she added, "your name."

"Jess," he said. The second it escaped his lips he wished he had said another name. Maybe being someone else was what he needed for awhile.

She wasn't looking at him when she replied, "Jo."

He stared at the back of her head, hair brown like mud, for a few seconds.

Finally, he mumbled, "That's an interesting name."

A flash of emotion lit up her dark eyes, and she turned to look at him, hands balled into fists on her lap.

"And what," she asked slowly, as if she was trying to make every word count, "is so 'interesting' about it?"

He shrugged, taking a drink of his beer, and then said, "It's not really a name you'd associate with a girl."

She smirked and turned away from him again.

"As if your name is one you'd associate with a boy."

He tilted his head, as if seeing her from a different angle would help him understand this.

"I do," he said. The confusion in his tone was painfully obvious.

She made a sound of disapproval, halfway between a sigh and a groan. Standing up from her stool, she leaned into the bar next him, chin resting on her hands, completely shattering whatever small amount of a personal bubble he had left.

"Let me guess. When you hear the name 'Jo,' you think of footballs and beer and making out with cheerleaders behind school buildings." There was a sly smile on her face, the smile of a person who knew how to get what she wanted.

"Maybe not to that degree, but sure. The gist of that," he said.

"Well, when I hear the name Jess, I think of little girls playing with little dolls wearing little dresses for little tea parties. Oh, and they're using itty-bitty little teacups," she said, showing the size by squeezing her fingers together.

The only sound that he emitted was a small "oh."

She grinned and sat back down.

She was definitely a girl who knew how to get what she wanted.

"What's supposed to be a good girl name then?" she asked, the knowing smile still on her face.

"I don't know," he said. This whole situation felt awkward to him now. "Katie, Emily, Lisa…. Amelia."

The last name stung. It stung worse than a shot or a bee. It burned like fire and tore through his heart like a bullet.

She made the same strange sound of disapproval again and said, "No, no, no. You apparently learned nothing from that entire long winded spiel. You're supposed to say, 'Why, Jo of course. Jo is a fabulous name for someone of the female species.'"

He laughed. He actually *laughed*. It felt so nice. It must have been the first time in weeks—months? He felt bubbly, like he had just drank a soda too fast. He felt happy and energized, like he did as a kid when he ate a chocolate bar on a hot Sunday afternoon.

"Besides," she said, "those names are *too* girly. Those really do bring to mind images of girls with tea sets. Jo is a nice name for a girl. It's strong but still feminine."

Even though she acted like she had come up with that conclusion off the top of her head, Jess assumed it was the product of many afternoons spent thinking, probably going through baby naming books. He supposed he wasn't one to talk.

"You're kind of quiet," she said softly. "I'm sort of uncomfortable with uncomfortable silences, so sorry if I talk too much."

"You're fine," he replied. She was more than fine. He was thrilled for a chance to escape the constant circle of guilt, despair, and sorrow that his mind had him running in before now. She smiled. Not at him directly—she kept staring straight ahead as if the wall was the most amazing thing in the world—but he felt like it was because of him. It made him feel surprisingly good about himself. Despite everything, he could make another person smile when he felt like crying.

"Please let me buy you a drink," he said. He sounded more pathetic than he predicted he would. She laughed, a strange and musical sound that seemed foreign to his ears, and gave him a pat on the back.

"Stop begging, boy. It makes you seem pathetic." She continued, "You can buy me a drink if you'll wipe that sorry look off your face."

"Consider it gone!" He said, a hint of a smile tugging at the corners of his lips. God, it felt nice to have that strange sensation again.

They spent the next few hours talking and drinking. He smiled, and she smiled. She laughed, and he laughed. He laughed and continued to laugh. Eventually, he cried, but it was laughter induced. He hadn't felt this good around someone in a long time. She told him stories about crazy people that she had met on her way to the city—apparently she lived a nomadic way of life, constantly moving because she couldn't stand to be tied down. She lived out of her car trunk, resided in motels, and was a connoisseur of diners. Her entire life could be thrown into one beaten up duffel bag. She admitted to him that her CD collection needed a box though, so it permanently rested in the passenger seat.

He stared at the empty glass in front of him, focusing on breathing as his thoughts raced past him. He felt a desperate need to be someone else, a raging desire to run and run and run as fast as he could until his legs gave out, and an insatiable thirst for a thrill. He met her eyes with a kind of passion and fire that he thought had burnt out long ago.

"How permanent is it?"

The knowing smile made its way onto her face again as she replied, "Not very."

He nodded and said, "Take me with you."

And just like that, the life that he knew and the person he was escaped into the humid July air.

Jess

It wasn't until they were four hours out of town that he realized he should have thought this through.

He had rushed home immediately from the bar and thrown everything he could fit into an unused suitcase he had bought years ago, his head still buzzing. He had been feeling pretty good about himself and his new found spontaneity. Jo, however, had looked at the black patent suitcase like it was pink with polka dots.

"You're bringing...*that*," she said, the disgust prominent in her voice.

He looked at it with a confused expression and said, "Well, yeah..."

She had made a humming sound and floated around front to the driver's seat. Jess climbed into the passenger seat, which was worn with age. Her car smelled like the ocean, all salt and sunshine. A lot like her.

When she turned the key in the ignition, the car made a sort of sputtering noise. She groaned, smacking the dash. After a bit of physical abuse, the car made a rumbling sound. A look of simple satisfaction passed over her face, and they were off into the dark night. The windows were rolled down—they didn't go up; she had told him when he tried to roll them up an hour later—letting the cool night air in. The sound of crickets outside and the rumble of the tires against the unpaved roads were enough to entertain him. She, however, was not satisfied with the simple sounds of the night.

She was constantly moving, even when she was driving. She would shift in her seat to get a better look at the right side of the road, as if she was making sure that she wasn't running off of it. Her mirrors would be adjusted every few minutes, and then quickly returned to their original positions. Her thumbs tapped a steady rhythm on the steering wheel. Every now and again she would start to hum a strange song that he had never heard before.

After ten minutes of "silence," she let out a groan. Reaching into the back seat, she grabbed a large box practically over flowing with CDs and passed it to him.

"Pick whatever. I can't stand this quiet."

He flipped through the different cases, trying to get a sense of her taste in music. After seeing two Dido albums, three Rolling Stones CDs, the Evita recording, and Benny Benassi's *Hypnotica,* he gave up. He was beginning to learn that there was no method to her madness.

He finally pulled out a Kansas album—thinking it was the safest bet—and put it in. The second the first song started all of her quirks faded away. Jo stopped squirming in her seat. Her thumbs no longer carried on their steady beat on the steering wheel. She finally relaxed into the sound.

It had been the strangest thing that he had ever witnessed.

"Hey," he said, after about thirty minutes, "Can you drive?"

She gave him the same look she had when she saw his suitcase.

"Watch as the car miraculously moves down the road," she snapped. Her brown eyes rolled up to the roof and then returned back to the deserted road.

"No, I mean... We drank. A lot."

She laughed. He noticed how her eyes sparkled; even in the darkness he could see the light from the moon hitting them.

"Oh, honey, I'm used to it."

The car didn't appear to be moving too far from where it needed to be, so he tried to relax. Every now and then she would hum along to one of the songs, but she never made any other sounds. No attempts at conversation.

It had been four hours when reality began to sink in. Suddenly, he realized he was sitting in a car of a girl he met a few short hours ago in a bar, heading for God knew where. He had left everything he knew behind. His stomach turned and knotted. Jo must have sensed the sudden tenseness in the car because she shot him a few quick glances.

Finally, she said, "You alright over there?"

He could feel his breathing becoming shallow, but he managed to say, "Yeah, fine. Just tired."

She made that weird sound of disapproval again; it completely puzzled him. *She* puzzled him. He couldn't understand what it was about this girl that possessed him to climb into a car with her and ride a hundred miles out of the city limits. He must have lost his mind.

"If you want breakfast," she said, "we could stop at a diner or something. It's almost six; almost all of them would be open."

He liked the sound of going to a diner, where there would be plenty of people around. People had cars; people had cell phones. He could probably phone a taxi and get his butt back to town in no time.

"Sure," he said. "Sounds good."

She pulled off of the road. The diner—if he could really call it that—looked deserted. He had never seen anything so pathetic in his entire life, except for maybe his own reflection in the mirror. Except for two lonely, beaten up cars in the parking lot, he could have sworn the place had been abandoned years ago. Jo didn't seem fazed by the appearance of the place. She was out of the car and opening the trunk before he could even unfasten his seatbelt. When he finally made it around to the back of the car, she already had money in her hand and was marching towards the door.

"Geeze," he mumbled, breaking into a jog to keep up with her. He reached her side when she was pulling open the door.

"You don't waste any time, do you?"

She turned her head to look at him, and even though the fake smile was plastered on her face, there was a look in her eyes that he thought felt far too familiar. It was cold and numb, the look of someone who had been through enough pain to be completely immune to it, of someone who had built enough walls around herself to keep the entire world out. A brief flash of a smiling face graced his mind with its presence, but quickly faded. He wondered what Jo's first blow had been.

"I move fast. I jump before I have time to think. If you don't like it, then leave," she spat.   She turned on her heel and headed into the diner. He blinked a few times, a bit taken aback. Shaking his head to clear the haze of confusion, he followed her. She was already seated at the bar, the back of her dark blue jacket facing him. He took a seat next to her, but she seemed to shift so she couldn't see his face.

For a fleeting second, he wondered if she had read his thoughts. He immediately dismissed the idea, realizing that it was ridiculous. As he stared at the plastic covered menu in front of him, he wondered if she was used to people leaving her. Maybe she could recognize the signs that people exhibited.

The more he watched her small frame, the back of her head, the side of her face he decided that it was just that. She was used to people leaving her. She expected it. She had known from the beginning that it was only a matter of time before he jumped ship.

In fact, she was probably so used to seeing people leave that she had realized he was thinking of it.

Biting his lip, he made his second rash decision in hours. He was not going to leave. No matter how stupid he had been getting himself into this situation, he decided that leaving wouldn't make it any better. He took another look at her face. She was trying to hide behind her knotted hair, but he could still see her eyes, eyeliner heavy and smudged, downcast. He tried to imagine the last person who had left her. He could practically hear the thoughts that would have been going through her mind when the person said he would come with her, a sudden small hope burning inside. He could imagine the devastation she must have felt when that person had left her. It was a never ending cycle for her—hope, devastation, hope, devastation. He couldn't believe she could manage to keep going on like that from day to day.

He would break the cycle. It was the right thing to do.

Looking at the quality of the food going past him to a table in the back, he wondered if he would survive this.

She ordered waffles, but he picked sausage. The second the word left his mouth she gave him another one of those looks that made him feel like he was completely insane.

"What?" he asked. "I like sausage!"

"Are you stupid?" she asked, one eyebrow raising as her voice went up. She leaned in close to him and mumbled, "Never order meat in shifty diners. You don't know where it comes from. You always pick safe foods. Your 'sausage' is probably a dead opossum they scraped off the road an hour ago."

A few seconds passed before he asked, "You're joking, right?"

"Do I look like I'm kidding?"

One look at her face proved that he probably was the crazy one.

He sighed, massaging his temples. "I hope I pick up some of this over time. Otherwise I don't think I'll survive."

She straightened up on her stool beside him, and he warily glanced at her face. There was a flicker of something behind those hollow eyes. He smiled to himself. Yeah, he had made the right decision.

"You can only hope that some of my brilliance will rub off on you," she said with a smirk. Jess realized that she was trying to keep up her act, but he could tell a change in her demeanor. There was now a glow beneath her pale skin.

When their food arrived, he realized right away he was an idiot. She watched him carefully with a grin on her face.

"So," she said, resting her face in her hands, "dig in."

He looked at the food with disgust. "Do I have to?"

He poked at the meat with his fork. It acted like rubber, and it was gray. He grimaced. Jo laughed at his pathetic state.

"Fine! Stop making that face; I can't take it," she said. "If you admit that I was right, I'll give you half of my waffles."

"Really?" he asked. He realized he must have acted a bit too excited when she started laughing again. Seeing her face scrunched together in a fit of giggles, he started to laugh too. Between chuckles, he choked out, "You were one hundred percent right. In fact, I think you might possibly know the most about crappy diners out of everyone in the entire world."

He waited a few seconds, letting the last part sink in, and then said, "Do I get a reward now?"

She grinned, and he noticed how real her smile looked. She stabbed one of her waffles, moving it onto his plate.

They spent the rest of breakfast cracking jokes about opossum hot dogs. She paid for both of them even though he had money in the car.

"It's nothing," she said with a shrug.

Whether it was his ego or maybe something more, he had a sneaking suspicion that it was thanks for staying, even if she thought it was only for now.

* * *

Jess learned early on that Jo only stopped twice a day: once for breakfast, and once for dinner. When he had brought up lunch around 2 PM, she had laughed at him.

"Don't you get it?" she had asked him. "The more you stop the less distance you cover."

"Where are we going?"

The roads she traveled were always empty, long, and seemingly untouched. Despite her desire to go farther and faster with each passing minute, she would take the long way around things just to avoid other cars. She would always choose a back road over a highway, a mess of gravel over a paved street. It confused him, and he was bothered that he couldn't figure her out.

"Everywhere," she replied, and when he looked at her face, he noticed the glow was back, the same one from the diner. "Everywhere and anywhere."

She flashed him a grin. As he looked out over the horizon, he tried to push the worries about gas and maps and home and lunch and *her* out of his mind. He tried to focus on the calming feeling of the car moving along the road and the sound of Jo next to him humming along to the music.

"You'll see," she said. "It takes a few days for it to sink in, the thrill of it. Then you'll get it. Everything makes sense."

He nodded in response, hoping she was right.

* * *

When night fell, Jo artfully located a motel. It was next to a diner and down the street from a club. Jess couldn't help but wonder if she knew where she was going after all by how easily she found the area.

"Food first or room?" She asked, turning the car off and unbuckling her seatbelt.

"Food, please. I've been wasting away in this seat for hours."

He couldn't help but stare as she climbed on to her seat. When she was bent over the seat digging for something in the back, he noticed how short her skirt was. He immediately averted his eyes once he realized he was gawking, but they ended up traveling back to her figure. His mind was assessing the sight, taking note of the differences and similarities between the last girl he had stared at like this.

The sound of Jo's laugh finally broke the spell, unabashedly loud and still strangely musical. She sat back on her heels as she rummaged through a wallet covered in duct tape.

She pulled out some money, threw the wallet back over the seat without much concern for where it landed, and said, "Like I told you, you'll adjust. Just eat a big breakfast."

"You don't have to pay for everything," he said. "I brought money."

She rolled her eyes as she said, "And it took you how long to tell me this? Chivalry really is dead."

She opened the car door and slid out, heading in the direction of Flo's, the diner down the street.

"You know," he said, once he caught up with her. "Every time I hear the name Flo I picture a morbidly obese person that you can't identify as a woman or a man, with a mole, hairy legs, and woman's clothing."

"Well, that's pretty much the typical diner crowd."

He made a face, and she laughed again.

He liked seeing her laugh. Her whole face would change. Her eyes weren't suddenly so overpowered by her heavy eyeliner: they stood out on their own as they caught the light. The glow would return to her face. A true, genuine smile would appear. It was wide and full, and almost didn't seem to match with her thin lips. If he looked at just one of her features at a time, she didn't seem that special. When he took in her entire face though as a whole, he was almost overwhelmed by her unique beauty. Even her messy hair and smudged eyeliner didn't detract from it; surprisingly, he felt like it added something. Whether it was character or mystery, he liked it.

The inside of the diner looked the same as the exterior: trashy. The counters didn't look clean. Cobwebs adorned every corner. A flashing obnoxious sign reminded the customers of the discounts on certain foods—Jo whispered to avoid them; they were probably weeks old. Cheap Christmas lights hung on the walls, and the booths were made of a green and brown plaid fabric. He wondered if they were originally another color, but he didn't really want to think about it. The dim lighting in the building left the faces of the diners dark and intimidating. There was a broken jukebox in the corner that covered a black and white poster of Marilyn Monroe. A torn, yellowed advertisement hung above it, informing the crowd of "the amazing crocodile man."

He suddenly wondered what he was doing here.

Jo gave his arm a tug when he appeared to be frozen to the floor, and steered them to a booth in the corner. Once they were seated, she passed him one of the menus, covered in fingerprints.

"I—" he started, but she held up her hand.

"Don't think about it. Don't look too hard. Don't try to take in anything. Just walk inside, sit down, order, eat, and then leave as quickly as possible. Otherwise you *will* be throwing up within the next two hours."

He sighed, opening his menu.

"This—"

"I know," she said, cutting him off again. "But trust me, you will get used to it. Before long a Denny's will feel like five star French cuisine, and this will feel like the place you took your girlfriend on the night of prom."

A strange gnawing feeling was in his stomach, chewing away at him from the inside out. He tried not to listen to her and focus more on her eyes, brown and dark, full of promises and secrets.

* * *

Motels weren't his thing. The second he stepped into the "lobby," he was greeted by a large, bearded man in a baseball cap chewing tobacco. His feet, covered by muddy boots, were propped up on the flimsy table where a very small television rested. The man's appearance matched the outside of the building, which made Jess wonder if the motel was even still in business.

It was beginning to seem like Jo wasn't fazed by anything. She strode into the building with astounding grace.

Pressing her palms flat against the folding table, she asked for a room.

The man hardly looked up from his television screen as he grumbled, "It's thirty bucks a night."

She threw Jess a sly look over her shoulder, one eyebrow raised. When he didn't move, she groaned. Her head fell forward in mock defeat.

"Do I have to do *everything?*" she whined loudly as he shifted nervously behind her. "Really, I drove, and I navigated. Without me, you would have spent the entire day hauled up in the bathroom because you were stupid enough to order meat. You are completely hopeless."

"Oh," he said, thrusting a hand into his pocket and pulling out three crumpled bills. "You want me to pay?"

She slapped her forehead with the palm of her hand.

"You are so dense!" she moaned. "There's no way I'm going to survive past a week with you around. I'll claw your eyes out in your sleep."

He grimaced, pushing the money over the table to the man, who had been watching them curiously. The man handed him a key in return, but Jo quickly snatched it from his hand. When he had stood there, admittedly a bit confused, she shoved him backwards with one hand. With the roll of her eyes, she headed outside to their room. Jess sighed, looking around the office nervously. Finally, he started off in the direction she had went.

He heard a gruff laugh behind him as he was leaving, followed by a low voice saying, "She's got you whipped, son."

Ignoring the man, he wandered outside. He caught sight of her messy brown hair five doors down with her beaten up duffel bag slung over her shoulder. When he jogged over to her, he was half expecting to get an icy glare. Instead, she smiled down at the doorknob, avoiding his eyes, and continued to fidget with the key in the lock.

"Do you want me to…?" his voice trailed off as he motioned towards the stuck key.

"I'm a big girl," she said sarcastically. He was beginning to find himself staring at the pout of her lips as she spoke.

With a hard push against the wood with her hips, the door swung open. The room was dark, and it smelled like a combination of mothballs and rotten food. He couldn't quite make out the outlines of all of the furniture inside, but he could still tell through the veil of darkness that it was a very small room. He hadn't really expected a condo though.

The room was suddenly illuminated by a small lamp in the corner of the room. She lifted herself off of the floor, brushing the dirt he couldn't see from her clothes.

"Well," she said, tossing her bag onto the lone bed in the room. The mattress squeaked under the weight. His eyes traveled from the brown carpet to the yellowing bedspread to the lamp in the corner. There was another door to his left, which he assumed led to a bathroom of horrors.

"This is one swanky place," he said flatly.

She thrust out her arms and said in a sing-song voice, "Welcome to your mansion, lover boy."

While he tried to relax onto the lumpy bed, she kicked her boots off and began to walk toward the bathroom. Her right boot ended up significantly farther away from the left on the other side of the room. With her head inside the bathroom, she called back to him, "Good news is that we have a shower. Bad news is it doesn't look like it works."

He heard a loud screeching noise, like nails on a chalkboard. The sound was enough to have him on his feet in an instant. He was by her side in two seconds, looking around frantically for the source of the noise.

Still crouched on the ground, she lifted one finger and pointed at the shower, staring at him with a peculiar look on her face.

"Oh," he said, feeling a bit sheepish as he looked at the pipes above. He rubbed the back of his neck.

She sat back on her heels and began to laugh.

"Thanks for… coming to my… defense!" she spat between laughs.

"Don't mock me," he moaned. "I didn't know it was the shower."

"What did you *think* it was?" she asked.

"I don't know!" he cried as his arms flew out in exasperation. "I was just worried!"

She rose to her feet, smiling from ear to ear, and patted him on the back. As she left the bathroom, he couldn't help staring. It was quickly becoming a horrible bad habit, like biting his nails or smoking cigarettes. He couldn't seem to help it. Something about her was so captivating that once he started looking he couldn't look away.

The squeaking of the mattress was the only thing that broke the spell.

"So," she said, looking up at him from the bed. "Where are you going to sleep?"

"I..." he glanced at the space beside her then back up at her face, where a sly smile was starting to show itself. She picked up a pillow and handed it to him.

"Sweet dreams!" she said. "Hope the cockroaches aren't too bad here."

He shuddered noticeably, and she started to laugh again. As he settled down on the filthy floor, he tried not to think about how dirty it was. He tried to focus on the slowing of her breathing as she drifted off to sleep. It was as melodic as her laughter.

* * *

His dreams were plagued by her presence. He could smell her shampoo encompassing him, filling up the room until he was choking. His body was overflowing with *her,* and it felt so good.

"Jessie," she said in her sing-song voice. *"You're such a slow poke. You just can't seem to catch me, can you?"*

He awoke with a start, panting and gasping for air, air that wasn't saturated with her.

"Oh, you're up."

He looked to his left and saw Jo standing by the bathroom door, toweling drying her dark hair. Her eye makeup was as wrecked as ever: black was everywhere around her eyes. Her clothes were new, but not really that different—a distressed denim jacket, another black mini skirt, and boots.

He didn't really understand why he cared this much about analyzing her wardrobe.

"Yeah," he replied, sitting up. "God, my neck feels like it was sucker punched by a kangaroo."

She looked at him curiously for a few seconds before bursting out laughing.

She had a pretty laugh. He found himself thinking she should laugh more.

Once she managed to regain her composure, she said, "The shower totally sucks, by the way. I washed my hair in the sink with a bar of soap. Talk about glamorous. This is totally what you signed up for, huh?"

She tossed the towel on the bed as she began to dig through her duffel bag. She pulled out a smaller bag, rooting through it.

"You mean life on the road doesn't mean five star hotels and room service? I got in the wrong car."

* * *

"I hope you're not expecting me to take you sight seeing or some crap like that. I don't *do* wax museums, historical sites, or biggest balls of yarn."

"You don't seem like the kind of person to appreciate knitters anyway," Jess said, gazing out the window.

He wondered why she never traveled on the highways. It was so strange.

A lot of things about her were strange though. It was hard to pick just one, sit back, and think, 'wow, that's a batty thing to do.'

It would have been like picking one chocolate bar from a box and saying, "Yup, this one is the sweetest."

Just impossible to do.

"Well, I've picked up the freaks who insist on stopping at Granny's Orange Orchard, Papaw's Nut Stand, and Uncle Danny's Crawfish Shack before. Before you know it, they want to stay at Auntie Dakri's Bed and Breakfast for the week, so they can participate in the apple festival."

"This sounds like a family friendly journey you took."

He noticed a small smile on her face. He was beginning to love it.

"You have no idea," she said, rolling her eyes.

He caught sight of a cow grazing in the distance. They were really far from the main roads, apparently.

Thinking about cows led him to thinking about milk, and thinking about milk made him realize how thirsty he was.

"Wait, people actually name their children 'Dakri?'" he asked.

"Moonchild, Destiny, Willow, Dawn… whatever."

He smiled as he said, "Rain."

"August." she said. "I will never understand naming your kid after a month."

"Back in high school I had to read this one book about bees, and all of the sisters were named after months."

"*The Secret Life of Bees*?" she asked.

"Yeah, that was it."

"It's somewhere in my trunk, I think." She continued, "Oh, you know what's a really weird name? Basil. Who in the right mind names someone after an herb?"

He laughed. "You're right, that's pretty bizarre. Not as weird as something like Karma though. Or Stormy. Charity..."

"I met a guy named Lennon once."

"Really?" He glanced at her box of CDs and said, "You must have geeked out."

She shrugged. "He didn't wash his hair. He had the good pot though. It was a beautiful friendship while I was high. Once it wore off, I realized his hairline looked like a vat of grease."

"Ew."

"Cherish is another good one."

"I wonder if they sell hippie name books somewhere. Like *5,000 Names for a Child That Make Sense While You're Trippin'*."

"Probably. *Full of classic, peace lovin' names such as Cloud, Coyote, Summer, Windsong, and Topaz*," she said in her best announcer voice.

"And Melody."

"Ooo, good one!"

"Or Skye."

"I knew a Skye once."

"Was he high?"

"...maybe."

"Treeflower."

She snorted.

* * *

"So, let me get this straight," he said, throwing his bag onto the motel bed. The mattress creaked—typical. "We wake up at the crack of dawn, eat food that leads to either premature death or life confined to the sofa, drive around killing the ozone, find a creepy motel that has a meth lab in one of the rooms, and repeat."

"Like washing your hair," she said sarcastically.

"I don't get it," he said, shaking his head. "Why?"

"Look," she sighed. "I didn't 'recruit you' or whatever. You chose this. You don't like it; you can leave."

"No," he said, lying down on the bed. "I don't mean it like that. I just... Don't you have a destination?"

She tilted her head, squinting her eyes at him. Shaking her head, she sat down on the corner of the bed by his feet.

"You don't get it," she said. "It's not about the destination. It's about the journey."

She smiled, lying back on the bed, the side of her hip against his.

* * *

He woke up in the middle of the night, desperately needing to pee. Opening his eyes, he came face to face with Jo, fast asleep. Her face was so relaxed that he hardly recognized her. She smiled in her sleep. She looked so... happy. It was kind of creepy. The Jo he had known for three days didn't seem anything like this during the day.

She seemed so hard when she was awake—stolid and detached. There were moments when he could see pieces of her —the real her—coming in through the cracks, but those moments were rare; he had to work for them.

While asleep, she seemed like an open book. All of her emotions, her fears, her desires, were played out on her face. She seemed so delicate like this, as if one wrong move from him could send her entire world into shambles.

Of course, there were the physical differences too. She was undeniably hot with her short skirts and dark eyeliner. Like this, however, she looked entirely different to him. She really was beautiful. Now she looked more like the girl you'd trust to babysit your children rather than the girl you lust over your entire high school career.

All of this analyzing was making him feel like a pervert, preying on some unsuspecting, sleeping girl. He rolled out of bed and padded across the disgusting carpet to the bathroom, trying to get her image out of his head.

* * *

The next time he woke up, she was gone. A momentary jolt of panic shot through him as he realized it was possible that he was stranded in a creepy motel in a strange town on a weird road in the middle of nowhere.

He grabbed his Converse shoes from their spot by the bed and struggled to get them on as he ran outside.

The second he opened the door and saw Jo's beaten up clunker sitting in its same spot in the lot, he let out a breath he didn't know he had been holding. She was still there.

Of course she was, he thought. Like she would leave him. She expected it to be the other way around. She must thank God every time she wakes up and sees he's still there.

He thought he was beginning to sound a little vain, despite the fact that his previous thoughts were most likely true.

As he approached the car, he noticed Jo was leaning against it, looking up at the starry sky. A cigarette was in her hand, the smoke trailing off into the night air.

"Hey," she said softly, without throwing a glance his way. It kind of freaked him out how she could do that.

"Hey," he replied, moving to be next to her. He looked up at the sky too, trying to figure out what was so fascinating about it that compelled her to stand outside at four in the morning.

"Isn't it amazing?" she asked, and he hesitated.

What was he supposed to say? 'No, sorry, I don't think it's really that special. It's always been there all my life. What's the big deal?'

"Yeah," he said, trying his best to sound convincing. The sky? Yeah, the sky was *awesome.* So were trees and grass and the gas mileage her car must be getting.

To his surprise, she laughed, turning to look at him. One eyebrow was raised, and she was smiling in this like-I-don't-know-what-you're-really-thinking way.

"Look," she said, pointing at a particularly bright star with her cigarette. "That's Venus."

He replied, "Cool," and then realized how uninterested he probably sounded.

"Someday you'll get it. One day you'll realize how miraculous everything is. I will never understand why people insist on living life confined to small houses and tiny backyards. Why would anyone ever waste their time worrying about taxes and offspring and higher education when they could be *living?*"

She turned her face back up to the sky, bringing the cigarette to her lips.

"This planet is so huge," she said, exhaling. "And there's so many more out there. You could never stop traveling if you wanted to. You could run forever and never slow down. I just... I want to see everything there is. I want to be everywhere and anywhere. Stories to tell, places to explore, adventures to have, all of that."

She pushed away from the car and started to walk back toward the motel. He stared at her back, speechless.

Finally, he called out, "You're kind of amazing, you know that?"

He could hear her laughing all the way back to their room.

* * *

They stopped to get gas the next day; while Jess was watching the numbers slowly climb on the meter, something hit him.

"Hey," he said, "what do you do about money?"

Jo smiled to herself, leaning against the back of the car. She looked different in jeans. It had thrown him off when she walked out of the bathroom that morning wearing them. *"What? Seen a ghost?" she had said, turning on her heel and walking out the door.* She said, "I'll show you."

A few minutes later they were back on the road. Today's music selection was different than the other albums they had listened to. The car shook with the beat of the electronic music. It wasn't really his thing, but he could get used to it.

* * *

They ended up in a bar that night, which Jess thought was strange, but he didn't object to it. He usually just kept quiet about things and let Jo take over. Whatever. It was her journey. He felt like he was just along for the ride most days.

"Follow me," she whispered in his ear. He watched as she scrunched her hair a few times and pulled her shirt lower to reveal her chest more than usual.

Interesting.

She threw a smile over her shoulder at him as she walked over to the pool table, where several guys were playing. She stood back for a few minutes, watching. The men automatically noticed her—it was hard not to, in all honesty—and motioned for her to come closer.

"Hey, sweets," one said, blowing smoke as he talked. "Want to play?"

"I would," she said, "but…"

She hesitated. Jo. Hesitating. What?

He felt like he was trapped in a *Twilight Zone* episode. Surprise! Everything was turned upside down! Now he was actually the one that was supposed to take the reins.

Or maybe she had a plan. He figured that was it. She always seemed to. So he stood back, far enough away not to be noticed, and observed.

He was getting a really bad case of déjà vu. The smoke in the air, the pool game, Jo looking sexier than ever. It was like a the day he first met her, drunk out of his mind in an attempt to get through another day. It was like some sick punishment. It always started with him trying to distract himself from thinking about it and ended with him drunk in a pool of his own sorrow. It was pathetic. If he could break the cycle just once, he would consider himself lucky.

That wouldn't happen though. He was doomed to suffer forever, haunted by the ghost of a girl he hardly knew.

He glanced at Jo at the pool table, twirling her hair and grinning up at the man like she did this every day. He wondered how much he actually knew about Jo. Maybe what he saw everyday was as much as a show as what he was seeing right now. He didn't really know. It could be. She could actually be a mass murderer who picked up victims in bars and killed them with rusty pipes from motel showers when they were sleeping.

It could happen.

He heard her laughing, and turned his head in time to see her taking the pool stick. She slid past the man—who took an extra second to check out her butt, he noted—and leaned over to hit the ball. She missed the first shot and pouted, arms crossed, eyes big and focused on the ground.

The man chuckled, coming over and patting her on the arm. He handed the stick back to her, and she tried again.

Another miss.

This time it was the guy's turn. He sent the balls flying.

The cycle repeated for a few minutes. Jo tried, failed, pouted, and the man succeeded. It was starting to look like Jo was really awful at pool.

Then something changed in Jo's eye.

Jess couldn't put his finger on it, but it was similar to the look she had when he told her he wasn't going to leave that day in the diner. She suddenly looked confident. Leaning over again, this time she hit two balls into one of the jackets.

The man cheered for her, as if it was thanks to his good teaching that she had suddenly had such a miraculous change in luck.

Jo's luck seemed to get better as the game progressed. In fact, she got so good that she won. She smiled as she grabbed the cash off the table, counting the bills. The man looked like he couldn't get more angry. Throwing a quick smirk at him, she walked away back toward Jess; she handed the money to him and raised an eyebrow in a just-look-at-how-clever-I-am sort of way. He shook his head as he counted the money.

"So you scam people."

"You make it sound so awful," she said, folding her arms across her chest. She glanced back at the man, who was playing with another guy now. It looked like he was slowly calming down. "We've gotta eat. I don't know what you expect me to do."

"Oh, I don't know. Get a job."

Jo snorted. "Sure. Like I can work as I travel the country. Right."

Jess shrugged. "Just a suggestion."

"I don't need your suggestions. This works fine." She waved the cash in his face and craned her neck to the other side of the room, where some poor, unsuspecting fellow was playing darts. She grinned, shoving the money into his chest.

"I'll be back," she said, and Jess rolled his eyes.

"You could always steal!" he shouted to her back.

* * *

She tossed the cheeseburger at his head, waking him up from his peaceful nap a bit too harshly for his tastes.

"Thanks," he said, unwrapping the paper and biting into it.

She nodded, sitting down next to him on the bed and stretching out her legs.

"Do you ever get tired of it?" he asked, mouth half full of cheesy cow.

"Of cheeseburger?" she asked, even though he knew she realized what he was talking about. She did that a lot. She liked to play dumb to stall for time.

"Of the journey."

She shrugged, fell backwards onto the mattress. Playing with a strand of hair, she said, "I get tired of some things, like dodging authorities during the days I couldn't get any money and the constant back pain from the beds. But most of it is fun. Not knowing where you'll end up next, feeling like it's just you and this huge canvas that you're going to explore." She shrugged again, and he hated it.

"So you do steal when you have to."

"I'm not really a person who wants to starve to death or beg for donations on a street with the cardboard sign and a sad face."

"Yeah, you seem like you'd get bored standing in one place for too long."

She smiled. "You're starting to get me."

He believed he got a lot more of her than she thought, but he didn't want to freak her out too early in the game. Scaring her off would be bad. She'd notice overtime. One of these days maybe she'd even notice that she didn't have to try so hard to put up the walls or shut people out. He wanted to believe everything was a matter of time. She'd discover these things when the time came, like maybe sticking in one place or with one person for more than five minutes wouldn't be that bad of a thing.

"Yeah." He repeated, "Yeah, I am."

She fell quiet, allowing his thoughts to drift off. He stared at the ceiling, his eyes tracing the outline of a mysterious stain. How did stains end up on ceilings anyway? They weren't on the top floor, and the room above wouldn't have a bathtub in that spot if the layout was the same as their room, so it wasn't a leak. Unless someone deliberately threw a drink upwards and ducked out of the way quickly, he just didn't see how it was possible.

He looked over at her and saw she was staring at the same spot. She was probably wondering the same thing. Anyone would. Still, he liked to believe this meant they were a lot more similar than he thought.

"How many people have you traveled with?" he heard himself ask. He stopped abruptly once the words were out, shocked that it came out of his own mouth. He had been wondering it since the first day, but he hadn't planned on saying anything ever. It seemed right up there with questions like, "How many pounds do you weigh?" and "How many times a week do you take a dump?" People just don't ask those uncomfortable questions.

Except apparently he did now.

She seemed frozen on the other side of the bed, not responding, not blinking. Even her hands had stopped twisting the end of the hair.

Great. Just great. Now he had done it.

"Sorry," he immediately blurted out, "I shouldn't have tried to—"

"A lot," she said, avoiding his eyes. "They all leave eventually."

He swallowed, making sure to watch his words. "How did you meet them?"

"All over. People in quarter life crises, guys who think I'm a prostitute, girls who have been dumped by their boyfriends and need to get away. They all think this is a temporary thing, like it's some kind of time out from real life and their problems. None of them understand this isn't some hiatus. It's a way of life. This is how I live. It's not something you can just walk out of once you're in too deep." She bit her lip. "Once they realize it's permanent, they leave. Usually when I'm not looking. No one has ever actually given me a heads up before. They just up and leave."

"That's horrible," he said.

She shrugged, and he wanted to throw something.

"You get used to it."

"But that doesn't make it okay," he said, brow furrowing. "You're not just some toy. They shouldn't just abandon you once they get tired of playing."

"But they do," she reminded him. "They always do. You will too. Just wait. It'll happen."

"No, it won't," he said, as firmly as possible. She rolled her eyes and flipped over onto her stomach so she didn't have to worry about looking at him.

"No, seriously, Jo," he said, putting a hand on her shoulder. She shrugged it off. He watched as his fingers curled into a fist on the mattress. He wouldn't leave her. He didn't want to hurt her. Why couldn't she understand?

"I'm not going to leave," he said slowly. "This isn't a vacation. This isn't a break. I want this. Maybe not the beds or the food, but… I couldn't stay where I was. Too much had happened. I couldn't keep living like that. It was impossible to be happy. I want to be a new person. I want to have a new life. And I think I can get everything I want from staying here with you."

She still didn't respond. He watched as her back rose and fell with her breathing.

"You don't have to believe me. You don't even have to want me along for the ride. But you should know I'm not leaving. I'm in. I'm all in. And nothing is going to change that."

He leaned back on the bed and looked back up at the ceiling. That stupid stain was still there. Not that he thought it would disappear, but people never know. He always heard stories about weird things happening: clothes going missing and ending up in some guy's yard across town. The same could happen with an ugly, unsightly stain.

BURNOUT STARS

He turned to his side, so he didn't have to look at it any longer. His back to her, he said softly, "And maybe one of these days, when you realize I'm here to stay, you'll let me in a little."

Jo

She woke up the next morning confused. It was a little weird to have someone traveling with her again, let alone someone sleeping in bed with her.

Who was she kidding? It was really freaking weird. This had only happened, like, twice, max, in her entire life. And one time the guy was drunk. Usually people freaked out once they saw the motel room.

Looking over at Jess' face, she wondered what he thought he was doing. Did he really think he could do this? She had her doubts. She would give him a week, two tops, before he bolted.

It was all a little depressing, really, waiting for someone to get out of her life. She told herself she was fine with it. What could she really expect? She wasn't stupid: she knew that people outside of her world had lives. They had family, friends, jobs, useless "real" things that she could do without. No one could really just give up everything to travel. Not permanently.

She padded over to the bathroom and looked at herself in the mirror. She had actually bothered to take her eye makeup off last night, a rare luxury. Usually she crashed once she found a mattress. Or a sleeping bag. Or any surface, actually. She liked sleeping on top of her car too, even though a bird once crapped on her and kind of ruined the experience.

The shower actually worked at this joint. The sound of the water rushing through the pipes made her want to scream "victory!"

She grabbed her clothes out of her bag while waiting for the shower to—hopefully—heat up.

Rooting through her bag, she stole a look at Jess' face. He looked troubled. He tossed and turned, mumbling incoherently in his sleep. His brow was furrowed. He must have been having nightmares. A little voice inside her head told her, *Probably about all of this.* Jo sneered.

It didn't matter. She didn't need him. She was completely independent. No one called the shots but her. She liked it that way.

Besides, what did he think he was doing turning last night into some sap fest? She didn't *do* emotion.

The water was lukewarm, and she loved every second of it. She hadn't had a hot shower in months. She followed a drop of water down the cracked wall tiles with her finger, thinking about how strange it was to have to lock the bathroom door for once.

Maybe... maybe she was kind of enjoying this.

It was nice to have someone to talk to, to fill the silence. She really hated the quiet. It was eerie. She always felt like she was half-listening for someone else's breathing.

Still, this couldn't last. She wasn't going to get her hopes up thinking that this would last more than a couple of weeks.

She shut the water off and went about the rest of her morning routine. She got dressed in a white v-neck and blue skirt, throwing her leather jacket on top of it. She french braided her hair and redid her eyeliner.

42

She was sitting on the edge of her side of the mattress, putting on her socks when Jess cried out. He was absolutely *freaking out*, thrashing one way and then the other. He kept screaming "no no no no" over and over again.

"Jess? Jess!"

She grabbed his arms and tried to hold them down against the mattress. He was still struggling to get away from her and continue his fit.

"JESS!" she screamed. "Wake up, jerk!"

He groaned, but luckily, started to stir. He stopped trying to break away from her, slowly opening his eyes.

"Jo?" he mumbled, blinking from the light. "Why do you have me pinned to the mattress?"

"Wipe that smile off your face, boy," she said, releasing her death grip on his arms. "You're not *that* lucky."

He chuckled, sitting up in bed. He yawned, stretched, and then looked back at her, smiling slightly.

"So, really?"

"You were spazzing out," she said, as she crossed her arms. "You kept screaming and taking it out on the pillows."

The look on his face faded immediately, replaced by a grimace as he looked at the bed: the covers had been kicked off, and the sheets were on the ground.

"Do you have night terrors, or something?" she asked.

Geeze, she hoped he wasn't hating this trip so much that he had to destroy the bed in his sleep just to send a message to her.

"I kind of do," he said, rubbing the back of his neck. "There's just this..."

He hesitated. She bit her lip, waiting.

She hoped he wasn't hating this. She really, truly did. As much as she liked to tell herself that she was totally okay with people leaving, she honestly didn't think she could handle one more.

And she liked him, in the totally platonic sense of the word. He was pretty funny, and while he was kind of quiet at times, he was better than nothing. Plus he seemed to like her music, so he scored brownie points on that one.

"Something really really bad happened back home," he said finally. He didn't meet her eyes. "It bothers me a lot, I guess. I dream about it all the time."

She nodded, but didn't pry. Things went wrong left and right in the "real world." Dogs ran away. Families fell apart. Jobs were lost, and people went upside down on their mortgages. The last thing anyone needed after a bad incident was to be forced to talk about his *feelings,* like they were all on Doctor Phil or some crap.

"Well, I've got good news," she said. He looked at her hopefully. He looked like a puppy when he did that. A puppy that had been abandoned, and then picked up by some random stranger on the street.

Even though in that scenario she was the puppy.

"We have a shower, and the water is a couple notches above cold."

"Am I supposed to be happy about this?"

* * *

She really hated traveling with girls. Most of them had been dumped by their boyfriends, and thought it would be fun to run away for a while. Once reality set in, they remembered they had daddies and universities. They cried too much and whined about what her broken windows did to their hair. It was too much for her. She hated the silence, but having someone to talk to who was as dumb as a brick really wasn't worth the constant fight with herself not to poison some blond chick's food.

The best part about having a guy around was that he didn't spend three hours getting ready in the morning. She needed five minutes; Jess, two. He jumped in the shower, was out in thirty seconds, put on his clothes, and was out the door. It was beautiful.

They were traveling down the road, music playing through the speakers of her car, when she caught sight of the look on his face.

He looked so…happy.

She wasn't used to seeing people so content when they were with her. Usually they looked like they were about to slit their wrists. This was strange.

She felt something strange inside her, a weird pressure in her chest. She ran through the symptoms of cardiac arrest in her mind. Chest discomfort? Check. Discomfort in other areas of the upper body? Some. Shortness of breath? Maybe a little. Cold sweat, nausea, or lightheadedness? Not really.

She declared herself fit to drive and able to feel.

While she didn't want to admit it, she was happy that he was happy. It gave her some bizarre satisfaction to see someone besides herself pleased like this—like she was.

But was she really that happy?

"I know I'm hot, Jo, but seriously. Stop with the staring."

Jess smirked at her, and she rolled her eyes, even though she couldn't wipe the grin off her face. Maybe this would work for once. Maybe she could—

Her car made a loud, horrible noise that she equated with the bowels of Hell opening up. Jess went into full-time panic mode, grasping at the seat and taking long, deep breaths like he needed to savor each one. She would have laughed at his pathetic state if she could think through the stream of obscenities running through her mind. Every dirty word she had ever heard, learned, or created was clogging her thoughts.

The car started to slow down. Jo could see smoke coming out of the hood, and she smacked the dash in frustration.

"No!" she screamed, hitting the dash again as they came to a complete stop. Her head fell forward and landed on the horn, alerting the cows of her current hopeless state.

She stayed like that for a while, thinking about how much this sucked and how much pool she was going to have to hustle to get this stupid thing fixed.

All of the sudden she felt a hand on her shoulder.

"Jo?" Jess asked hesitantly.

She groaned in response.

"You okay over there?"

She groaned again.

"Does this happen a lot, or is it a special occasion?"

"It's all because of that stupid shower. I can't have one good thing. The shower worked, and the water was practically warm, so now my car has to break down. God, I hate the balance of the universe."

She threw her seatbelt off and the car door open. Smoke was flowing out of the hood like it had been pinned up in there for years, and it finally just now was getting to escape. She coughed as she opened it, trying to fan away the smoke that was in front of her face.

"Can I help?" Jess asked.

"Yeah, buy me a new car," she replied.

"Do you want a plane and a yacht too, or just the car?"

"Car is fine. I can just attach some floats to it like I'm the *Wild Thornberrys*, and then I've got a boat. Don't need a plane if you have a boat."

He leaned against the side of the car while she attempted to fix the piece of junk. She glanced over at him every once in a while, taking note of the short blond hair, the dull eyes. She was still stuck on what she saw that morning. Whatever went wrong at home, it must have been serious to bother him like that. Still, it wasn't her place. Unless he decided to tell her on his own, she wasn't going to bother asking. She had her own secrets and her own problems.

One of them being this stupid car.

She kicked the tire, letting out a scream.

"This sucks! This sucks! This *sucks*!"

She moved next to him, and hit her forehead against the roof again and again until he eventually pulled her back.

"Okay, okay, don't give yourself a concussion," he said.

"This sucks."

"Yeah, well, you can add this to the f-m-l collection."

"My life is one big f-m-l collection," she said plaintively.

He laughed and said, "I thought you loved this. I must have you mixed up with another Jo who actually enjoys life on the road."

She pulled her duffel bag out of the backseat. One of the stickers she got in Vegas was falling off. There were empty places where some of them used to be before they peeled off. New York, Colorado, and Kansas were gone. Honestly though, she didn't really value anything in Kansas besides the open spaces.

"I guess we're walking," she said, walking over to the road. "Hopefully, we'll find a town with a repair shop."

"Oooo a real adventure!" he said, throwing an arm around her shoulders playfully. She shoved it off. "I hope we get to camp."

"This pretty much *is* camping," she reminded him.

"Camping is cleaner, I think."

She looked up the dirt road as far as she could, but she didn't see anything in sight. It was funny; in all of her years of traveling, she had longed for open spaces like this. Now she wanted nothing more than to see a huge metropolis, buzzing with people and cars.

* * *

"So, do you hate people?"

"What?" she responded, giving him a bizarre look. This boy was full of surprises.

"I'm just trying to figure you out."

He smiled at her slightly, and she looked away. He made her feel weird, not like super-creep-gonna-do-bad-things-to-me-in-my-sleep kind of weird, but definitely not a normal kind of weird. It was kind of a I'm-getting-attention-and-don't-know-why-it's-warranted weird.

"I only hate people who slow me down," she replied, looking up at the sun. It had to be around three, judging by where it was in comparison to the horizon. It was impossibly hot: she was pretty sure sweat was dripping from every pore on her body. This is what she got for driving through a desert.

"What about the people you leave behind, though?" Jess asked, watching her carefully. "Family? Friends?"

"Yeah, don't have any of that."

This boy was annoying—creepy and annoying. He was getting nosier by the second. A week ago, he had seemed too quiet for her; now she couldn't get him to shut up.

"I could say the same for you," she pointed out. "You must have been drunk out of your mind that night. You didn't even think about it."

He shrugged, suddenly looking uncomfortable. She wondered if she overstepped her boundaries, but he was the one who started it.

He was a mystery to her, surprisingly enough. Usually, she had a sob story by now, a reason why a person's life was oh so awful. Never had she had someone who *didn't* complain about his life or his problems.

It was bizarre.

Maybe he was more like her than she had first thought. Maybe he *did* get it, get this.

Get her.

The thought was overwhelming to her. She couldn't tell if she was thrilled or nauseated. Her head hurt, and her heart ached almost as badly as her feet.

"How long do you think we've been walking?" he asked, breaking her out of her thoughts.

"A few hours."

"Do you think there's really anything out here?" he asked, and she doesn't know the answer to that.

"Well, we're out here," she answered. It was the best answer she could give him.

Jess smiled as he looked out over the empty road.

"We should play a road trip game."

* * *

They gave up around eleven. Jo's feet hurt. Jess kept complaining about his back. She was getting fed up with everything that moved, which was a sign that she *needed* sleep.

"Where are we going to sleep though?" Jess asked.

"Look around!" she exclaimed, walking behind some bushes and dropping her bag on the ground. She made her own little sleeping spot on the ground and settled in for the night. Jess, on the other hand, stood there stupidly, looking out at the road.

"What's wrong with you?" she asked, watching him from her spot on the ground.

"Aren't there, like, coyotes? Crazy, axe-wielding murderers?"

She started cracking up. She laughed until she couldn't breathe, and the world was spinning faster than it should. When she looked up at him, the look on his face was a combination of satisfaction and panic. She patted the ground next to her. He tentatively sat down, glancing over his shoulder into the darkness.

She laid back down, using her bag as a pillow. The stars seemed so much brighter when she was away from the city. It was amazing. She could always get lost in them, even when she was little.

"You really like stars, don't you?" asked Jess.

She shifted her gaze to the person next to her and smiled slightly at him, looking back up at the sky.

"You know what I think is amazing?" she said. "They're so far away, but they still shine brightly enough so we can see them."

She continued, "But they don't last forever. They burn out. They're all just burning stars, dying so we can see them. Isn't it kind of ironic?"

"I guess," he said. He appeared to be thinking for a few minutes before he finally added, "Yeah. You mean, like, they kill themselves trying to live."

"Exactly!" she exclaimed. She turned to him, feeling lightheaded, and repeated, "exactly."

Maybe he wasn't as dumb as she thought. Maybe he really *did* get this. She smiled at the thought. Maybe this would work for once.

"They're a lot like people," he said, catching her off guard. "They want to live so badly that they end up killing themselves in the process."

"We're all just burning stars," she said with a small smile. "Eventually, we burn out. Some just shine brighter than others, burn faster."

"You know," he said. "You're pretty smart, Jo."

She laughed, elbowing him in the side.

"You're not too bad yourself."

* * *

The next day, they finally reached civilization.

Well, sort of.

It was an old, small town, but all she really needed was to find someone to tow her poor, sad car. Jess seemed overjoyed at the thought of hot food though.

"Is there a diner? Do you see one?" he asked excitedly, turning around in the street a few times. She laughed, pointing to the right.

"Over there. I just need to get my car taken care of before someone jacks my CD collection."

"I wonder how long it will take to fix it," he mumbled.

"Sounds like someone is a converted nomad."

He smiled.

They walked into a gas station because it was the closest building. Jess was lagging behind, and she was starting to get worried that he was going to keel over. Some people couldn't skip a few meals; their feeding clocks get out of whack, and before she knew it, she had people puking all over the back seat of her car.

Given, she didn't have a car for him to puke in right now, but she did have her last clean outfit.

"So you'll get someone out there?" she asked again.

The man nodded, looking a little annoyed, and directed them toward the local motel.

"We're getting food now, right?" Jess asked eagerly.

"Cool your jets. I can only walk so fast after this journey."

The diner looked more like a McDonalds than a no-name, low-budget crapfest. Admittedly, she liked the crapfests. They had character. Each one told another story. Just as musicians geeked out over tiny clubs littered with graffiti and posters, she loved the tiny diners that were scattered across the country.

"Is it safe to eat meat at places named after meat?" Jess inquired. He held up the plastic menu with *The Cow's Head* printed in bright red text.

The entire dinner was decked in red and white. The plastic furniture was bolted down to the floor like it was some kind of asylum.

"Hey, you okay?" Jess asked, setting down the menu and leaning in toward her. "They'll fix your car in no time. You won't be stuck here."

"I'm fine," she said, looking up at him. She must look awful. She can see it now—raccoon-like eyeliner, messy braid, pale skin. At least she didn't smell. Hopefully.

"And I don't know. I just know to avoid meat at breakfast because that's when they scrape the roadkill off the road."

She opened up the menu, glanced at the food, and added, "You can risk it if you want, but you might spend the next two days crapping your brains out."

"That…" He scrunched up his face. "Sounds really unpleasant. Where's the grilled cheese option?"

"Not available."

"Kids' menu?"

"Nada."

"Healthy eaters' corner?"

"Nonexistent."

"Safe choices?"

"Zilch."

"Nearest Pizza Hut?"

"Now you're just kidding yourself."

"And I wasn't before?"

"You know what, Jess?" She propped her aching feet up on the available seat next to him. "I like where this is going."

* * *

The motel was one of the creepiest she had ever seen. She had been to a *lot* of motels. She was pretty sure if she ever stayed in an "exclusive" vacation destination, she would panic. She liked the smelly, cheap rooms and bad mattresses. They weren't meant to serve any purpose besides a quick rest before embarking back on her journey, and she liked how insignificant they were in the grand scheme of things. She didn't worry about getting a "good" room or a "bad" room because it never mattered. As long as she got some sleep, she was satisfied.

This motel, however, was giving her the creeps. She was expecting rapists to jump out from behind corners. The wallpaper was falling off the walls, the ceiling in the closet was caved in, and there was a mysterious dripping sound that she couldn't find the source of. Surprisingly, Jess seemed less shocked than she did. He leapt onto the mattress and settled in right away, leaving her standing in the middle of the room, looking at the door nervously.

"What's wrong?" he asked, sitting up on his elbows.

"I don't know," she admitted. "It's weird. I just don't feel right."

She sat down on the edge of the bed, and he scooted in next to her, putting his hand on her leg.

"It's just your car," he said. "You'll feel better once it's fixed."

"I don't know," she said again, biting her lip. "I don't think that's it."

"I'm sure it is. It's practically your house. You want your CDs and your torn seats and your broken windows— speaking of which, I wonder if those will get fixed."

"I don't want them fixed," she said stubbornly as she crossed her arms.

"I have a feeling that they won't be, anyway." He glanced out the window at the small town. The repair shop looked dead.

She looked carefully at the bathroom from her spot on the bed. Something was definitely off. She just didn't know what it was.

"We need to do something to get your mind off of it. Are you tired?"

She shook her head no. Electricity was zinging through her veins. She didn't know what was going on with her, but she knew there was no way she could possibly sleep when she was like this.

"Then I have an idea."

She looked at him expectantly, and he grinned. Part of her wanted to protest, "No. *I'm* the one with the ideas." The other part of her wanted it to shut up.

* * *

There was a tiny pool behind the motel that looked like no one had swum in it for years. Jess seemed unfazed by the murky water, throwing his shirt and shoes off without a second's thought.

"Come on!" he said, snapping in the air. He had certainly adjusted fast. He was hardly the same person she'd met that night in the bar.

"I don't know about—"

"Since when are you the one to hesitate?" he asked, crossing his arms.

His words struck a chord with her. What was wrong with her? This wasn't her. This was some wimp that had possessed her body. She took a step and plunged into the water. He followed suit.

The bottom of the pool was littered with leaves, and the water smelled wrong. Honestly though, the cool water felt so good that she was just happy to finally put an end to her melting state.

Hours flew by. She didn't realize how long they had been swimming until they got back to the motel room. The fat, bright red digits of the clock read 8:46 PM. For a few minutes, she thought the clock must be wrong. Then she looked back outside and realized she had just gotten lost in the amount of fun she had been having.

Fun. She couldn't remember the last time she thought about *her* having *fun*.

"You know what we should do?" Jess said from the bathroom. His voice was followed by the sound of running water and a cheer. He reemerged from the bathroom grinning.

"Well, first, we need to take advantage of this shower. Then we should go rent a movie."

"A movie?" she asked, squinting her eyes. She couldn't remember the last time she had watched a movie. She usually didn't have time to kill like this.

"Yeah," Jess said, digging through his suitcase. "I saw a movie store when we walked into town. This place has a VCR —even though I didn't even know that VCRs still existed. I thought they had all been destroyed once DVDs came out, but whatever. We can probably find a movie on tape in the back of the store."

One thing Jo had learned over time was that these small towns always seemed to be stuck in a time warp, untouched by advances in technology. Diners didn't keep up with the new health laws that had been passed, motels were never up to inspections, and the people were usually old, high-school dropouts that couldn't get work doing anything else but working at gas stations.

"Like what?" she asked, sitting down on the bed.

"Anything that can take your mind off things," he said with a shrug. "That's what movies were invented for anyway, escapism. But yeah, I think we should rent a movie and get a pizza somewhere."

She laughed. "I don't think there's a Pizza Hut close by."

"Yeah, but that diner probably could make one. Pizza is like the easiest thing ever to make. Well, not *good* pizza, but bad pizza is easy."

"You aren't making any sense right now," she said, rolling her eyes.

"Good pizza is *hard* to make. You have to make sure the crust isn't floppy. The sauce has to be tangy, and the cheese has to be more than just American." He pulled out some clothes and shut his bag again.

"But bad pizza is simple. All you have to do is make some dough, squash some tomatoes, and melt some cheese. Easy."

"You seem to know a lot about pizza making," she said, lying back on the bed. The ceiling was cracked. She wondered if it would fall in on her in the middle of the night. That would really be a crappy way to die. Young woman killed by falling ceiling in motel! Name unknown. Motel owner refused to speak to press—was too busy counterfeiting.

It would be quite the headline.

"Yeah, well." He shifted awkwardly, looking down at the red carpet. "My friend's parents were in the business."

"That always sounds so cool," she noted. "'In the business.' It makes every job sound like the mafia."

"They were in the business of causing premature heart attacks and clogged arteries, not the business of busting kneecaps."

"When you put it that way, it's kind of the same thing."

She smirked at him, then looked back up at the ceiling.

"So are you claiming the shower first? Or do I get the pleasure?"

"Are you kidding me?" he said. "It is *so* my turn."

He half-walked, half-ran toward the bathroom, shutting the door behind him. She rolled her eyes.

Boys.

She stared up at the ceiling and listened to the sound of rushing water. It was strange; she didn't feel anxious anymore. In fact, she felt better than she had in a really, *really* long time. She glanced at the closed bathroom door and smiled. Maybe she was better off with someone after all.

* * *

They walked to the video store in sweatpants and flannel. Pajamas were good enough for a late-night movie run.

Just as she had expected, the rental store was lost in the tides of time. There was only one rack of DVDs, accompanied by a huge sign that read, "Just In!"

Jess seemed shocked and appalled by this new development.

"What's wrong with this town?" he whispered in her ear, carefully eyeing the cashier to make sure she wasn't eavesdropping. What Jess didn't realize was that no one cared.

"What's wrong with all of them," she said back with a smirk.

He shook his head in exasperation, staring at the sign.

"I feel like I'm trapped in the 90s."

"I think if you mentioned Apple around here, people would cry 'witchcraft!'"

"Are they all like this?" he asked, flipping a video over and reading the summary on the back. He grinned and tucked the case under his arm.

"The towns? Pretty much. Some are more remote than others."

They checked out the movie from a middle-aged woman with too many tattoos and a nose ring. Jess had seemed uncomfortable talking to her, answering all of her questions with "mhm" and looking toward the door too often. Finally, Jo decided to spare him from his pain, and linked arms with him, steering him out of the shop.

"That was traumatic," he said, eliciting a laugh from her.

"You're always laughing at me," he said thoughtfully, looking up at the stars.

"You're amusing," she said with a smile.

"So have you started to believe me yet?"

They turned a corner. There was a shack up ahead that claimed to sell pizza. Whether it was pizza or smashed rats was yet to be determined.

"What?" she asked, clearly confused.

"Have you started to believe that I'm in for the long haul?"

"Oh," she said. "I—"

The strange thing was she *did* believe. If he was willing to hike forty miles in the blistering heat with her, he must be serious about this. Plus he had tried so hard to get her to take her mind off things.

Trust was a difficult thing for her. Her life followed a pattern. She met someone, she started to trust him, he left, and she was devastated. Somewhere along the way she decided that enough was enough: she was tired of being hurt. She hadn't allowed herself to trust anyone else since.

This, however, felt different. She *wanted* to trust him. She wanted to believe the good in him.

"Yeah," she said finally. "I do."

"Good," he said, grinning. "Because I am."

Every single drunkard in the pub turned around and stared the second they walked in. They probably weren't used to having visitors. This was one of those towns that people moved to when their lives were washed up: they came, they lived, they died. The end.

She ordered a pizza to go from the bar, and flirted with one of the guys while she waited. She watched the way his face lit up while she talked. She had a God-given gift for deception. It was far too easy for her.

Jess, however, was proving to be the most awkward person to ever walk this planet. He looked so out of place in his body, eyes darting around the room like he was mad, fingers tapping an unsteady rhythm on the bar's counter.

"What's wrong with you?" she whispered sharply.

He shrugged, not looking at her. She rolled her eyes. It must have been his time of the month.

When they finally got their pizza, Jess practically *bolted* out of the building. She walked calmly after him, trying not to make a scene. He was waiting outside for her, pacing back and forth.

"Are you possessed?" she asked.

"I'm fine. Let's go."

He snatched the pizza from her and started walking down the sidewalk. Then it hit her.

"Oh my God," she said, catching up with him. "You're jealous!"

"No, I'm not!" he spat. He began walking faster in a futile attempt to get away from her.

"Yes, you are, and you're going the wrong way."

He abruptly turned on his heel, and started walking the other direction. She snorted.

"Come on, *Jessie.* I didn't mean anything by it."

He stopped dead in his tracks. Great. Now what?

"You okay?" she asked hesitantly. He looked crazy, like he was about to rip off his clothes and transform into The Incredible Hulk or something. He shook his head, snapping out of his trance.

"Yeah, fine," he said. "Don't call me that."

"Fine, fine!"

She threw her hands in the air.

"Are we good then?" she asked, watching his face carefully. "I'd hate to lose my nomad buddy."

A small smile appeared on his face.

"Yeah, we're good."

* * *

The movie was awful in the best kind of way. The acting was corny, the writing was awful, and the music was too dramatic. They were constantly laughing. Jess had rolled off the bed twice during hysterical fits of laughter.

The empty pizza box was on the floor, torn to pieces. They had both tried to argue that it was not the pizza box's fault for the crime that was the pizza, but they had to let their anger out on something. They had finished the pizza off by a series of dares. It started when he declared that he was going to vomit, and she bet him that he couldn't eat three more pieces. He did, and bet that she couldn't eat two more. The game went on until the pizza was gone, and they were both 99.999% sure that they were going to hurl.

"This is what death feels like," he said, lying on his back. His head was hanging over the end of the bed, and he was watching the movie upside down. She was on her stomach, moaning in pain.

"Oh look, here comes Brows," she said, pointing at the small, fuzzy screen.

Every character in the movie had a ridiculously long name that neither of them could manage to remember. Instead, they decided to create their own names for them based on physical features. It made it much easier to remember who was who.

They had Brows, the protagonist with extremely hairy eyebrows; Chin, who had a chin sharp enough to cut through cement; Guy with Huge Freaking Scarf, who was wearing a huge freaking scarf every scene; Curly, who had curly hair; and Not Tiny, who was probably too large to fit through the doorway. They were originally going to name him "Huge Dude," but felt like it didn't suit him well enough. "Not Tiny" just felt right.

"Brows is so annoying," she said. "'Boohoo I'm rich and unloved. Boohoo boohoo my privileged life is just so hard.' Find yourself a purpose."

"I'm so thirsty," Jess whined. "That pizza is really messing me up. I can't stop sweating."

"Ooookay, bordering on t-m-i," she said, scooting away from him.

"The tap water is too hot," he whined again.

"If I go get ice, will you shut up?"

"Yes!" he cheered. She rolled her eyes, but smiled.

"Fine, but you owe me."

She climbed off the bed and put on her boots.

One could always judge how classy a motel was by the room keys. If the room had a keypad, it was seriously fancy, like mint-on-your-pillow, free-massage-upon-check-in fancy. If the key was a plastic swipe card, the room was up to date. If one received a metal key upon check in that he needed to physically stick into a lock and turn, he was screwed.

This swanky joint used metal keys.

The door to the room was light, and she had no doubt that someone could kick the door in if he wanted to. The ice box was on the first floor next to one of the rooms. She half-walked, half-trotted down the stairs, looking up at the stars. It was almost August; she hadn't seen a calendar lately, but she could plainly see the summer triangle up above, three bright, white stars in a sea of darkness.

It was amazing how much one could figure out just by looking at the stars.

She opened the lid to the ice machine and blinked. Something wasn't right. She tilted her head to the side, looking at the way the ice had a faint, tan glow to it. It wasn't just dirty. There was something else going on.

Her heart started to hammer in her chest as she pushed back the ice. Before long, she started frantically digging, throwing ice chips onto the ground. When she pushed back some ice on the left side, she let out a gasp.

There was a hand, a cold, dead hand, sticking out of the ice.

She couldn't breathe. She couldn't think. She pushed back more and more until her hands were numb and a face came into view.

"It can't be," she whispered in shock. She stared at the girl's face, with it's small, delicate features, her mouth open in shock. Not knowing what else to do, she slammed the lid back down.

Then she started running. Her feet pounded up the stairs, the sound resonating off the concrete walls. She slipped on one of the top steps and scrambled to get back up. She couldn't get the key into the lock fast enough. Her hands were shaking. She couldn't see. This was so bad. She didn't—

"Jo?"

Jess was standing in the doorway of their room, holding the door open for her. She looked up at him, her mouth open, just staring. The shock must have been written all over her face, because he pulled her inside without a second's notice, shut the door tightly behind them, and latched the chain.

She leaned against the wall, desperately trying to inhale. She couldn't *breathe*. How could this be happening? How could *she*—this didn't make any sense.

"Jo?" he asked again, putting his hands on her shoulders. She jumped. "Jo, look at me."

She reluctantly met his gaze. With all of this adrenaline pumping through her veins, she couldn't stop shaking. She felt like her legs were going to give out.

And they did. She fell to the floor, landing in a heap. She pulled her knees up to her chest, trying to breathe normally. Jess crouched down next to her, putting a hand on her knee.

"Jo," he said slowly. She looked up at him, shaking her head. "What happened?"

"There's—I—and she—oh my *God*."

She didn't realize she was crying until he wiped away one of the many tears trickling down her cheek. It would have been cute if she wasn't so freaked out.

"Th-there's—okay." She took a deep, shuddering breath and tried to calm herself down. She stole a look at his face, his eyes wide, concern written into his features. For a split second, her thoughts cleared enough for her to think about how worried he looked. *Wow,* she thought. *He cares.*

Then, as quickly as it came into her mind, it was gone again, replaced by a pale, motionless face, tinged slightly blue.

"There's a, a dead girl in the ice machine."

"What?" he asked incredulously. He must have thought she was joking, but one look at her face must have assured him that she was dead serious.

"A dead girl," he repeated. She nodded.

"Well," he said, biting his lip. "We have to call the police."

"No!" she shouted, grabbing his wrist. He looked at her like she was crazy. "We can't!"

"There's a dead girl in the ice machine. We can't just let her stay in there. There will be people who actually get ice from there without noticing."

"No, I... we *can't*."

"Why not?" There was a hint of laughter in his voice. He thought she was crazy. She sure was acting like it.

"I—I knew her."

Jess

There are certain things in life that are supposed to change a person: college, marriage, mid-life crises, whatever. No one had ever told him that what would *really* change him would be getting in the car with a girl he didn't know.

It was funny how different he felt now compared to then. He felt lighter, freer, happier. Life didn't seem so bleak anymore. He wasn't upset when he woke up every morning. Things were better now.

As far as regrets went, he regretted a lot in his life. He regretted blowing off his high school graduation. He regretted giving up on college after two months. He regretted ever letting *her* leave. He didn't regret getting into Jo's car.

She was moody, rude, and downright impossible to predict, but he couldn't help but like her. There was something about her, something buried below the surface. She was mysterious. She was interesting. He felt a strange, innate desire to figure her out.

Looking down at her now, he realized there was a lot about her that he didn't understand.

"The girl in the ice machine?"

She nodded, biting her lip.

"You knew the girl in the ice machine?" he repeated, confused. Did she put her in the ice machine? Was she one of those lunatics that shoved their victims into ice machines as a surprise for the next poor unfortunate soul to find them?

Looking at her wet face, he very much doubted it.

"Yes!" she shouted, hitting the floor with her fists. She was coming apart at the seams before his eyes. Her hands were in her hair and on the ground and hitting the walls. She was crying hysterically, and he was starting to see the fine cracks in her soul that she had artfully tried to conceal growing larger and larger until they were impossible to overlook.

"How?" he asked.

She fell silent, gathering her hands in her lap, and averting her gaze.

Maybe she *was* a serial killer.

"Jo, talk to me," he begged. "You can trust me, promise."

"I—" she hesitated, looking at the ground.

"Come on," he said softly.

She took a deep breath, looked at him, and said, "She traveled with me, not for very long though. We didn't get along.

"We can't tell the police," she said, releasing a shuddering breath. "They could trace her back to me. I didn't do anything wrong, Jess! She left *me*, but I… I don't want to be blamed for anything!"

She looked so desperate like this, crying on the floor of a nasty motel room. It was such a contrast from the strong Jo that he was used to seeing. It was unsettling.

"Calm down," he said quietly, squeezing her knee. She was shaking. "Nothing bad is going to happen to you, okay? We *have* to call the police; the girl's family deserves to know at the very least."

Jo looked like she really didn't like the sound of that.

"Jo, I promise you," he said. "Nothing will happen to you, okay? I won't let anything bad happen."

She slowly nodded, chewing on her thumbnail.

"Come on," he said, pulling her up. He directed her toward the bed. The movie was paused on the tiny TV: Huge Freaking Scarf was perpetually stuck arguing with Chin and Not Tiny. He was a bit surprised that the three of them could all fit in the frame—Not Tiny was the size of a barn already. He guessed this was the magic of the movies.

"We could watch more of Brow's amazing adventure on the farm if you want," he offered, gesturing with the remote.

"I really kind of hate this movie," she said softly.

"I really kind of do, too."

"But I really hate the silence more," she said with a sigh.

He hit the play button without another word.

* * *

Okay, so when he woke up the next morning with sunshine pouring in through the windows, he realized he might have made a mistake by falling asleep.

A dead girl in an ice machine was probably more pressing than sleep. Then again, who knew how long she had been in there. If she lasted this long, she could probably last one more night. It's not like she was keeping track of time.

He glanced over at Jo, who had fallen asleep not too long after the movie started playing again. She was mumbling about how annoying Chin was before she passed out. She looked stressed even in her sleep. Her fingers were curled into tight fists, and her brow was creased. He pushed a strand of hair out of her face then stopped.

He was pushing major creeper boundaries at the moment. Watching someone in her sleep wasn't exactly comforting for the person being watched. He couldn't really help it. There was something about seeing her like this that made him want to do his best to return her to her strong, sarcastic self. She was too vulnerable like this. It wasn't right.

He tossed his cell phone back and forth. It was funny. Back home, it was always glued to his hand. He was hardly ever seen without it.

He hadn't even thought about it once in the past few weeks.

His priorities had really changed a lot recently.

He looked back over at Jo and sighed. Should he call now, while she's asleep? Should he wait until she's awake, so she could brace herself? It was a tough call. He always hated decision-making. How did he ever know if he made the right choice?

The glow of the screen seemed so bright compared to the dim lighting in the room. If the sun hadn't already blinded him, he wouldn't have been able to read his screen. He had six voicemails and four texts which he blatantly ignored.

It was good to know that after going missing, the most anyone cared to do was call him six times. He wasn't expecting a search party or anything, but a text message just felt like a slap in the face.

His contacts were as boring as ever. He wasn't the most popular, the most charismatic, or even the most involved. Was it really a shock that no one cared that he was missing?

He scrolled through the list, reading the names of the people that didn't care. Aaron, Abby, Ade—he stopped on one name.

Amelia.

He would never understand how one name could send shock waves of pain and excitement through him. It had to be a mystery to modern science. It didn't make any sense to him how she *still* had complete control over him.

He wondered where she was: New York, London, Paris? She had always seemed like the type of girl to want to live in Paris, high fashion, high class. She would have fit in nicely.

He wondered how she was: happy, sad, tired, awake, sick, well, good, bad? There were too many possible answers to that question. They made his head spin.

He wondered who she was. She was always a person who could be anything she wanted to be. With her effortless command over people, she could have ruled the world.

Could have, would have, should have.

She could be dead, but that thought killed him. It made him want to scream and cry and throw up and *run*. He glanced over at Jo again, who looked as stressed as ever. He adjusted her covers like a doting father would.

She was probably alive. She wouldn't have accepted death. She wouldn't have given up so easy.

Wherever she was, he hoped she was happy.

* * *

"Jo, slow down!" he shouted, jogging after her. She was a beast when she was angry. He hoped to catch up with her sometime between tomorrow and next week.

She stormed through the town, bursting into the repair shop and marching up to the counter.

The man behind it didn't even look up from his magazine. Why was it that no one in these small towns ever looked like they bathed?

"Yeah, hi," she said. "You guys are supposed to be fixing my car."

Before his very eyes, he saw her hoist herself up onto the counter and look down at the man's magazine.

Jess quickly grabbed her hips, trying to pull her back down.

"What the heck do you think you're doing?" he whispered in her ear. She elbowed him in the stomach, so he promptly let go.

"'Sexy' has a 'y,'" she pointed out, looking at the magazine casually. The man pulled it away from her, stashing it under the counter.

"While I'm sure your magazines with plastic barbies are riveting, I was hoping you were actually earning your paycheck the fair and honest way. If you wanted to steal my money and my time, you could have just mugged me when I walked in."

The man's eyes narrowed.

"Yer car ain't done just yet," he said, and she rolled her eyes.

"Yeah, thanks, Sherlock," she said. "I put that together. When will it be done? I'm hoping sometime before Armageddon."

Jess was torn between laughing and running away. If Jo would have been a Joe, she would have been beaten to a pulp by now.

"Check back Thursday," he grumbled, reaching back behind his counter.

Jo, with her reflexes of a ninja, snatched the magazine out of his hand before Jess even saw it reappear.

"Customer service fee," she said, turning on her heel and walking towards the door. Jess quickly followed.

The second they were outside, she tossed it into the nearest trash can. She stopped, turning to him.

"Wait, did you want that?" she asked with a sidelong glance to the trash.

"Nah, I'll pass this time around," he said, earning a smirk from her.

As they were walking around the town, Jo said, "Fine, you're right."

"Right about...?"

"I hate people," she said with a sigh. "Everyone is so incompetent. I could fix my car faster."

"I think this is probably just an exception to the human race. I mean, if we were near civilization, we could probably find someone more qualified to fix your poor baby."

She stopped and gave him a dirty look.

"Don't. Mock. My. Car."

He put his hands up in mock surrender. Or maybe it wasn't so mocked. She was a little scary when she was like this. Okay, a lot scary.

She turned back around and started walking again. When she realized he wasn't following her, she called over her shoulder, "Come on, nomadic friend!"

He quickly caught up with her.

* * *

He let out a long sigh. His cell phone was sitting on the small table in front of him, waiting for him to pick it up and dial three numbers. It was a simple task on paper, but in real life, it seemed much more difficult.

One, there was Jo, who became a nervous, shaking wreck every time she saw his phone out. She didn't have too much to worry about if she didn't claim to know the girl; it's not like the girl was going to speak up.

Two—well, he guessed there was really just one reason: Jo. He just didn't want to upset her. He hated seeing her anything besides her snarky self. That was the whole problem.

This was stupid.

He grabbed his phone, accidentally hitting the internet button. Stupid touch screens. He was about to close out of it when he dropped his phone. It clattered to the ground, followed by him.

Wireless Connection Found:
Amelia's Wireless Card.
Password required.

"*What?*" he whispered, staring at his phone in shock.

Four months. It had been *four* months. It had been four months with no word from her, no sign that she was still alive. And now this.

Part of him reasoned that it wasn't the same Amelia. She wouldn't be *here* of all places. Paris, Florence— those were places where she belonged.

But a small voice inside his heart whispered, *"But what if it is?"*

"Jo!" he screamed, beating on the bathroom door. "Jo!"

He heard her shout back through the door, "Jesus Christ! Keep your pants on!"

"No, I—"

She threw open the door and glared at him.

"What the *heck,* boy?"

"I have to go!" he said, whirling around and darting towards the door.

She immediately paled.

"What?" she said quietly.

"No!" he said quickly, grabbing her shoulders. "No, not like that! I'm not *leaving* leaving. Just going out. I'll be back."

"Oh," she said, not looking convinced.

"I mean it, okay? I'll be *right* back."

Before he knew what he was doing, he kissed her on the forehead and dashed out the door, cell phone in hand.

He didn't have time to think about what demon had momentarily possessed him. He just had to find her. There was no one outside in the parking lot: there were two cars, but no one was in either. He looked through the windows to see if there was a red laptop sitting there, but his search proved fruitless. No one was outside on the first or second floors.

This was getting tricky.

He glanced back down at his phone. He must have been out of range now: there wasn't anything about a wireless connection on his screen. Interesting.

"Can I see the room next to mine?"

The motel manager pointed to a sign on the counter: "Rooms: $25 a night."

"Great," he mumbled, digging through his pockets. He threw the cash down on the counter, snatched the key out of the wo(?)man's hand, and ran back up to the second floor. He fumbled with the key in the lock, shaking too badly to get it in, and gasped when he heard the *click.*

"Hello?" he said softly, slowly pushing open the door. He didn't want to walk in on anyone naked, assuming someone was in this room. It was a little unsettling to him that the motel owner was completely willing to give serial killers the chance to waltz in and strangle their victims for twenty-five bucks.

He got no response, so he stepped inside.

"Amelia?" he called out again.

The lights weren't even on in this room. There was no way she was here. Still, he flipped them on, holding his breath.

The room was completely empty. The bed hadn't been slept in. The bathroom looked like no one had touched it in years.

He tried to keep his hopes up, even though he knew the hazards of it.

"Can I see the room on the opposite side?" he asked the motel owner. He already had his money ready. She handed him the other key, raising an eyebrow at him.

"Problems with your gal?" she asked.

"Sort of, kind of," he replied, running toward the door.

He didn't take as much time getting the second door open. He stuck the key in the lock without a moment's hesitation and threw the door open.

His heart fell.

The room was dark. He flipped on the lights with a sigh. The bathroom was empty, of course. The bed was clear. He was about to give up when he saw something. On the small table in the corner, there was a bag, half unzipped, with a chord hanging out of it.

He thought his heart was going to burst out of his chest as he walked toward it. He unzipped the rest of the duffel bag —why did everyone on Earth have a duffel bag besides him?— and saw a red laptop, still plugged into the wall.

* * *

He shut the door quietly behind him as he re-entered their room. Jo was sitting cross-legged in the middle of the bed, biting her nails.

"Oh, thank *God*," she said. She let out a relieved sigh and grinned at him. "I'm *so* glad I was wrong about that one, and I hate being wrong. I was really worried that you were going to—hey, are you okay?"

He nodded, leaning against the closed door. His hands were clutching the bag to his chest. Was he okay? No, far from it. He thought he was going to faint, actually.

"What's that?" she asked, climbing off the bed. She tried to pull it away from him, but he refused to let go.

"Okay, fine," she said as she took a step back. "Personal space. I get it."

"I—uh—huh."

"M'kay, right." She walked back to the bed. "Let me know when you start thinking again."

He stepped back outside the room again, looking down at his phone. Maybe it was stupid, but he felt like he should try.

BURNOUT STARS

He always got nervous when he dialed her number. He always felt his throat freeze up, and his brain slow down. This time was no exception; in fact, it was worse. He paced back and forth, hoping he would hear her voice on the other end of the line.

When he heard the familiar *beep* of her voicemail, he let out a sigh. Of course. He couldn't have honestly thought this would work, could he?

"Amelia, I don't know where you are, or what's going on, and I know it's been four months but I—" he tried to swallow the lump in his throat. This was opening up one wound too many. "I'm at this sketchy motel in the middle of nowhere, and I found some of your stuff. So if you ever feel like coming back down to Earth, call me. Bye."

He hung up before he could make even more of a fool out of himself. Running the message over in his head, he started to panic. Did it sound too rushed? Too cold? Too impersonal? Was it really his fault if it sounded bad? She was the one to disappear out of the freaking blue.

He sighed. Why was he even worrying? It wasn't like she would ever hear the message. It had been four months without one phone call, text message, fruit basket, or smoke signal, and Jess had realized that she was never coming back.

She probably had an international phone, so she didn't have to deal with every single person from her old life in Kansas trying to reach her. That made sense. She didn't respond because she couldn't.

It was sad that this was what his life had become: him telling himself lies, fallacies, and exaggerated half-truths in an attempt to make himself feel better. Then again, wasn't that what everyone did? Survival was getting through from day to day, not always telling the perfect truth.

He dialed another number as he examined the key in his hand. He hoped he could get a refund on this.

"Hello, what is your emergency?" said a voice on the other end of the line.

* * *

"Okay, I'm back for real," he said, shutting the door.

"Oh, you left?" she joked.

"Haha," he said as he carefully sat down the gray bag on the table. "I know you missed me."

"Did you finally get yourself a suitable bag?" she asked, looking over it carefully. "You couldn't have picked anything less girly?"

"I called the police," he said, pulling the bag away from her. It was strange how protective he felt of a piece of canvas. It had suddenly become his most important possession, and he couldn't let anyone, not even Jo, bother it.

"Oh," she said. She was chewing on her lip again as she sat back down on the bed, looking at the door nervously. "I guess you had to."

"Yeah," he said. "Just sit tight. It's not a big deal. They're not going to interrogate you if you just sit here."

She nodded.

They stayed in the room for the rest of the night, watching a basketball game, even though he was almost one hundred percent positive that there was nothing he hated more in the world besides *basketball*. At some point during the night, they stopped watching. She stared up at the ceiling and fiddled with her hair. He stared at the same spot, listening to her steady breathing. Even though he wanted to believe that they got some sleep during the night, he knew that he was kidding himself.

Around three in the morning, she mumbled, "I want to know what happened to her."

He rolled over onto his side to look at her and said, "This isn't *Pushing Daisies* though. We can't just bring her back to life and ask her what happened."

"But we *could* find out, Jess. We could start off where she left me, and follow in her footsteps."

"Look for clues?" he said, raising an eyebrow.

"Don't make it sound so hokey," she said with a sigh. "I just want to know."

They fell silent again. Jo hummed a few bars next to him. The air conditioning rumbled above them.

"Part of me feels like I should be happy," she said softly. "Like I was finally vindicated. She was a jerk. She left me. It killed me."

She took a deep breath and continued, "But another part of me feels terrible, like whatever happened to her has a huge effect on me. I'm just so *bothered*."

"You found a girl that you knew dead in an ice machine," he reminded her. "You're not supposed to feel warm and fuzzy."

"I know, but—" she flipped over and screamed into her pillow.

He stared at the back of her head, her dark hair sticking out in every direction, and sighed. He put a hand on her shoulder.

"Can I be Freddy in this Scooby adventure?"

* * *

Jo was a force to be reckoned with when she had her mind set on something. She was absolutely impossible to stop when she was like this. She walked into the office of the motel, not slowing down until she was face-to-face with the motel owner.

"Yeah, hi," she said, waving a hand in front of her face. The woman reluctantly looked at her.

"Oh, it's you two. Hey, did you see the po-po here last night?" the woman asked excitedly. "Heard we was on local news!"

"That's great," she sad flatly. "I was actually wondering if you knew what happened to that girl."

"Well, I suspect she's been buried by now," the woman said, scratching her chin.

"No, I mean…"

Jo was visibly growing more and more frustrated. When she got like this, Jess always panicked he was going to have to restrain her, and he really didn't know if he could do that. She looked really strong.

"How did she die?" Jo asked, gritting her teeth.

"Oh, well, I heard she was in the ice machine. You know, I'm really mad about that. Everyone expects me to buy a new one now. Those things is expensive!"

Jo rested her head on the counter. This wasn't going well. Jess moved next to her, just in case.

"Was she stabbed? Was she poisoned? Strangled?"

"Oh, I don't know," the woman said with a shrug. "She was in the ice machine."

"Yeah, but the ice machine didn't kill her," Jess said.

"Could of!" the woman said. "Might of fallen in and hit her head!"

"M'kay, well," Jo said, pulling back from the counter. "If you hear anything, let us know."

She left the office so quickly that Jess stumbled a few times trying to catch up with her. Once they were in the parking lot, Jo let out a scream of frustration.

"What has my life become?" she moaned.

"I think it's probably always been like this," Jess said smartly.

"I miss my car," she whined.

"I missed breakfast."

She groaned, grabbed his shirt sleeve, and dragged him into town.

* * *

"Washing machines are calming," he said, leaning against a dryer.

"And noisy," Jo said with a smile. "Laundromats are awesome."

"Except for the sketchy people."

So far today, he had seen three almost muggings, four homeless men, and two guys that had to be dealing drugs. And to think: they had just had lunch.

"I like the sketchy people," Jo said. She was sitting on top of a dryer, her legs crossed. "They're colorful."

"Their knowledge base of murder is colorful," he replied. "I'm not surprised that girl was killed. If you weren't so mean, you probably would be dead by now too."

"Thank you, thank you," she said with half a bow. "I have worked very hard to cultivate this fierce, angsty image of an empowered young woman who can kill you in your sleep."

"You've definitely done a good job. Once anyone gets to know you though, they find out that you're not that scary."

She crossed her arms and glared at him. He had gone from finding it frightening to finding it slightly endearing.

"Oh, so I'm just a big pussy cat, hmm?"

"Maybe an old pussy cat. You know, one that attacks you out of nowhere because it's ticked off at the world."

She smiled. "That sounds just about right."

"Hey, how do you think we'll find this girl?" he asked. "Do you even know her name?"

She hesitated as she said, "Kind of? I never really believed her. It was one of those names that sounded too good to be true."

"Like Treeflower?" he joked. She smirked.

"Not quite. It was such a rich girl name, like part of me thinks she probably made it up."

"What was it?" he asked, playing with their spare change.

"Amelia," she said, rolling her eyes. "Talk about names that evoke images of girls at tea parties, right?"

He thought his heart stopped.

Jo

"Okay, okay, this is so not good," she said, staring at his body sprawled out on the floor. She snapped in his face—no change.

"So, so, so, so, *so* not good," she mumbled. She shook his shoulders. Hadn't she seen something like this on television before? Then again, she didn't really watch much television. She wasn't sure she had learned any life lessons from it. Do people wake up on their own after fainting, or do they need special medical attention?

She stared down at his face.

"Uhhhhhhhhhhh."

She glanced around the laundry mat.

"Hello?" she called out. She had sworn there was someone else in there earlier. "I could really use some help!"

A figure in an overcoat emerged from behind one of the washing machines. Thank you, higher powers.

"Hi, my friend fainted," she said, feeling stupid. Wasn't that obvious? Duh, he fainted. He didn't fall asleep standing up. "I don't really know what to do."

"Did you try slapping him?" the guy asked.

"What?" Jo said, face scrunching up in confusion. Was he serious? Was that a legitimate way to get someone to "come to?" It didn't seem right.

"Slapping them works sometimes," the guy said. "Well, it does on TV."

That was good enough for her. It seemed like most people got through life with help from life lessons learned from *Full House* and *The Brady Bunch*, or whatever else was airing these days. She didn't really know. She just wasn't up to date on these things. Technology wasn't her thing. Neither was medical knowledge, apparently.

"I guess I can try," she mumbled, staring at Jess' face. He really wasn't that bad looking when he wasn't tripping over his own words.

"Sorry, bud!" she said before she slapped him clear across the face.

"Mmm huh?" Jess mumbled, slowly opening his eyes.

"Oh, thank God," Jo said, exhaling. "Don't ever do that again. I almost crapped my pants when I saw you going down."

"Wait, what happened?" Jess asked.

"You fainted. No idea why."

"What were we even talking about?"

He was grabbing his head. Was that bad? Did he hit his head? Was this going to lead to a concussion? She was definitely panicking. She made a mental note to pick up one of those *For Dummies* books on everyday disasters. She didn't know if there was one, but it seemed like there was one for just about everything by now.

"Dead girl," she responded. "You wanted to know her name. I told you. You passed out. Probably from the sheer stupidness of a name like that. All little girls should be named Jo, I know, I know."

Jess looked absolutely awful, and she had a suspicion that it was caused by more than just fainting in a dirty laundromat.

"Are you okay?" she asked, trying her best not to keep talking.

"I—uh—I don't really know," he said honestly, rubbing his temples.

"Did you hit your head?"

"Worried about me, huh?" he said with a grin. She had to resist the urge to slap him again.

"I'm fine physically," he said.

"Only physically?"

"For the time being."

He looked so uncomfortable at the moment, fidgety and so *small*.

"What's wrong, Jess?" she asked. She knew she didn't do the whole sympathy thing very well, but she was trying at least.

"Do you know what that girl's last name was?" he asked. He looked so serious.

"No, I don't. We were never really that close. She whined about her dad a lot. Then she left. That was the extent of our beautiful friendship."

Jess looked like he was thinking. She didn't understand what the big deal was. She just wanted to know how she died. Was she hit by a car? Poisoned by something at a diner?

"What did she look like?" he asked.

"Redish wavy hair, curvy, air of superiority?" she offered. She hadn't known her for very long. She didn't commit the girl to memory, really.

"Oh my God," Jess mumbled, running a hand over his face. "This isn't happening."

"I don't know what 'this' is, but it's probably happening."

"I knew her, I think," he said.

"*What*?!" she shrieked, grabbing the attention of the guy who had helped her earlier. He poked his head around a washing machine, saw Jess conscious, and gave her a thumbs up. She heard the door open and wondered if he was heading home to learn more medical knowledge from whatever was on TV.

"Yeah, she was my....well, my neighbor."

She wasn't a person who believed in fate or destiny, but this was pretty creepy.

"And?" she asked, raising an eyebrow. He blushed. That was what she thought.

"She was in my class," he said.

"And?"

He sighed.

"You were totally in love with her, weren't you?"

"Maybe," he said, looking even more uncomfortable than before.

"I see, I see," she said. "Well, isn't this a 'Small World' moment."

"Haha," he said as he finally got off the floor. He brushed off his pants and sighed. "So you didn't like her, huh?"

She shrugged. "Like you said, I don't really like people all that much."

"Everyone loved Amelia," he said.

"Let me guess: most popular in high school?"

He nodded.

"Called it. She had seemed like the type who gaged her self-image on what others thought of her."

"She was only like that around everyone else," he mumbled. She had to resist rolling her eyes.

"Look, Jess, people like her always make you think you're special. Then they crush your heart when they leave."

"She was different," he said quietly.

"Whatever you say," she said, seemingly unconvinced.

"Wait," he said, pulling his wallet out of his back pocket. He pulled a picture out and held it up to her face. "This her?"

"God, you keep a picture of her in your wallet? What's wrong with you?" She sighed and grabbed the photo from him. It was definitely her. The only difference was this Amelia was smiling, while the one she had briefly known hadn't smiled once. She was always complaining. When she left, Jo was upset because she was alone again, not because she had enjoyed the girl's company one bit. Still, she felt obligated to figure out what happened to her. She might have been the last person to ever speak to her.

She shuddered.

"Yeah, that's her."

"Are you positive?" Jess asked, looking nervous.

"Yeah." She paused and then added, "Sorry."

He nodded. He was staring at his feet, and it was enough to make Jo feel guilty.

"You're not going to go all suicidal on me, right?" she asked jokingly. "You'll be alright?"

"I just...I was hoping she was still alive. People disappear all the time, rarely turning back up, but the people who knew them always get by by living in denial. It's sort of like what you said about the stars: people will do anything to live."

He gave a fake laugh, and she felt something in her chest again. The two of them weren't really that different at all. He did get her, even if he wasn't one hundred percent sure of it.

"We'll figure out what happened to her," she said in her best reassuring voice. She was sure it didn't sound that convincing, but she was working on the whole sympathy thing.

Baby steps.

* * *

When the motel owner saw them enter, she shouted out, "You two *again?*"

"I feel so very welcome," Jess mumbled under his breath. Jo ignored him, walking up to the counter and handing the woman a picture.

"Oh yeah, she was here," the woman said.

"How long ago?" Jess asked.

"A couple of weeks?" the woman offered, not sounding particularly sure herself. Jo glanced at the computer screen then looked away again. She wasn't foolish enough to think it was actually used for actually keeping track of reservations. It probably was only used for solitaire and illegal downloads.

"Was she with anyone?" she asked, and the woman feverishly nodded. Jo raised her eyebrows at Jess, who looked like he was going to puke. He must have had one heck of a crush.

"Had to be about your age," the woman said, tilting her head towards Jess. "Dark hair, tan skin, weird beard."

Well, that narrowed the search down to all of the males in the population, along with the women with facial hair.

"Anything else?" Jo asked, feeling desperate.

The woman scratched her head.

"Sorry, sweets. It's been too long. They didn't hang around as much as you two folks do."

Jo opened her mouth to ask another question, but Jess quickly put a hand on her shoulder and said, "Thanks for your help."

The motel owner nodded, and Jess walked Jo to the door. She pulled away from him once they were outside.

"I can find my way out of a building, thank you!"

"I have an idea," he said flatly before he started walking off towards their room.

When did he become the one in charge?

"Do you recognize this bag?" he asked when they were back in their room. She squinted at it, waiting for it to unfurl its wonders. When it didn't, she shrugged.

"Not ringing any bells."

"It was Amelia's. She had the room next to us. My phone picked up the wifi connection from her wireless card yesterday morning."

"God, way to leave me in the dark!" she exclaimed, making a grab for the bag. He quickly moved it out of her reach. She rolled her eyes. So he was one of those nostalgic people.

"Oh, that's where you went," she said as she thought back to how paralyzed she felt sitting in the room, stuck staring at the door.

He pulled out the red laptop and hit the power button. When it booted up, she found herself staring at a Juicy Couture desktop. She felt the urge to vomit. Stupid stupid stupid girl.

Jess opened up the internet and loaded Facebook. The log-in box came up, and Jo wondered what his plan was.

He typed in an email and password that she honest to God hoped was not his. *qtpi2256@aim.com* did not seem like a fitting internet personality for him.

"She was my neighbor," he reminded her. "She was at my house all the time: I saw her log in to her email account more times than I can count."

"Got it. Good to know you have a more masculine email address."

Amelia's Facebook homepage informed them that she had 12 new messages, 47 new wall posts, and a million other notifications. Jo had actually never used Facebook before. There was an ad on the side of the page advertising some farming game.

"Why would people want to play a game about a farm?"

Jess blushed. She smirked.

"I hope your little character got to wear a straw hat."

"Shut up," he said, clicking on Amelia's profile. It was what Jo would have expected. There was a picture in the top left hand corner of a cute girl in a bathing suit—no wonder she got herself killed. When Jess scrolled down, she saw a ton of wall posts asking Amelia where she was, what was going on, and if she was going to so-and-so's party Saturday night.

Boring, boring, boring.

Jess brought up a box labeled "Amelia's Friends" and started scrolling through them.

"You're going too fast!" Jo groaned. "I can't see who you're moving past."

"Anyone she didn't know," he replied, scrolling past four shirtless guys.

"But they're her friends," she said, pointing at the box's name. Jess grinned.

"You've never used Facebook, have you, Jo?" he asked, turning around to look at her. She shrugged, crossing her arms.

"I don't have any desire to be a farmer."

"Okay then," he said. "Facebook is forty percent you keeping in touch with people you know, and fifty percent strange people who think you're hot trying to get access to your profile and your pants."

"And the other ten percent?"

"Is you making yourself feel validated."

"I see," she said, leaning over his shoulder to look at the long list of guys. "So it's almost completely pointless then."

"Pretty much."

Jess clicked on a guy named Scott.

The picture in the corner seemed to match the motel's owner crappy description; he even had a strange looking goatee.

"Think that's him?" Jo asked, looking at Jess' face. He looked *angry.* It was bizarre. She was used to passive Jess, who seemed okay with everything.

"They dated back in high school," he said, and Jo could hear the hatred in his voice.

"What's that?" she asked, pointing at some text at the top of the page.

"His status."

*"**Scott Lansing** mexico loosers!"*

"Did he fail 9ᵗʰ grade English?" she asked, more for Jess' benefit than her own. He cracked a smile, and it was enough of a reward for her. It was strange how badly she wanted him to smile. Usually she didn't give a crap if the people she was traveling with were happy or not.

It must have been because she knew this was different. Even though there was still the risk of it, she had a feeling he wasn't leaving anytime soon. No one else really understood why she did the crazy things she did. They assumed she just liked wasting money on gas and taking long road trips. Jess actually got it; he even understood the stars. That's why she felt so desperate to make him happy. Even though she hated to admit it, she liked the guy. He was actually becoming her friend.

"So I guess we're going to Mexico," she said a few minutes later when he appeared to be frozen to the spot, stuck staring at Scott's shirtless profile picture.

He looked up at her, looking more surprised than what was necessary, and said, "Yeah, guess so."

* * *

The next day she showed up at the repair shop at opening. However, like the low lives the workers in this town were, no one showed up until noon, and by then, she was absolutely *raging*.

"Just calm down," Jess said. She let out a scream of frustration as she kicked over a tower of tires.

"Okay, okay," he said, grabbing her by the shoulders. "Just breathe."

"Just *breathe?!*" she shrieked. "This is my car we're talking about! It's practically my house! Some girls have walk-in closets filled with shoes; I have my car with its piles of CDs and ripped backseat. I *love* my ripped backseat, Jess!"

She groaned, hanging her head. This sucked more with each passing day.

"I know, Jo, seriously, I do." He gave her shoulders a squeeze, and she reluctantly looked back up at him. "But you just have to accept the fact that it will get fixed eventually. Things will get back to normal for you. These guys will eventually die and rot, and their horrible shop will probably go under in the recession."

Even though she tried not to, she smirked. Just a little bit.

"Aha!" he said with a grin. "I saw that!"

"You didn't see anything," she said, quickly frowning again. "You're blind. Delusional. All of this diner food is making you hallucinate."

"Whatever you say," he said, still grinning.

"Stop," she said with a frown, pulling away from him. She sat down on the curb, and he quickly followed her.

"Stop what?" He grinned bigger.

"That. Stop that," she said, pointing at this smile.

"I have absolutely no idea what you're talking about."

"You did *not* make me feel better. Don't get that idea in your head."

"Whatever you say," he said, putting an arm around her shoulders. She shrugged it off. He put it back.

* * *

"How hard is it to get anything done around here?!"

"Jo," Jess said calmly, reaching out to her. She smacked his hand. He took three steps backwards.

"You incompetent idiots!" she screamed. The worker was staring at her, looking uninterested. He must get this kind of reaction a lot in order to be completely immune to it.

"I mean, really," she said, continuing her tirade. "It's been a week. Maybe even longer. I've lost track of time because I've been stuck in this wasteland, festering in *Hell*. I know you're angry at the world because you're stuck here too, but you could at least help a brother out by getting us out of this hole."

The guy looked off toward the horizon. Jess looked worried, and he had good reason to be. She was positive that any minute she was going to punch this guy. She might not look strong, but she had three times the typical girly upper body strength. She was contemplating which eye would be better to hit when she heard Jess' stupid voice.

"How long is her car going to take to get fixed?"

The worker shrugged.

"I don't know, man. Could be today. Could be next week."

The next time he opened his mouth, he was on the floor, clutching his left eye. The left one had just seemed better. She hated punching things that were directly in front of her. It always felt wrong. The left eye offered a better stretch for her arm.

Jess was absolutely freaking out, with both hands clutching her arms, holding her back from the sorry mass of a human on the ground.

"So you'll have it done today, right?" she asked cooly, lifting an eyebrow.

The man nodded.

"That's what I thought. Come on, Jess."

Jess

Jo had definitely gotten inside his head. As he watched the landscape change outside the car window, he realized how *right* this felt. Being on the road was the best thing he could imagine. It wasn't the same as family road trips that resulted in arguments and motion sickness. This felt like an amazing dream that he never wanted to wake up from.

"Have you ever been to Mexico before?" he asked her. She seemed much more at peace now that she had her car back. The scene back at the repair shop that morning had been enough to jump start the repair staff. Her car was ready a few hours later.

"Yeah, a couple of times," she said. She changed the song without taking her eyes off the road. Today's music selection was an obscure indie band he had never heard of. Jo had apparently seen them play a gig out in the desert once, which was enough for them to win her heart.

"It's pretty," she said. "But don't drink the tap water."

She shrugged. He couldn't help but wonder how much dirtier things could get. The last motel hadn't exactly been cleaned thoroughly. Shockingly enough, cobwebs and mold didn't really surprise him anymore. It was funny what a difference a few weeks away from home made.

"Is it any worse than what I've already seen?" he asked, half-joking and half-dead serious.

She thought for a few moments and then said, "That's kind of subjective. I'm so used to the grime that I really only notice it in passing, you know? I don't know if walking barefoot on motel carpet still freaks you out or not."

A few weeks ago it definitely did, but now? Not so much.

Geeze, it was like he was a different person.

"Is it hard to drive to Mexico?"

She smiled and said, "You know me: it stinks, but I love it."

You know me. He smiled to himself. She finally believed that he wasn't going to leave, and the strange part was, he no longer wanted to. He wanted things to never change.

"Driving gets so horrible once you cross the border. People walk along the road like there's no way they could ever possibly get hit. Cattle take their dear sweet time walking down the road. It's horrible, but hilarious."

"Do people ever hit the cows?" he asked curiously.

"No idea. They're probably too busy hitting each other." She gasped and then added, "Oh my God and the tolls! They're so horribly expensive. Plus the potholes make the road seem like a thirteen-year-old boy's face."

"Any less of a woman wouldn't have survived those two trips."

She laughed. "God, I know. They don't use headlights down there! Isn't that complete crap? I almost hit a semi the last time I was there because the Einstein decided he wanted to save gas that day—and yeah, you do get better mileage without your headlights on. Who would've thunk it."

"Wait, seriously?"

"Headlights are optional!" She smacked the steering wheel. "Isn't that the dumbest freaking thing you've ever heard? Plus the cops don't really do anything. If you get pulled over, you can bribe them with a couple of bucks. Now that's classy."

He snorted.

"Mexico sounds amazing."

"I love the crazy," she said excitedly. She was grinning from ear to ear, bouncing in her seat a little. She was cute when she was like this.

"Crazy is good," he said, because he knew that he liked her brand of crazy.

* * *

They pulled off around three thirty in the morning because she was falling asleep at the wheel. In order to prevent a *National Lampoon*-esque sleeping-while-driving scenario, they decided it would probably be the best if they stopped for the night.

The only problem was that the area they were driving through was deserted, and not just "deserted" like the last town was deserted. This was truly desolate. He would have jumped for joy at the sight of a motel, but he wasn't that lucky of a guy.

Jo was shoving clothes and bags off of the backseat and onto the floorboards. When she was done, she climbed out of the car. He waited for her to come back, but after five minutes, he started to worry that she was grabbed by some creep.

"Jo?" he called out, scanning the area around the car.

"Roof!" she said joyfully. He looked up and lo-and-behold, there she was, lying on top of the car, staring at the stars.

"Does your astronomy obsession ever interfere with your sleep cycle?" he asked.

"*Please,*" she said. She extended her hand, and he took it, climbing up next to her. "Sleep is for the weak."

"Look!" she said, pointing up at the sky. "There's Cassiopeia."

"How can you tell?" He squinted at the bright dots. They all looked the same to him.

"It's a 'W,'" she said, tracing the outline of it with her finger. "Cassiopeia was the queen of Ethiopia. She was gorgeous and knew that she was, and her vanity eventually led to her daughter being sacrificed to a sea monster."

"That sounds…harsh."

She laughed and said, "Those crazy Greeks liked blood and gore. Her daughter was saved though. Cassiopeia wasn't as lucky. You see, she pissed off Poseidon by bragging about how she was prettier than the sea nymphs. After her daughter lived, Poseidon decided to put her in the sky in a way that she would be upside down for half of the year."

"When did you start loving stars?" he asked her. She subconsciously tried her best to tilt her head while lying down: it was her signature thinking pose.

"I don't know," she said. "I know I did in high school. I'm sure I loved them before that."

He couldn't picture Jo in any kind of institution, being forced to sit still and stay in the same classroom for hours at a time. He hoped for her sake she didn't go to a stuffy private school with uniforms. She probably would have been in prison by now if that had happened—she would have strangled the principal in a fit of rage after being told her skirt wasn't long enough, and she wouldn't have had Jess there to hold her back.

He wondered if she was different now. Maybe it was selfish to think that he had changed her, especially since he wasn't sure that anyone could really *change* Jo. She wouldn't let them. She was too headstrong and too stubborn. Still, he thought she seemed different now than she was when they first met, and he desperately wanted to think he was the cause of that.

"What were you like back then?"

She rolled her eyes. "Boring."

"I doubt that."

"No, trust me. I was just a stubborn girl who wanted nothing to do with education and everything to do with getting out of town. I hadn't seen anything. I had spent my whole life in a small town reading books. I was incredibly boring."

"But you were still you, experiences or not."

"I was different though," she said. "Not really *me* yet. I don't know." She shrugged, lowered her gaze to the horizon, and continued, "It wasn't my shining moment."

"Were you the chick who wrote poetry about death during class?" he asked jokingly.

"Nah, I was a party monster." She paused. "That was a movie."

"With the *Home Alone* kid?"

She frowned and said, "He got ugly."

"I can't see you going to parties. Were you popular?"

"People knew me, I guess," she said. "Some probably thought I was a dealer. I was always on *something.* That's why parties were better when I was around."

Everything seemed better when she was around, but he didn't say that. He didn't want to freak her out. What they had now worked. He didn't want to mess anything up. He *liked* sleeping in creepy motels and hunting down links to his first love by her side.

"What about you?" she asked, elbowing him. "I know you had a major crush on Amelia."

"I was a nobody," he said flatly. "I had a couple of weird friends."

"And spent all your time lusting after Amelia?"

He sighed. "Okay, not the way I was going to phrase it, but pretty much."

He could see her smirk in the dark.

"What do you think happened to her?" he asked quietly.

She hesitated. "Do you want to know my honest opinion?"

He nodded, but then realized she couldn't see it. Feeling stupid, he said, "Yeah."

"Okay," she said, taking a deep breath. "She was probably murdered by this guy. I didn't know her well enough to know that there was anything going on between them, but they probably had a fight. He decided to solve the problem by getting rid of it. The ice machine was just there."

He shivered, falling silent.

"Hey," she said softly, grabbing his hand. She squeezed it. "I could be wrong. We'll figure it all out."

"Hey, Jo?"

She looked over at him, and the way the moonlight lit up her face gave him trouble processing his thoughts.

"I'm really glad I got in your car that one night."

She looked a little embarrassed, biting her lip as she looked away from his face.

"Don't get all sappy on me," she said, and he smiled.

It just had to be said.

"Hey, Jess?" she said later when he was starting to dose off.

"Hmm?"

"I'm glad you did too."

* * *

He woke up the next morning with Jo kicking the back of his seat. He lifted his head off the window pane, wincing at the pain in his neck.

"Rise and shine. Thanks for reclining your seat onto my feet!" she said sarcastically.

"Sorry," he mumbled as he rubbed his neck. He couldn't remember moving inside to her car. When he tried to think back to last night, all that came to mind was an image of the starry sky with Jo's laughter still ringing in his ears.

She let out a yawn, rubbing her eyes.

"I have some food—" She yawned again. "Somewhere."

A box of Cheez-Its and two bottles of water emerged from underneath the back seat.

"How long have they been in here?" he asked hesitantly, and she shrugged. The Cheez-Its didn't show any obvious signs of mold, so he figured they were probably safe to eat.

"Oh, by the way," she said, sitting up and cracking her neck. "We need to find out where exactly this guy is. We're almost to Vegas right now. I can keep driving and go down through Baja, or we can head to Texas and cross the border there. I just need to know."

She yawned again and said, "One of those crossroads in our lives."

He pulled his phone out of his bag and stared at his contacts list. It had been years since he had really talked to anyone from his high school. They probably didn't remember him. They didn't know him back then: why would they know who he was now?

He hit the "call" button and held his breath.

"Jess?" asked a voice from the other end of the line.

"Hey, Kyle," he said, looking over at Jo. She was watching him too closely. It was freaking him out a little. "Are you still in touch with Scott?"

"Scott Lansing? Man, why do you *want to talk to* him?"

Kyle laughed, and Jess sighed. He hated these people. They were horrible to be around back then, and apparently, they still were now.

"Do you know where in Mexico he went?"

The other end of the line fell silent, and Jess wanted to bang his head against the dash. The quicker he got the answer the better. He had no desire to relive all four years of high school in one phone call.

"He's surfing at deserted beaches on the Baja peninsula," he said slowly. Jess could hear the reluctance in his voice.

"Well?" Jo whispered, leaning forward on her seat.

"Baja," he said to her, and to his horror, she let out a loud groan.

"I *HATE* DRIVING ALONG THE BAJA PENINSULA."

"...is that a girl *in the background?"*

"Shut up, Kyle," Jess muttered, watching as Jo jumped out of the backseat, got into the driver's seat, and slammed the door. The whole car shook with the force of her tantrum.

"It's probably your sister," he said with a laugh. Jess hit the "end call" button without another word.

"He sounds like a jerk," Jo noted as she put the car into drive.

"That's because he is," he said. He turned his phone off and hoped he would never have to turn it back on again.

He glanced over at her relaxed state and noticed she looked *calm.* Pleased, even. A smile broke out over his face. She really didn't hate Baja. She just wanted to make Kyle think he had a girl with him. She looked over at him and grinned.

Looking back at the road, she said, "Stop giving me that look."

* * *

Jo wasn't kidding about the roads being horrible. The highway was impossibly narrow and packed with cars. There were bumps that shook her little car so hard that every time they hit one, he thought they had been in a crash. The cars passed so closely that with every lane change he was clutching the seat and leaning toward her, trying to put some distance between himself and the other cars. He hadn't seen any cows yet, but the day was still young.

In every movie he had ever seen involving Mexico, the sun was always blazing in the sky, and the characters were always without air conditioning. While Jo's air conditioning wasn't that great with the windows perpetually rolled down, it was good enough, and she had a handheld fan in the backseat. However, the sun didn't pierce through the clouds once. It was drizzling in the morning, but now they were trapped in a complete downpour. Jo's car wasn't exactly built to withstand strong storms. Her way of dealing with the rain getting in the car was to tape trash bags over the open windows, which, while it looked "trashy enough to make her want to die," was surprisingly affective. He hated how it prevented him from seeing out though. He craned his neck for a chance to see to the right out of the front glass. The cars were so close that he could reach out and touch the driver if he wanted to. He was shocked that it didn't make Jo feel claustrophobic.

"Would you rather be in a big city surrounded by people or in the middle of nowhere?" he asked her curiously.

"It depends," she said, which figured. Everything that came out of Jo's mouth was hinged on ambiguity. "I grew up in the middle of nowhere, and it seemed awful. Looking back though, I wonder if I only hated it because I wanted to see things, and that tiny town was preventing me from doing that.

"I've been to big cities," she continued. "And I like them well enough. I like how fast they are. They're always busy, always alive. I really don't like all the buildings though. I always feel like I'm trapped in a concrete jungle. I really wish there was more of a happy medium, where there's a big city in the middle of a corn field, or something strange like that."

"Big cities make me nervous," he said with a laugh. "I don't know what it is."

"Fear of getting mugged?" she offered, but he didn't think that was it. He obviously didn't want that to happen, but it really didn't cross his mind too often.

"I guess I don't like all the people," he said. "Ironically enough, I am one of the Jo species."

"I don't hate people," she said quietly. "I just hate being let down, and I'm *always* let down. The worst part is I set myself up for it. Like with Amelia? I knew she wouldn't stick around, but I still let her come along with me. Look how well that ended."

"It's not your fault that she's dead, Jo."

"Then why does it feel like it is?"

They fell silent after that.

* * *

When Jo wasn't around—which was rare, so it was more like whenever Jo was asleep—he went through Amelia's things. He couldn't look at them when Jo was awake, watching over his shoulder. There was something about holding her things that felt so private and personal that Jess couldn't bring himself to look into her bag without being alone. He felt like it was his personal duty to preserve her memory and her presence, despite how foolish it was.

Her clothes still smelled like her, even though the scent was intermingled with the smell of mothballs. It still brought back so many memories, even after all these years.

She had a few things in her bag, but they were mostly predictable. He would have guessed that she would have her makeup, her hairbrush, and her iPod along for the trip. There was a pair of Coach sunglasses, which would probably make Jo vomit if she saw them, and her wallet, complete with pictures of her dog and some guy he didn't recognize.

Her laptop was a scary thing. Every time he opened it up, he quickly shut it again. It felt wrong: he felt like he was invading her privacy, even if she was—God, it killed him to think about it—dead and gone.

He knew he was being stupid. If he would look at her files, her internet history, or her email, he could find out so much more about the mystery that always surrounded Amelia.

He closed her laptop once again and put it back in the duffel bag in the backseat. He promised himself that someday he would look at everything, but right now, he didn't really think he could.

* * *

He must have dozed off at some point during the night because he was awakened by Jo screaming "WAKE UP WAKE UP WAKE UP!" at the top of her lungs.

"What? What's happening?"

Were they lost? Were they in a wreck? Did someone steal their hubcaps? Did that really happen in real life or only in movies?

He suddenly felt very awake.

"Morning, sunshine!" she said excitedly. There wasn't any music playing, which struck him as odd.

"How long have I been sleeping?" he mumbled. He was already falling back asleep now that he knew they weren't in eminent danger.

"Too long," she whined. "I'm bored."

He smiled, leaning his head against the headrest.

"I've been trying to stay quiet," she continued. "This is pretty much my version of Hell on Earth, just so you know."

"Oh, trust me, I know," he mumbled as his eyes started drifting closed.

"Wait wait wait wait!"

"Noooo," he said. "Quiet! I'm tired."

"No!"

He was drifting back to sleep after a few seconds.

Then the tapping started.

"Hey," she said, poking his shoulder. "Hey, you. Wakey wakey!"

"Shut up," he moaned, smacking her hand away.

"Noooo, Jess! Jess! I'm so bored. Come on!"

He had no idea how he managed to fall back asleep with Jo freaking out like she was, but the next time he woke up the sun was straight overhead, and Jo was angry.

"About time," she mumbled, eyes fixed on the road.

"Don't hate me. I don't sleep much anymore."

"Hung up on Amelia?" she asked softly, and he nodded. He couldn't tell if he liked or hated how well she could read him. "At least you weren't the one who found her. I think I almost peed in my pants when I saw a hand sticking out of the ice."

Jo made him feel all mixed up. When she was around, everything he felt or thought was met with an opposing emotion, and it was really frustrating. He felt like he was always against himself these days. While part of him was glad that he didn't find his long lost love dead inside an ice machine, he also wished that he had just so Jo didn't have to go through it. She had been such a mess that night. Seeing someone that always put on a strong face suddenly so

108

distraught was terrifying for him. If she could crumble like that, what was holding him together?

"I guess," he said, which didn't sound convincing in the least.

"We should get tacos," she said about an hour later. "I'm starving."

"I have those Cheez-Its somewhere," he said, glancing around.

"I'm pretty sure they've been in here since '08. I want something that was made in this decade, at least."

He shuddered. He had eaten them.

At some point along the way in their journey, Jo had given up her no lunch rule. The café that they chose looked surprisingly clean, but it wasn't until he saw a waitress heading their way that he realized they had overlooked a huge, significant detail.

"I don't speak Spanish," he said alarmingly, looking at her like a deer in headlights. Her face mirrored his.

"You couldn't have told me this earlier?" She whispered conspiratorially, leaning across the table.

"You don't know Spanish? You know *everything!*"

"Yeah, and don't you forget it!" she said, sitting back against the seat, pleased with herself. Then she looked up at him. "Wait, what were we fighting about again?"

The waitress was at their table now, saying something in Spanish. Jess looked at Jo nervously, and she bit her lip. This detour was going *so* well.

"Um, sí," Jo said, and Jess wanted to hit his head against the table: they were so screwed.

"Quiero tacos," he chimed in with what he had learned from Taco Bell commercials. There wasn't a crazy dog around, but he would have to do.

The waitress didn't look too thrilled with them, and he had absolutely no idea what she was saying. He was positive that Jo didn't either, but she was still saying "Dos? Sí? Sí?" in a failing attempt to get through this. When the waitress finally walked away, he let out a sigh of relief.

"Oh my God," she moaned, resting her head on the table. "That was so horrible."

"I feel like I'm trapped in my high school Spanish class again, only this time I can't leave after half an hour," he said.

"We need to get a *500 Helpful Phrases to Make Sure You Don't Get Killed in Mexico* book stat," she said.

"I hope it's next to the hippie naming book."

When their tacos arrived, he realized they were going to have a lot of problems in Mexico. There were at least twenty tacos on their table, if not more. Jo stared in awe of the spread in front of them.

"I thought you said 'dos,'" he said.

"I guess they changed the meaning of 'dos' from two to twenty five," she said flatly, picking up a taco.

All of them looked different. Some were definitely beef. He thought that maybe some were fish, but he couldn't really tell what the mysterious meat was without eating it.

"So what's the verdict on meat in Mexican cafés?" he asked.

"What?"

She gave him a weird look.

"No meat in shifty diners first thing in the morning," he dutifully recited. "What about Mexican cafés mid-afternoon?"

She tilted her head to the left slightly as she chewed her taco.

"I figure you're not going to get out of Mexico without getting explosive diarrhea," she replied.

Was that supposed to make him feel better? He looked down at the tacos suspiciously. This didn't seem promising.

"You can avoid the tap water and try not to eat chicken for fear of salmonella, but it doesn't really make a difference in the end." She tilted her again and added, "Well, I guess it can make the difference of a day off from work versus a week spent in the hospital, but either way, you're going to be crapping your pants."

"I'm so glad we're having this conversation over lunch," he said.

He didn't think his sarcasm was really as convincing as hers, especially since it always made her laugh *at* him.

"You brought it up!" she exclaimed. "This wasn't my idea!"

"I still don't know if they're safe to eat," he whined, poking at one.

"I'm eating one!" she said, waving it in front of his face.

"I know, but I'm convinced you're immortal. I don't know how else you would have survived so many months on the road. Aren't there statistics about how much time one spends in a car versus how many wrecks he has?"

"There's also a study that says most accidents happen within ten minutes of your home," she said. "But I don't have a home, so I guess that's why I've never had an accident."

"Interesting." He glanced down at the tacos and then added, "So are they safe to eat?"

Jo

"So what *are* we going to do about this language barrier?" he asked.

Her car hit another pothole, causing Jess to swear and grip the seat. He was so jumpy compared to her, who hardly flinched with each break in the road. The holes were everywhere: she had stopped acting surprised hours ago.

"What *are* we going to do about the fact that we don't really know where this kid is?" she said, mimicking his tone. He groaned; she laughed. She liked giving him a hard time. He was cute when he was frustrated.

"Wing it," he said simply.

"Wing it," she repeated. Then she added, "Actually, there might be a Spanish phrase book in my trunk if we're really lucky."

She didn't count herself as a lucky person, but she didn't see herself as necessarily unlucky either. Some things went wrong, like finding dead chicks stuffed in ice machines and being stranded in a town for a week without a car, but some things went right. She was free, after all. The good tended to balance out the bad in her life. Rather than being incredibly lucky or horrifically unlucky, she was just…neutral.

"He's most likely in Tijuana if he drove," she said.

"Are we heading that way?"

"Yup."

There was really only one road through the Baja peninsula, Mex 1, and it was awful. It zigzagged back and forth the whole way through, and Jo hated how hard she had to focus on driving. Driving was supposed to be peaceful, not overwrought with fear of running off into the prickly, cactus-filled desert.

She stopped at the first store she saw to stock up on supplies. She couldn't remember the last time she bought anything besides diner food, so she figured it was probably about time she made a supply run. Inside the store, she grabbed a cheap tent, two sleeping bags, and too many water bottles for her to carry.

"Jess?" she called out. Looking over the top of a shelf, she saw him looking at the back of a book. "Are you ready?"

"Oh," he said when he finally looked up. "They have some Spanish books over there."

She rolled her eyes as he took the water from her.

"I'm a big girl."

"You were going to drop them!" he protested.

"Was not."

"Was too."

"Was not."

"Was too. Do you know if you have that Spanish book in your car?"

"We should just get one," she said, then lugged her items over to the cash register. She turned around and pointed a finger at him. "And was not."

The store was incredibly hot. The doors were propped open, letting bugs and heat inside the small space. There was a rickety old fan sitting on the counter with the cash register, but it wasn't doing much to help with the heat.

"Summer in Mexico sucks," Jess noted, positioning himself in front of the fan.

The cashier rung up their purchases and gestured to their total on the small screen, rather than wasting his time trying to communicate with them. It was great to see that some people still had sympathy toward failed Spanish class students.

"What's the tent for?" Jess asked when they were back in the car.

"Just planning ahead," she said. She tied up her hair into a high ponytail. When she turned around, she noticed him staring. He looked away immediately, and she was about to make a snide remark when she thought better of it. He had probably just zoned out for a minute, no big deal.

"How long until we get to Tijuana?" Jess asked.

"Don't tell me you're getting impatient already!" she joked, throwing a smile his way.

"Can we have a sing-a-long?" he asked. She had no idea if he was serious or not, but she really didn't want to take the chance to find out.

"Not on your life."

* * *

They stopped at the first beach they saw on the outskirts of Tijuana. The sun was beating down on their faces through the windshield of her car, and the smell of the ocean permeated the space inside. The beach was a bit of a walk from where she had parked, but as she pointed out when they started hiking, they needed the exercise: diner food didn't exactly promote healthy living. The second the ocean was in full view, Jess let out a surprised "wow."

She turned her head to look at the crazy smile on his face. "Never been to the beach before?" she asked. He shook his head, still staring straight ahead in awe.

"In pictures," he said. "But I guess that doesn't really count."

"Well, don't hold back then," she said, gesturing toward the beach. "Let loose! Run wild! Go frolic in the sea!"

He looked from her to the ocean and then finally, with a childlike air of splendor, darted towards the ocean. He stopped before the water touched him, standing awkwardly at the point where the water met the sand.

"Go on!" she called out to him. He threw his shoes and a grin over his shoulder, tentatively taking a step into the water. She watched him carefully as she weighed things out in her mind.

Her emotions were her worst enemy. She grew tired of constantly being let down, constantly feeling like she wasn't good enough. She had spent years trying to build a wall around her heart, but it seemed like the fortress was destroyed by raindrops—never mind a cannonball. Watching him with brown eyes, she felt a flutter of something in her chest that she very much did not want to feel, not again. She wanted to stop staring at him and how adorable he looked as he made his first foray into the ocean, so she looked up and down the beach for signs of life. There were a few deserted camp sites and forgotten souvenirs littering the sand. There was a scuba mask half-buried in the sand near her feet and a broken fishing pole near Jess. The beach looked like a picture that belonged on the front of an overpriced "Wish You Were Here!" postcard.

Far up the left side of the beach, there was someone moving. She practically jumped with excitement. She flew toward Jess, not bothering to take off her tennis shoes. Her fingers curled around his arm, and he looked at her expectantly, probably thinking there was a shark in the water. She pointed toward the figure.

"Look!" she cheered, bouncing on her heels. She was awkwardly balanced on the sand, his arm the only thing keeping her from sprawling into the ocean. It was weird, this feeling: somehow she knew he wasn't going to let her fall.

"Is that…" he said slowly. "A person?"

"Yes!" she squealed. She couldn't help it. It was getting exciting now. They were done with the training wheels: this was the real deal. They were actually doing this, investigating murders, playing private eye. Hopefully, they had their first suspect.

"Maybe he'll know something about Scott," she said. He looked pretty uncertain, but in all fairness, he wore that look two thirds of the time.

He carefully pushed her back onto dry land as he walked out of the ocean. He cast a forlorn look toward the water the second he was back on the sand.

"I can't believe you've never seen the ocean before."

"I grew up in the middle of farmland. There isn't a whole lot of beaches." He glanced at the man on the beach and then added, "Now, what are we doing?"

She rolled her eyes. Sometimes she couldn't tell if he played dumb or if he was just plain stupid.

"Okay, listen closely," she said slowly, just in case it was the latter—she doubted it, but that wasn't the point. "We're going to ask that nice man if he has seen Scott around here. If it's a yes, we have a trail to follow. If it's a no, we go to the next beach."

He looked back at the ocean and said quietly, "But I like this one."

"But if Scott wasn't here, there's not really a point in us being here," she said.

He pouted, looking out at the sea. He was like a kid sometimes. She half expected him to stomp his feet and to demand to play longer.

She started walking toward the man. Sand was in her shoes, and more poured in with every step she took. She had always been amazed by how such little specks could cause so much discomfort.

"Wait, wait, wait," Jess said, grabbing her arm and spinning her around to face him. She looked up into his face and *felt* something again in her chest. It was starting to scare her a little. Usually when she started to feel this attached to something, whether it be a cute town or an appetizing diner, she ran. It didn't make sense for her to get too invested in it; it would all end eventually. She hated how she was slowly letting more of her guard down with each passing day. The walls of her fortress were crumbling, and no one was bothering to rebuild them.

When it came down to it, Jo was a masochist, for no matter how many times she tried not to, she always sacrificed her heart for a chance to live.

"What are we going to do about our language barrier issue?" he whispered.

Hadn't they already discussed this? What was wrong with his brain? She could have sworn he was awake during that conversation.

"I told you this already," she said simply as she attempted to turn back toward the stranger. He refused to let go of her, which wasn't so much cute as it was infuriating.

"Jess," she growled. "Let go of me."

"We're not going to be able to talk to this guy!" he reasoned.

She hated reason. Reason and logic seemed like worthless inventions that—while they served their purpose for making sure no one died doing something stupid—were constantly insisting what things people could and could not do. Jo hated boundaries, and hated feeling trapped. She hated people who tried to tell her she couldn't do what she wanted.

"We'll be fine," she said when she finally broke away from him. The guy was already walking their way, so meeting him halfway wasn't hard. Jess lagged behind her, watching the suds that formed with every wave crashing against the shore.

"Hola," she said, and the guy looked the two of them over. She hoped he wasn't one of those drug dealing kidnappers that were always talked about on the news.

The guy didn't look very menacing. He must have figured out they needed something from him because he stopped in his tracks, waiting for her to speak.

"Uh… we," she said, gesturing the two of them. She really shouldn't have slept through all of those Spanish classes back in high school. What was "we" in Spanish again? "Nosotros… are looking for our amigo."

Jess snorted behind her. She glared at him over her shoulder.

"What does he look like?" the guy asked.

And she wanted to die.

"You speak English," she said flatly. The guy nodded. "You couldn't have said something *before* I made a fool out of myself?"

The man smiled, and she had seen that smug look one too many times. She could see Jess out of the corner of her eye, still watching the ocean. One thing that she really liked about him was that even when he was right about something, he didn't gloat. The vindication didn't surround him like an aura, intoxicating everyone who came near him. He took his small victories and stashed them away inside himself for times when he needed the happiness, and she appreciated that.

"I just wanted to see how well a lovely señorita like yourself could speak," the man said, practically oozing with overconfidence. His brown hair almost matched his tan skin, his jeans stopped above his ankles, and his white shirt was stained with sweat.

Jess looked up from the ocean then, over at the man, and then at her. She couldn't tell if she felt excited or nauseated, but the feeling was definitely new.

"Not very well, obviously," she said. She shot a look at Jess, who quickly appeared at her side, standing a *bit* too close. "Like I said, we're looking for someone."

Jess pulled out a picture, one he had magically come up with during the night, out of his back pocket and held it out to the guy. His grip was tight, and his face was serious, a complete 180 from the kid who had been playing in the ocean a minute ago.

"Oh, yeah," the man said immediately. "I know him. He used to surf out here."

"Used to?" Jo said before she let herself get excited. She could see Jess about to jump up and down with joy, so she had to do *something* to avoid that public embarrassment.

"Yeah, he got into some trouble with la policía," the man said, rubbing the back of his neck. Jo slowly turned her head to look at Jess, praying that he wasn't going to hyperventilate. Finding out that some jerk you hated in high school killed your one true love was one of the biggest slaps in the face she could imagine.

Jess' voice shook as he asked, "What happened?"

"I dunno, man. He went to the police station less than a week ago and never came back."

"Where is it?" she asked. The guy scratched his beard, then grinned mischievously.

Her bad feeling senses were tingling.

"I can show you, señorita," he said, and maybe she was hallucinating because of the heat, but she could have *sworn* she saw Jess visibly tense.

They walked back to her car, where the trouble really started. The guy—Ricardo, he said—decided he wanted to ride shotgun. One look at Jess' face, and she knew they were in for a fun ride.

She imagined Jess as the whiney, loser kid who was thrown into trash cans in high school, mainly because he didn't seem to have one self-respecting bone in his body.

He didn't argue, didn't protest, just accepted himself as excess baggage, and climbed into the backseat. It made her so ridiculously angry. She couldn't even pinpoint what was making her mad: Ricardo, Jess, Jess' refusal to stick up for himself, or Jess' apparent indifference to sitting next to her.

The last thought was too scary for her to dwell on, so she quickly pushed it out of her mind.

She looked down at the front wheel of her car and decided, yup, they were definitely in for some "fun."

"Jo?" Jess asked with his head out of the back window. "Did you see a rat or something?"

She just pointed at her front wheel, or rather, where her front wheel *should* be. She heard a car door open and close somewhere off in the distance, but she didn't process that it belonged to her car until Jess was standing next to her with a hand on her shoulder.

She couldn't tell if she loved or hated how well he understood her and her attachment to her stupid car. Jess made her feel so mixed up inside, and she really, truly hated it. She wasn't sure of anything at all anymore, not of herself, not of her feelings, and certainly not of her utter lack of dependency on anyone. He was slowly but surely erasing her perfectly drawn picture of herself so that he could dip his hands into outrageous colors and sling them onto the canvas.

And she hated it.

"Jerks," she mumbled, not entirely sure who she was addressing as she whirled around and marched toward her trunk. Jess was hanging back as usual, staring at the spot where her tire was before their beach excavation.

"They're fast jerks," he said, sounding more impressed than disgusted, unlike her. When she returned to the front of the car, she pushed him out of the way, getting right to work on getting them moving again.

"Do you need any—"

"No," she said quickly. Loudly. Strongly. She might have been overrun with self doubt and confusion, but one thing she knew she could do was change a stupid tire.

"Okay," Jess said with a smile—a freaking *smile,* like he knew exactly what was running through her mind and was thoroughly amused by it, and she just couldn't *take it.* She needed to run around the block, clear her head, take a long, cold shower, throw herself into that ocean, scream against a pillow, *anything.*

Or maybe she just needed to smile back at him.

* * *

She thought she could probably find someone at the police station who spoke fluent English, or even maybe just disjointed English, but she decided it would probably just be easier if she let their new pal Ricardo take over, considering he was so eager to please.

He immediately started gabbing to the nearest cop, flashing Scott's picture in front of his face, and gesturing wildly. They talked back and forth too quickly and too fluently for her to be able to catch anything, so she opted to nudge Jess with her elbow. He was leaning against the counter at the entrance of the police station, lost in his thoughts.

He nudged her back immediately, a small smile threatening to make its way onto his face.

"Nice job with the tire," he said teasingly. "Not that I'm surprised or anything."

"Wait until you see me wrestle a grizzly bear," she said. "Then you'll be impressed."

She knew he couldn't tell if she was joking or dead serious, and she liked it better that way. At the end of the day, after her vulnerability had reared its ugly head and her emotions were kicked into overdrive, all she really had left was her air of mystery.

"He's back there if you guys want to talk to him."

They both looked up at Ricardo, who was obviously trying to make his best sexy face. She patted him on the back as she walked past, figuring it would give him enough satisfaction to fuel his ego for the rest of the week.

"This would never fly in America," Jess said absentmindedly as they walked down a hallway.

"Oh my God," said a voice the second they came into view. "No way. Jess? Is that you, man?"

Usually in circumstances like these that were bound to be full of reminiscences and nostalgia, she would purposely fade into the background so as not to be a bother, because nothing was more awkward than trying to include someone that was currently in a person's life in a conversation with someone who used to be. However, in this circumstance, she decided it would be better to stay right with Jess, for her freaky Jess senses were telling her he was even more uncomfortable right now than she was.

"Yeah," he said slowly, weighing out his words, not wanting to screw up. It was excruciating to watch. "Um, this is Jo."

Awkward. Awkward awkward awkward. This would have worked out better if he hadn't said anything at all, but she guessed Jess either saw her as the elephant in the room or wanted to deflect the attention off onto her for a second.

"Charmed," Scott said to her, waggling his eyebrows. He looked over at Jess and said, "Is this your sister? She's a lot better looking than you."

"Girlfriend," she said quickly before Jess had a chance to say anything at all. She was praying that he wasn't about to faint behind her, because she really wanted to give him one good memory from this experience, since Scott definitely wasn't it. Besides, nothing stunk more than seeing the guy one hated behind bars and finding out he still had the power to make a person feel like crap.

"No way," Scott said. When Jo tilted her head to the side, he kind of looked like a Ken doll, all plastic and fake with too orange skin. When she looked at Jess, she saw the opposite. He didn't seem all that special at first glance. He didn't look like Chad Michael Murray or Taylor Lautner. His grin was lopsided, and his features didn't really fit his face. However, he was handsome in a unique kind of way. As corny as it sounded in her head, she felt like his personality was what made him stand out. How many people would get into a car with a stranger? How many people would stay?

"Believe what you want," she said with shrug. "How'd you end up in the pokey?"

He rolled his eyes in an overdramatic way that caused his pupils to stick to the ceiling for far too long.

"Cops think I killed a chick. Still waiting for the U.S. cops to come get me, but I think they put me on the back burner. Whatever."

"Amelia?" she said quickly, because she had a feeling if Jess started asking about her, he would endure a horrible rain of criticism from Scott, whose family probably owned four yachts and a beachfront home.

"Yeah," Scott said hesitantly, eyeing the two of carefully. "How do you know about her death? What are you doing here?"

"Not breaking you out, so don't get your hopes too high," she said with a fake smile. She saw Jess smirk out of the corner of her eye.

"Look, Scott, let's make this short and sweet, okay? I've had my tire stolen once today, and I'm half-expecting the rest of them to be gone by the time we get through this."

"Still counting on a girl to do your dirty work for you, huh, Jess?" Scott sneered.

"Scott, are you deaf or just stupid?" she asked flatly, snapping in his face. "I said I don't have time for this crap, so let's get started."

"You said you didn't kill Amelia," Jess said, much to her dismay. Jo wished he would just be quiet and try to keep himself out of trouble.

"Why would I have killed her?" Scott half-shouted, red faced. "She was the one who decided to disappear on *me*. If anyone would want to kill her—"

"It would be you," Jo finished cheerfully. "Because you're mad that your girlfriend left you."

"But I didn't!" he exclaimed, exasperated. His hands were in his hair. It stood up straight, making him look even more mad than he already seemed.

"Then who?" Jess asked.

Scott's eyes narrowed. "How do we know it wasn't you who killed her? You were always trailing after her like a creepazoid stalker."

"Just answer the question, Scott, so I can go get a taco," Jo said with a sigh.

She was getting too old to deal with this crap. Bratty little boys who broke their toys didn't deserve her attention.

Scott was quiet for far too long, and Jo was about to take that as a sign of guilt when Jess put his hands on the bars and said, "I don't think you killed her, Scott."

Scott looked up at him all of the sudden like he was his freaking Messiah.

"Really?" he asked quietly, and Jess nodded.

"You cared about her too much," Jess said, reluctantly.

Scott was looking down at his feet when he said, "Yeah… You did too, man."

Jess nodded, but didn't say much.

"So are you guys trying to figure out what happened?" Scott asked, looking back and forth between the two of them. They both nodded simultaneously, and Scott sneered, "Cute, you two."

"Do you know anything at all?" Jess asked, sounding a little too desperate for her tastes.

Scott glanced down at the hallway before saying, "I have a theory."

"I love theories," she said automatically, linking arms with Jess and leaning toward the bars on Scott's cell.

"She went to Vegas one weekend with some of her friends, and she met this guy there. He always seemed pretty shady to me, man, I don't know."

"Do you know his name?" Jess asked, and Jo chimed in with, "Face? Address? Place of occupation? Favorite bar? Anything?"

"Do you have any paper?"

* * *

When she saw that all four of her wheels were still on her car, she let out a sigh of relief.

"So is this it for Mexico?" Jess asked, climbing into his rightful seat beside her.

"Not quite," she said with a devilish grin. "I have an idea."

She drove back toward the way they came with the sun in her eyes. It was at that perfectly awful position where no amount of opening and closing her visor was going to make a difference. When she stopped the car back where they were an hour ago, Jess gave her a suspicious look.

"What are you doing?" he asked, and she simply smirked as she climbed out of the car and walked back to her trunk. By the time she had the trunk open, Jess was standing next to her, eyeing her carefully. She thrust the sleeping bags into his arms and grabbed the tent, being sure to lock her car as she walked away.

She dropped the tent in the sand and got to work putting it together. Jess stood there stupidly, looking from her to the ocean.

When she was done, she turned around to watch the sun set over the sea.

"I don't get you," Jess said, and she laughed—she didn't really get herself either. "Why did you do this?"

He was looking at her like he wanted a straight answer, rather than just a snappy one liner with a touch of sarcasm. The problem was she didn't think she could give him that.

She wasn't entirely sure how she felt about him, but she knew she did have feelings, even if she had tried to burry them.

She was always slow at this kind of thing: she certainly hadn't just decided that she was heads over heels for this guy. It was the little things, like the way she wanted him to have something good, not just because he deserved it, but because she just wanted him to.

"I like the beach," she said flatly, hoping that would put an end to this conversation that was pushing the boundaries on comfort.

He growled, actually *growled*, her name. She stared at him, a bit taken aback.

"Why do you have to be like this?" he asked. His eyes were boring into hers, and she was as far from comfortable as she could get.

"I just am," she said, and he shook his head feverishly. She looked up at the stars, which were already starting to come out, and thought of how much simpler things were a month ago.

But was simple better?

He sighed and said softly, "Will you answer one question for me? Just one?"

She didn't like the sound of that. It sounded far too much like a trap she didn't want to get caught in. He must have sensed her hesitation, because he looked at her with those big green eyes of his all sad and puppy dog like, and she broke.

"*Fine,*" she said. "Whatever. Ask it. This better not be something emotionally traumatizing for me."

He took a deep breath, and suddenly looking very serious, asked, "Why did you pretend to be my girlfriend?"

Oh *crap*. He must have been a freaking psychology major before he dropped out of college, because this was just too much. She wondered momentarily if there was any point in running away.

"I didn't want him to make you feel worse," she admitted, saying each word slowly. "Because…"

"Because?" he egged on. He looked so impossibly adorable right now that she couldn't even look at him for fear of doing something stupid. She kept her eyes fixed on the ocean, which was getting darker and more mysterious with the impending night.

"Because you don't deserve to endure his crap," she said. "Because you're a good person, and your first reunion with your high school frenemies is supposed to be when you show them how much better you are without them around."

She could see him grinning through the darkness, and she was pretty sure that if she had a mirror, she would see herself blushing.

All of the sudden, out of the darkness, he just *grabbed* her, wrapping his arms around her back and burying his face into her shoulder. She was in a panic. She had absolutely no idea what she was supposed to do. When was the last time she was hugged? Years? Decades? She had no idea, and this was so incredibly unfamiliar and strange.

"You're supposed to hug back," he reminded her, and it suddenly struck her that she had control over her limbs. She awkwardly put her hands on his back, and hoped he couldn't tell how fast her heart was beating right now.

"This got really sappy *really* fast," she said, causing him to laugh.

"Thanks, Jo," he whispered in her ear, and *wow,* her personal bubble wasn't just popped at this point: it was completely obliterated.

She awkwardly nodded against his shoulder, and he finally pulled back, smiling at her sheepishly.

"Sorry about your personal space," he said.

"How do you do that?" she shouted.

"Do what?"

"That... *thing*! That thing where you know what I'm thinking!"

He was smirking at her. Smirking! At her.

"I'm just good," he said.

Jess

He woke up the next morning to the sound of the ocean. When he peaked through the flap of their tent and actually *saw* the sea, he realized he wasn't just dreaming. This was too crazy.

The ocean was warmer than he thought it would be, but he figured it was probably just because of the time of the year.

He looked down the beach. There was no one as far as he could see. It was just him, the sand, and the sea. He would miss this when they left. Twenty one years without even one thought about the ocean, and now he couldn't imagine ever leaving it.

"Having fun?"

He turned around to see Jo, still looking half-asleep. He grinned at her.

"Morning, sunshine."

"Don't get cheeky with me," she said, pointing a finger at him. She stifled a yawn.

"Not a morning person?" he asked.

"I've tried and tried, but I don't think it's in my genetic code."

A wave hit him from behind, and he fell forward into the water. When he finally got back to his feet, she was doubled over in laughter.

"Not funny!" he cried, shaking the water out of his hair.

"You are not a dog!" she said, shielding her face, but not backing away.

"Oh yeah?" he said, splashing her. He was expecting her to shriek and run off, like another girl he knew, but she retaliated immediately, jumping straight into the ocean.

They spent the rest of the day at the beach, which he really wasn't expecting. They had more splash fights than he could count, took turns fishing, and made their own fish tacos. Around sundown she started packing up, and she didn't ask him to help.

He liked to think that he understood her better than he thought, but Jo was a slow process with a steep learning curve. He understood her a bit better every day, but it definitely wasn't something that came all at once.

He didn't really know much about her. He knew she loved obscure bands, snuck out of their motel rooms in the middle of the night to look at the stars, and tilted her head to the side when she was thinking: he only knew what he observed.

He didn't know her whole life story, her favorite color, or her hometown, but he wasn't sure that any of that mattered. Was the past really important if they were moving toward the future?

He didn't think so. Staring out the window as her car rolled down the road, he mulled over the past month. Jo was definitely more open now than she used to be, and he took every conversation of theirs as another small victory, proof that he was doing something right. He loved it when she opened up to him, when she chose to *trust* him. He knew he wasn't all the way there, but he had a feeling that they would get to a point very soon where she stopped hiding her thoughts from him, especially since he was getting so good at predicting her thoughts and reactions these days.

"What are you thinking about?" she asked, a hint of amusement in her voice.

"You," he said simply. He wondered which Jo he'd see in response to that. The Jo he had first met would have made a snappy, sarcastic comment, but the Jo he was seeing lately would probably just look uncomfortable.

She shifted in her seat, focusing too much on the road. He was right yet again.

"You're freaking me out a little," she said, and he laughed.

"I don't *mean* to!" he protested.

"Well, you are, so try to be less creepy," she said.

"Noted," he said. "I will try."

"Seriously though," she said. "You're one step away from spying on me in the shower."

"Oh come on," he said. "I'm far from that. I'm hardly a pervert."

"Yet."

He had no idea why he loved joking with her like this. He guessed he liked to judge her reactions, but he felt like there was probably something more beneath the surface. Maybe he just liked her company; she was definitely a fun person to be around. Maybe he was just grateful because for one of the first times in his life, he wasn't *hurting*. Maybe he just desperately wanted to prove her wrong by showing her that not everyone in this world wanted to hurt her, because that was what she was showing him.

Or maybe it was something else.

He really didn't want to fall for her, because he didn't want to be *that guy.* He didn't want to win her trust and then ruin it by doing something that was driven more by his testosterone than his brain. He just wanted her to trust him, but he couldn't help feeling something more. The thing was it was different than what he felt for Amelia—which he really couldn't explain, and he wasn't sure that he wanted to. He was afraid of the revelations he might have if he read too much into it. With the focus on figuring out who killed Amelia, his thoughts were preoccupied with ideas about murder weapons and police interrogations. His dreams were overrun with games of Clue—it was the mystery man in Oklahoma with the ice machine.

He couldn't help but feel like he should be more distraught over Amelia—poor, dead Amelia. For some reason though, he had spent more time thinking about Jo and trust, rather than his high school fantasies. Maybe Scott was right after all those years; maybe he really didn't love her like Scott loved her. He spent so much time dreaming about Amelia, and now it was certain that none of those dreams would ever come to fruition. Why wasn't he more upset about this?

"I should be more upset about her," he said softly. Jo glanced at his slumped figure and then back at the road.

"She had been gone for awhile. You can't tell me that you didn't think at least once that she had bitten the dust."

"I… I…"

He had thought she had gone to Paris, or London, or Harajuku. But hadn't he spent the vast majority of the year living in denial, telling himself that she was fine and happy? That was why he drunk himself into a coma every night: denial.

"God, my life was depressing before this," he mumbled, and Jo laughed.

"Guess it's a good thing I came along, huh?"

"Yeah, no joke," he said. "I'm glad."

* * *

They stopped at a gas station after a few hours because he was pretty sure his bladder was going to burst if they didn't. He kept squirming in his seat, thinking about UTIs, weak elderly bladders, and those commercials with the leaky pipe people.

"*Jooooooo,*" he whined.

"No."

"But—"

"No."

"Please?"

"No."

"Pwetty pwease, Jo? My favoritest cuppy-cake in the whole wide world?"

"I'm going to kill you if you ever say that again," she had said, pulling off the road.

The car hadn't even come to a complete stop before he jumped out, which he figured was probably a safety violation, but he really didn't care at that very minute.

Gas stations were all the same, much like diners and bars: unhappy cashiers that hated their lives, shelves full of food that lead to childhood obesity, and bathrooms where every surface was wet and toilet paper was a foreign idea.

"I need a shower," he announced the second he came out of the filthy restroom. Jo ignored him, or at least, pretended to. She bought trail mix and granola bars, which gave him an interesting image of her as a soccer mom. The idea was horribly flawed, filled with cracks that let the light of reality in. He didn't think Jo would ever be caught dead watching a soccer game. He also didn't see Jo ever having kids.

"You would probably kill them," he said out loud. She turned around to stare at him, and he nervously laughed, wondering what was wrong with him.

It was true though. Jo would probably freak out the first time she found out she couldn't shove a newborn in the front seat of her car, and even if she made it past that part, she would probably forget to feed it. Him, he meant, or her. Whichever sex the baby decided to be.

God, why was he even thinking about this?

"Do you ever think of really weird, inappropriate things?" he asked when they were back in the car.

"Please don't tell me you were undressing me with your eyes," she said.

And with that, he decided to drop the conversation, because he really didn't want to explain to Jo why he was picturing her at a soccer game with children who made her Mother's Day cards out of macaroni.

Instead, he decided to do the unthinkable. He pulled out Amelia's laptop, and turned it on. Over the past few hours, he had realized that she died a long, *long* time ago. The Amelia he knew was long gone, even when she was still alive. She had been replaced by a hollow shell of her old self that was pretty to look at, but had nothing beneath the surface.

He pulled up the menu and stared at the different folders. He clicked on the pictures folder, deciding that would probably be the safest. It was what everyone's picture folder looked like: a ton of pictures taken on Photobooth with tacky effects, pictures from vacations, and a few with her friends. Nothing too exciting. He clicked around for a bit before finding a picture of a group of people that he didn't recognize, standing outside a casino. Amelia was off to the right in a short, red dress. Scott was on one side of her, and a guy he hadn't seen before was on the other. The other people must have been friends of theirs that he never had the pleasure of meeting. There were tall, slim girls in skirts and handsome looking guys, the typical crowd she hung around.

"I wish we knew what this guy looked like," he said, examining the guys in the picture. If only pictures could talk, he would know all the answers. He looked the guy on the other side of her right in the eye and telepathically drilled him. *How well did you know her? When did you last see her? Did you kill her? Did you love her? Did you know she only ate the orange jelly bears out of the package because she said they were the unloved ones? Did you know she never left the house on Friday the 13th, even if she had a math test that was worth half of her grade?*

Jo probably hated orange jelly bears.

No matter how hard he tried, he couldn't stop comparing the two of them in his mind. It was horrible, he knew, and unfair to the both of them. It was unfair to him. Still, he couldn't stop. He would lie awake at night and think about how even though Jo wore skirts, she wore different ones than Amelia, who liked flowy, floral printed pieces of fabric. Even though Jo knew she was beautiful and used that her advantage, she didn't use it the same way that Amelia did, to attract everyone's attention and bend them to her will. Jo used her assets in stride, saving them for dire situations like when they ran out of cash or when the motel didn't have any vacancies.

The worst part was that he didn't know why he did it. It wasn't as if he was trying to choose between the two of them. He was pretty sure he couldn't have either of them—well, he *knew* he couldn't have Amelia, but he didn't see Jo as an obtainable girl. She was completely out of his league.

And he didn't really want to *obtain* her. He didn't think anyone could have Jo. She was too wild, too free. He didn't think she would ever allow herself to feel like she belonged to anyone, and she shouldn't. It didn't fit her.

"Yeah, that would help," she said, breaking him out his thoughts. "We'll just ask around. Someone always knows something, even if they don't let on about it."

* * *

Vegas was prettier than it looked on television. He had only seen it before in movies, and the cameras could never capture the exact feel of a city like this one. Music was flowing into the car through the open windows. People were laughing and dancing—they were everywhere. The lights and the colors burned his eyes against the dark sky, but he didn't mind. It reminded him of sun on his face. The air smelled like smoke and pollution, but he couldn't get enough of it.

"This is *awesome,*" he said, half-hanging out of the window. This was a million times better than he had imagined it would be. He was overwhelmed by the burning passion he felt inside when he thought about how great it was to be alive.

He was glad Amelia had seen this before it all ended for her. She had experienced more of the world than he had, but she ended up in an ice box for it. He was sure that there was some kind of twisted lesson about karma in her story, but he couldn't be bothered to think about it when he was trying to read all of the signs passing by his window.

"You haven't been to Vegas before?" she asked, always surprised by his lack of worldly knowledge.

"Look," he said. "I'm from Kansas, okay? I've seen some cows and some corn. That's it."

She stared at him from across the car, unblinking. She seemed to not be processing this information.

"No California?" she asked, and he shook his head no.

"No New York? No mountains? No Disney World?"

No, no, no. He wasn't kidding about leading a sad existence.

"Ohmygod," she exhaled. "...did you ever get off the farm?"

"Don't joke about it," he said seriously. "This is the first time I've had 3G on my iPhone in my *life*."

She laughed until she was having trouble driving across the flat road. Every once in awhile she managed to choke out a word, like "awful" and "life" and "you" and "too cute." He didn't see what could possibly be "cute" about him never using his phone's full capabilities, but whatever. He wasn't going to turn down a compliment.

"Like you're from anywhere better," he said.

"California."

His jaw dropped.

"Really?"

"Yup."

"You're a California girl," he said, and he must have sounded about as unconvinced as he felt.

"Like the Beach Boys song," she said, and he could tell she was getting impatient by the way her voice was tight and tense, impeccably controlled. He wasn't completely stupid; he knew when to quit while he was ahead, especially considering she just willingly told him a fact about herself.

"Hmm" was all he said.

"I know," she said with a groan. "I'm not tall, blond, or perfectly tan. Whatever. I like my antisocial lifestyle better than I do beach parties."

He laughed at the thought of her as a tan blond who engaged in normal, age appropriate activity.

"What?" she said.

"Nothing," he said immediately, trying to straighten up and failing to do so. She shot him one of her smoldering glares, and he said, "I just can't see you like that. I don't know. It's too out of character."

"Man, I would *hate* to have to wear those skimpy beach shorts with 'juicy' printed on the rear," she mused as they passed a huge hotel. He had a feeling they were going to get stuck in the outskirts in a rundown crap fest.

"You'd have to buy Juicy Couture flip-flops," he said.

"Can you imagine how much pool I would have to hustle?" She shook her head. "What has happened to the world? People need to rise up and realize that Tar-Jay isn't that bad."

He watched as the city came and went. Feeling a bit deflated, he turned around in his seat to look back at the lights.

"We'll go down the strip, calm down," she said, managing to read his mind. Maybe he wasn't the only one who had that freaky ESP thing down. "We have to go to Fremont Street to get a room. Those hotels are way too overpriced, even if they do have jacuzzi tubs. Besides, I want to drive through old Vegas first."

"Jacuzzi tubs?" he repeated, suddenly feeling a little less okay with a motel away from the flashing lights and music. "I like a good jacuzzi tub."

"Get a job, and then we'll talk," she said.

"I can say the exact same for you," he said as he narrowed his eyes.

The old part of Las Vegas was what he usually saw in the movies. There were hundreds upon hundreds of old wedding chapels and other buildings that looked run down, but still managed to keep that Las Vegas feel. They passed another casino, and he saw a guy getting escorted out the front door.

"He must have been underage," she said, tilting her head toward him. "Or, like, beating up people. You be the judge. I didn't see his face."

"Didn't Britney Spears get married at one of these chapels?" he asked, reading their names as they drove past. Chapel of the Flowers, Cupid's Wedding Chapel, A Special Memory Wedding Chapel—

"Like I'd know," she said as she flipped on her turn signal.

* * *

For one of the first times since they had met, he got his own bed.

It wasn't really a surprise when he didn't, and he didn't really blame the managers, because when a girl and a boy came in together and asked for a room, they were most likely together or related. It just made sense. He had always hated those people who made poor desk girls' lives living hells, and he really didn't mind sharing a bed with Jo, so he never said anything. He realized he was pretty lucky that he got in a car with a girl, rather than a large, burly man who snored and hogged the blankets. That would have just been awkward.

"Hey, Jess," Jo said, her palms pressed against the window in their room, "Come here."

He obliged, and when he looked out the glass, he was glad he did. The whole city was lit up in different colored lights. He had never been to New York, or Tokyo, or Hong Kong, or any other big city pictured in *Time Magazine*, but he thought that the view right here was a million times better than any of those. All he could get out to express his feelings was a small, quiet "wow."

She laughed, turning away from the window.

"Are you tired?" she asked. He knew there wasn't any way he could sleep with excitement like electricity zinging through his veins.

"Nah," he said. He tried to make out what each sign was for, but there were so many that it was difficult. He could read "casino" on one particularly large one, but besides that, they were just little LED lights, shining brighter than the stars.

"Good," she said, pulling out clothes from her bag. "Because I want to go out."

* * *

Vegas was huge: absolutely, undeniably huge. The buildings were crammed together on the flat strip of land, and people were everywhere. Taxis drove down the road, advertising shows and strip clubs.

"There's a castle," he said, fully aware of how stupid he sounded. Hey, Jo, it's dark out here! This sidewalk is hard! There's lots of people! I like pointing out the obvious!

"Yup," she said, unfazed, and continued walking.

"But there's a castle!" he repeated. It didn't look like a well constructed castle, more like it was made of legos rather than stone, but still, there was a *castle.*

"There's a pyramid too, but you don't seem as psyched about that."

He looked up and sure enough, there it was: a pyramid. He wondered briefly if this counted as seeing a real pyramid, because he would really liked to mark that off his bucket list.

"Wow," he said, and she laughed again. "Don't laugh at me!" he said, his face serious. "I know about haystacks and water towers, I kid you not."

"You're cute in your childlike wonder," she said, nudging him with her elbow. "Like a little kid on Christmas Eve."

"I hope we have to go to New York next," he said. "Or London. Africa… Always wanted to go to China, even though I hate Chinese food."

"We better get those floats," she said, sounding serious. "Tie them to my car really, really well. Otherwise we might not make it across the pond. And besides," she said, giving him a bizarre look. "You hate Chinese food? What else do you hate? Children? Christmas?"

"You're really hung up on these kids during December," he said jokingly.

"Ha ha ha," she said, abruptly stopping in the middle of the sidewalk. "Okay, you have a choice."

He looked at her questioningly, and she pointed at a different hotel with both hands.

"Castle or pyramid?"

* * *

He was surprised that the inside of the pyramid managed to keep with the Egyptian theming. He had expected it to just look like any other casino, but instead, he saw hieroglyphics—that might have not been real, but were still impressive—painted on the stone walls and fake pharaoh thrones. Breaking away from the theme, there were slot machines lined up throughout the space, complete with bright lights and loud sounds. People were winning, cheering and jumping up and down. People were losing, crying and screaming. Some people were obviously drunk, but the whole atmosphere was so intoxicating that he couldn't help but get wrapped up in all of it.

"Are we going to gamble?" he asked excitedly, linking their arms.

"Oh my god!" she laughed. "You seriously have to stop this. I'm going to go into cuteness overload."

He gushed and said, "I can't help it. So are we?"

"Yes," she said, and he grinned wider. She said in her best announcer voice, "Pick a game, any game!"

They were halfway through a game of Poker when he caught something out of the corner of his eye. He turned his head to get a better look, his heart absolutely *hammering* in his chest, and that was when he saw her standing across the room.

Before he knew what he was doing, he was on his feet.

"Jess?" he heard Jo say, but he didn't respond. He started running after her, through the mass of people hanging around in the casino, through the rooms and the sound and the haze in his brain. She was always too far away for him to grab a hold of her, always across the room or down another hallway, red hair flying behind her as she moved through the building.

When he finally got to an end of a hallway, it was just the two of them. His heart was going to jump out of his chest at any second. Slowly, he reached out to grab her shoulder. The girl whipped around, the scent of cinnamon hitting him in the face, and jumped back.

His heart fell.

"Get away from me, creep," the girl spat, shoving him to the side as she passed.

"Sorry," he whispered.

"Jess?" He heard Jo's footsteps behind him, getting closer and louder until they finally stopped.

He didn't know how she knew what was going on, but when he felt her hand on his shoulder, he knew that she did. He was shaking from the adrenaline that was still pumping through his veins, and he couldn't catch his breath.

"I... She... I'm really... You're not..." Jo groaned, growing frustrated because she couldn't always put what needed to be said into words, especially not when it was something as delicate as this. Instead, she walked around to his front and wrapped her arms around his back. At first, he didn't know what to do. He was still trying to grasp the fact that he had just seen a dead girl run through an entire casino and then turn into someone else before his very eyes, but for that moment in time, he pushed the thoughts out of his head and hugged her back.

* * *

They tried to play a few slot machines after that, but neither of their hearts were really in it. They walked for awhile before stopping in front of the Belagio, one of the hotels he had always seen on television.

He watched the water shoot up into the sky, and thought about how amazing this city was. If he ignored the reason why they were there and what had just happened, everything seemed perfect. He leaned against the railing, listening to the music that was playing loudly in the background.

"I kind of hate big cities," she said suddenly, catching his attention. She was looking down at her drink, one she had taken with her after they left the pyramid, as if it was the one having a conversation with her. She always did that when she was talking about something that actually mattered, something significant to the entire being of Jo—avoided his eyes like she was too nervous to see his reaction.

"Too many people, right?" he said, trying to make it sound like a joke, but knowing he was failing.

"No," she said with a smile, and *God,* she had the prettiest smile. "I mean, well, yes, no, I…"

She laughed at herself, shaking her head. "I hate how you can't see the stars," she said. "It's like they've faded out, and I hate that. I guess it's because of the number of people that it's like that."

"All of the lights," he added, and she nodded.

"I know it's silly," she said, swirling the liquid around in her glass. "But it still bothers me."

"It's not silly," he said immediately. "You just want to make sure they're still burning."

"Yeah," she said, smiling, but still not looking at him. "So are you okay?"

He really wasn't sure, but he also really didn't want to make a big deal out of it. He was seeing a dead girl run through a casino, which he knew was the complete opposite of okay. He probably should be on medication or something.

"Yes and no," he finally admitted. "That was just… but I'm fine out here. Here, you can't see anything besides what's already there."

"Do you ever wonder if everything is one big facade?" she asked. She had that same dreamy look about her that she always had when she was looking up at the stars.

"What do you mean?"

"Like," she said, turning around and facing the street, still filled with people who were walking by. "All of these people. How many of them are actually who we perceive them to be, who others think they are? I look at that couple and think, 'People madly in love.' But maybe she actually is using him to get a promotion, and he's only in on this for the lip action."

"You're really depressing," he said. "Anyone ever told you that?"

She laughed. "A few people, believe it or not."

"I never wonder about those things," he said, back to addressing her question. "But maybe I'm just gullible."

"You're the best kind of gullible," she said, and she was back to not looking at him again. "You want to believe the best in people."

"It bites me in the butt though," he said with a laugh. "But thanks. You're a good person too, you know?"

She rolled her eyes.

"Let's stop the chick flick while we still can, okay?"

"Whatever you say, Jo."

"Hey," she said, her eyes lighting up. "Maybe you saw a ghost!"

He was trying his best to forget about the whole experience, and he had been hoping that she was too, until now.

"I don't know, Jo," he said with a sigh. "Maybe I'm just losing it."

"I doubt it," she said, looking up at the empty sky. She frowned, looking obviously bothered. "You seem normal. Aren't crazy people supposed to have trouble dealing with everyday conversation and expressing their feelings?"

"I wouldn't know," he said reflexively.

"Aha!" she said, jumping off the rail that she was sitting on and jabbing a finger into his chest. "See? You know you're not crazy. You admitted it."

She looked proud of herself; with her hands on her hips and a smug smile on her face, she was the picture of triumph. He felt something right then, something deep inside his chest that was new and different, yet all the same. It was so strong and overwhelming that he almost needed to look away from her face.

When he started walking back toward the hotel later, she fell into stride with him, as if she had always been there. She hummed as she walked and stared up at the sky. Every now and then her shoulder would brush his arm, sending goosebumps across his skin even though it was incredibly hot outside. People passed them by, not sending one look their way, but he liked it. It was as if they were in their own little personal bubble, where the outside world couldn't get in, and it was just him and Jo, who wasn't walking in a straight line and kept crashing into his side, giggling quietly as she tried to right herself. Sometime after their fifth collision, he realized that he had fallen for her.

Jo

Hotels in Las Vegas were noisy at every hour of the night. People were incessantly cheering and screaming, and the slot machines shouted about jackpots constantly.

She could tell Jess wasn't a fan of it, judging by how he kept tossing and turning, sighing every so often. She, on the other hand, loved it. The sounds made it easy for her to fall asleep, much easier than when she slept in her car with the radio static sounding in the background. At least, they usually did.

She kept thinking about what had happened at the casino—the way Jess had taken off without saying a word, the look on his face when he knew Amelia wasn't there, the panic that seized her almost immediately when she realized something wasn't quite right. She couldn't shake the eerie feeling that had passed over her since then, and she was surprised that he had managed to.

Denial, it was funny like that.

* * *

She woke up around four—why, God?—to a dull light on the other side of the room.

"Hnrghhh," she managed, swatting at the air, trying to flip the light switch off.

"Sorry," Jess said quietly, and the light dimmed slightly. She opened one eye to try to figure out what had happened, and noticed that the stupid laptop was on, the lid half closed, sitting on Jess' bed.

"Why are you awake?" she asked, stifling a yawn. "It's so late… or early. Depending on your point of view, I guess."

"Couldn't sleep," he said, keeping his voice down. She had no idea why he was bothering: she was already awake, and it wasn't like the people next door would wake up if he used his normal register. "So I looked through Amelia's files."

"Find anything interesting?"

"I found out she changed her Travelocity password, which is proving to be a problem," he mumbled.

"It's probably something about a boy band," she grumbled, pulling the covers up to her chin. He laughed softly from his spot, and she smiled to herself.

"Just go back to sleep, Jo," he said. "I didn't mean to wake you up."

"Mhmmm."

A few seconds later, she opened one eye again, and said, "Hey, Jess?"

"Hey, Jo," he chimed.

"Are you okay?" she asked.

He hesitated for a second, staring at the bright,—*so* bright, ridiculously bright—laptop screen.

"I don't know why I thought she was Amelia," he said. "But I don't think I need to line up for an electric shock treatment, or anything. I could probably use the therapy, but I think it's probably a waste of money."

She "hmm-ed," her eyes already shut again.

"Yeah," she mumbled. "I can be your therapist... tomorrow...or today. Whatever it is now. Just go to sleep, *please.*"

He laughed again, thankfully shutting the screen of the laptop. She would have cheered if she wasn't so tired. She heard him get up to put the laptop back in its cherished overpriced bag. He must have stumbled over something on his way back to his bed, because she heard him get a few steps off track before the mattress finally squeaked, the covers rustled, and his breathing slowed down. She fell back asleep shortly after, thinking about how if Amelia really was a ghost, she hoped that she was more fun in the afterlife.

* * *

She woke up before him around seven the next morning. After taking a warm shower—*lucky*—and putting on some clean clothes, she sat on her bed, waiting for Jess to get up. The thing about Jess though was that he was a really deep sleeper. So much so that she thought she could probably jump up and down on his bed, and he wouldn't stir. After waiting for at least twenty minutes, she started to feel like a major creep.

She was sitting in a room, watching a sleeping boy. How the mighty had fallen.

"Jess," she said, poking his shoulder. He didn't show any signs of life. She sighed.

"Is it okay if I look through Amelia's laptop?" she asked.

No response.

"Because I want to figure out what happened to her fast, so I can go stargaze somewhere."

Nothing.

"And then once I discover that they're still up there, I thought we could go to New York, since you haven't been."

Nada.

"Okay then," she mumbled to herself. She sat down at the small table in the room, opening the lid of the laptop. It was still on from a few hours ago—Jess hadn't turned it off, probably because he was planning to try to sneak back on once she was asleep again, but he ended up passing out too.

It was all the better for Jo, who didn't have to waste time trying to guess Miss Popular's computer password. She rested her cheek on her palm as she clicked on Amelia's document folder. Most of it, surprisingly, was school work: papers for biology classes and a few analyses of literature. She clicked on one paper that was written May 11, 2009, and started to skim through it.

She really just wanted to know if Amelia was a person who had it coming. She could live with herself knowing she dug a girl's grave who deserved it, because she killed puppies and stole from homeless men. She wasn't so sure she'd feel the same if she had built houses in Haiti.

After reading the first few pages of the paper, she had to admit she was impressed. Amelia didn't seem like a complete baboon: her argument was clear in the paper, and her grammar was much better than in conversation.

Her documents folder didn't have anything too incredibly telling, besides the fact that the number of biology assignments pointed to Amelia being a bio major, which was, to Jo, a shocker.

She didn't waste time going through her programs, which she was sure were probably the same as everyone's. She went to the movies folder instead. There were a few scattered episodes of *The Big Bang Theory* from different seasons, which once again, surprised Jo, because the results of her sleuthing were showing that Amelia actually might have been pretty bright. She also had a download of *Love Actually*, and a couple of other movies Jo hadn't heard of before. There was a quicktime file that she clicked on, and was immediately greeted with a loud *"Okay, okay, go!"* erupting from the computer speakers. She quickly lowered the volume, glancing toward the lifeless mass that was Jess, but found him still sleeping—of course.

She recognized the voice immediately. In the short period of time she had known Amelia, she had cried and whined and complained constantly, so Jo had really grown accustomed to hearing her high pitched voice at all hours of the night.

What was really a surprise was the second voice.

"Are you sure?" someone said with a laugh, waving the lighter in the air. Amelia giggled with excitement, and Jess beamed at her, bending down to light the firework. He darted away just as it exploded, much to Amelia's excited cheers.

"Jo?" Jess mumbled, sitting up on the bed.

Really? She couldn't wake him up for the life of her, but the second he heard Amelia's laughter, he stirred. All of the sudden, she felt rage bubble up inside her, even though she wasn't sure why.

Stupid Jess and his stupid way of messing up her stupid emotions.

"Hmm?"

"What are you doing?" he asked, rubbing his eyes with the backs of his hands. His hair was sticking up in odd places, and she couldn't help but notice how adorable he looked like that.

"I tried to ask you," she said immediately, gesturing toward the laptop sitting on the small table. "You wouldn't wake up though, so I just took your silence as a 'yes.'"

"Got it," he said with a yawn. "How long have you been up?"

She could tell his lack of control over the laptop was making him uncomfortable. His eyes kept going from her face to the table, over and over again, even though she was pretty sure he didn't know he was doing it. She couldn't really blame him. It was probably the equivalent of someone else driving her car.

He finally stood up to go shower. The second she heard the bathroom door click shut, she turned her attention back to the laptop. Amelia and Jess actually were friends. She had halfway believed that it was a crazy fantasy he had concocted in his head, especially considering the way all of his high school "buddies" seemed to act about it. But she saw now that she was wrong. She played the video again, and paused the screen the second Jess grinned at the camera. He looked so *familiar* there, if she disregarded the weird hair and the flip-flops. There was a look in his eye, accompanied with his lopsided grin, that she had seen a lot of recently.

As she studied the screencap, something suddenly hit her. She had seen that look when her car died a few weeks ago when they were watching the *Adventures of Chin*. She had seen that look back on the beach in Mexico when he pulled back from their hug. She had seen that look just last night when they were walking back from the Belagio.

She let out a gasp, pulling her hands back from the laptop immediately. Jess was in love with her.

This was going to be awkward.

* * *

He decided over an all-you-can-eat steak buffet that their best bet to finding this guy was to go to really *big* casinos, as if every casino they had walked past since they arrived in Vegas was just training for the real deal.

"Scott said he was a big gambler," he said, stabbing at his steak. A $6.99 steak buffet was proof that human beings were, underneath the nice clothes and perfect composure, animals. People everywhere were tearing into the meat like savages, cramming as much food as they could onto one plate as if the apocalypse was nigh, and this was their final supper.

She hadn't known Amelia: she had known her face and the sound of the voice when she was whining, but she hadn't really *known* her, not like Jess had. Despite this, she couldn't help but imagine Amelia with them, along for the ride. It's not that Jo thought Amelia would be their third musketeer or anything like that; she just liked to take what she knew and what she was learning, and put her imagination to good use. For example, Amelia probably would have been disgusted at everyone in the room. She probably would have cut her *one* steak into tiny, bite size pieces and would have proceeded to slowly, delicately consume them while she looked around the room, her nose wrinkled in disgust.

Jo believed that picture fit perfectly.

Jo wasn't a big fan of ignoring reality: she took the real world in large, long strides, and accepted what came her way.

She wasn't a big fan of a dish of lies with an extra helping of denial, but there was definitely something therapeutic about picturing Amelia that way.

It was easy to not feel guilty when Jo was imagining Amelia walking down the street with them, complaining about the heat and attracting the attention of too many people she had yet to meet.

Jo wasn't like that: she didn't like having anyone's attention unless she needed it for something. It was different when she was out of money or in trouble. Those were times when she welcomed a few staring gits. On a day to day basis though, she tried her best to avoid it. That was one good thing about big cities, as far as Jo could tell. Cities were loud and crowded, and the air was always heavy with exhaust fumes and pollution, but she was always felt comfortably invisible in the throngs of people going about their days, who kept their heads down to avoid making eye contact.

As they walked down the Strip, the sun beating down on them—the two of them—Jo thought it was always nice to just fade away, to not have to worry about preconceptions or expectations.

They walked into a casino with a man outside screaming "Win money, money, money!" Jess quickly slowed to a stop once they were inside the air conditioned building, and she turned to look at him, his face completely blank.

"You alright?" she asked hesitantly. The events of last night were still buzzing in her head, not to mention her mini discovery this morning. She was going to go into a Jess-induced seizure if he clogged her thoughts any more.

"I, uh." His fingers twitched absentmindedly as he shifted his weight from foot to foot; he was the picture of nerves standing in a buzzing casino in Las Vegas. "I just realized we don't really have a game plan," he said with a laugh.

She didn't find it as funny.

"Sure we do," she said, because what they had now was more of a plan than she had had for the past four years of her life. "Ask around, find out who he is, see if he chucked Amelia in an ice machine or not. Sounds like a plan to me."

"I know, but…" his voice trailed off, and for a moment, she panicked. Did she upset him? She knew she was lacking the whole empathy thing, what with her sisters jumping in the "warm and fuzzy feelings" line while Jo went back to "survival skills" for a second helping. Still, she should probably start thinking before she spoke, especially when dealing with the delicate topic of a dead girl that was once his never-gonna-happen dream prom date.

"I guess I'm just used to things that are rooted in certainties," he said slowly, and she watched his face closely, took note of the shadows on his face. "I like to be sure of things. This 'plan' is based more on chance."

"That's reasonable," she said. "But nothing in my life is based on guarantees, apart from things like, I'll always have to pee every hour on the hour."

A small smile crossed his face, and every thought in her mind turned to *job well done, Jo.*

"At some point, you just have to take caution to the wind," she said to him. "Cliché and all. You can't plan everything out."

"I know," he said quietly. "I just feel like…"

This is important; you're not taking it seriously enough; this is a dead end—all of it remained unspoken, but she understood others' silences well, for she was constantly trying to find the sound in them she ached to hear.

She responded with a squeeze of his shoulder, all *I know it is; I'll try harder; everything will work out; just trust me.*

Jess smiled at her, offering his arm for her to take. She linked arms with him and headed toward the first Black Jack table she saw.

* * *

Either the workers at the casino were right about the two of them being completely crazy, or Scott was a major jerk.

Jo believed the latter.

"We should have known better," Jess said quietly, slumped at the bar in the lobby of their hotel. "Nick Papagiorgio was Rusty Griswold's fake name in the Vegas *Lampoon* movie."

"'Holy crap, Wayne Newton's hittin' on mom,'" she quoted, echoing his tone of voice.

"Yeah, that one," he said with a sigh.

Jo had hit some pretty pathetic lows in her life, so she didn't want this to become another one. She didn't plan on spending the rest of the night drinking in a Vegas bar, and having to drag Jess back up to their room. She drew the line at puke.

"Look," she said, pushing away her drink. "This isn't the end of the line."

Jess made a gurgling noise in response to voice his disagreement.

"No, bad Jess," she said, grabbing his drink from him and moving it out of his reach. He made grabby hands at it from his spot next to her, but she ignored him.

"Just listen to me for a second," she said, and he finally met her eye.

"*Scott'sanidiot,*" Jess mumbled, and *wow,* he really couldn't hold his liquor. His words were already slurring.

"One, you're *such* a lightweight!" she said in dismay. He grumbled something under his breath that she couldn't make out and put his head down on the counter.

"Coooooold," he mumbled, rubbing his cheek against it.

"Two," she said, poking him in the shoulder. He groaned, rolling his shoulder blades back. "We've got to find something on Amelia's laptop. No one's life is really private anymore. There's Facebook, Twitter, and a million other websites where people blab about their lives," she said. He turned his face so he could look at her from his place on the counter. He looked hopeful all of the sudden: there was a glint in his eye that made something in Jo's chest let go, just a little bit.

"Hey, Jo?" he said, and he was face down on the counter again. She shook her head, throwing back the rest of her drink.

"Hmm?"

"Was the Vegas movie the one where Audrey got really, *really* hot?"

She laughed.

"Yup, she was ugly and annoying in the European one."

"We should have watched *Lampoon* instead of *Chin*," he said.

* * *

"What is wrong with your *legs?*" she half-shouted later that evening when she was stuck dragging him toward the elevator, and *oh my God* she had *not* wanted this to happen. Stupid, *stupid* Jess. Didn't she meet him in a bar, anyway?

She punched the button for the elevator with her knee, attempting to keep Jess upright. His head lolled to one side, resting on her shoulder.

"Mmm," he mumbled, and she couldn't tell if he was asleep or just really, really drunk. "You smell nice, Jo."

"No news to me," she said as the elevator doors opened.

Elevators in Vegas were ridiculous, at least the ones in their hotel. They were staying on the 17th floor, which sounded perfectly okay during check in. However, as usual, things didn't quite work out.

Even though the buttons in the elevator ranged from one to forty five, the elevator only went to the fifteenth floor. She had discovered this right after they had checked in, when the elevator doors were pinging loudly to signal *hey guys, we're open over here! Yoohoo!* Jo, feeling quite tenacious that day, had stood in the elevator, punching the button labeled "seventeen" over and over again, trying to figure out why it refused to stay lit up.

"This is absolute bull," she had declared, and Jess had reached around her all, *no fear, the man is here,* and started pressing the button too. After a few seconds of persistence, he had sounded defeated as he mumbled, "Must be broken."

That was when someone outside of their little world had finally decided to save them from ripping out the elevator buttons in fits of rage.

"Oh!" an elderly woman exclaimed, standing in the hallway outside of the elevator. She was wearing a plastic visor and a Hawaiian shirt, and Jo really hoped someone would do her a favor and shoot her if she ever left the house like that. "The elevators only move fifteen floors at a time. You'll have to get out and go to the one next to it."

"Thank you!" Jess had called out, the picture of a perfect, polite grandson. Jo, on the other hand, had given her best snarl as she stomped out of the elevator and into the hallway.

"Like I said," she had mumbled. "Complete bull."

Now here she was, holding up a stupid, drunk Jess, who was giggling quietly every few minutes at nothing important. Getting him out of the first elevator and into the second was a struggle, but things got easier once they got to their floor.

"Okay, lean against the wall," she commanded, carefully letting go of him. He started sliding down the wall immediately, and kept going until he hit the floor with a less than dignified thump.

"Or do that," she said, fishing for her room key in her pocket. She made sure the door was open before she pulled him back up on his feet and attempted to get him through the doorway. She suddenly felt like she was caring for a really big baby. She let go of him once they were by his bed, and the springs of the mattress squeaked as he fell back onto it.

"Nighty night, drunkard," she said teasingly, but before she could get away, he grabbed her wrist.

"Hey, Jo?" he asked, and she could tell that he must be really, *really* drunk, because that look was not one that any sane, sober person would wear.

"Yeahhh?" she replied, and it came out like that, slow and unsure.

"I really, really like you," he said, and she rolled her eyes, wrenching her wrist free.

"Okay, too many mushy gushy chick flick moments for one night," she said as she started to move away. She heard the mattress creak, and so help her, if he was going to get up and stumble across the room toward her she was going to kill him.

Luckily, when she turned, she saw that he was just sitting up on the bed, chewing on his lip and looking at the floor.

"I really do though," he said. "I don't think you really know."

"No," she said softly, because she was pretty sure he was falling into the stage between sleeping and waking, and she didn't want to knock him out of it. "I know, Jess."

He fell back against the mattress, the sound of his heavy breathing deafening to her ears.

* * *

Jo read an article once that claimed the statistic about humans needing a full eight hours of sleep was complete bull. It had said that all people really needed was three or four hours of sleep to "keep on keepin' on," so Jo had taken that advice and ran with it.

Tonight, she was spending five of the eight hours Jess would be getting by the light of Amelia's laptop, regardless of what any studies said about using computers in dark rooms.

Amelia's laptop was a scary place. If she went too far, and she hit a folder of pictures of *nail art*—yes, nail art, pictures of her fingernails with cutesy designs drawn on them after hours of focus, concentration, and steady hands. At the other side of her hard drive, there was an endless mass of carefully written papers on genetics and philosophy.

Jo was starting to wonder if maybe Amelia shared her computer with someone else.

She flipped through bookmarked webpages aimlessly, looking for some clue about what had happened to this girl, because she knew the second Jess woke up sans alcohol he would be panicking about their failed "plan."

Amelia's internet favorites were about as confusing as her files. There were online stores and blogs in a language that she couldn't understand, but suspected was Portuguese. She stumbled across a page halfway down Amelia's long list of favorites, a blog titled "Larger than Life Size."

She was about to quickly hit the back button, because it sounded like she had stumbled onto a blog about obesity and McDonalds, when her eyes caught something off to the side of the page. Jo's eyes widened as she read the "About Me" box.

amelia. practically imperfect in every way from head to toe. bio-american history double major. chronic liar and wannabe jetsetter.

Too many thoughts were running through Jo's head, such as classics such as "who the heck is this girl?" and a series of obscenities because really, how was Jo this awesome?

She glanced over at the lump on the mattress that was either Jess or a small mountain, and thought about waking him up right now. She probably couldn't wake him though, and even if she could, she wasn't sure that she *wanted* him awake.

He would probably throw up and then try to kiss her, and Jo wasn't mentally equipped for that level of gross at two in the morning.

She scrolled through the entries on the blog, wondering how many there were. The handy archive button on the side of the screen told her that entries dated back to 2006, so Jo settled in for what would inevitably end up being a long night.

She decided it would probably be best for her to have a fully formed plan on hand ready for whenever Jess decided to greet the day, so she clicked on "recent entries" and scanned those first. Amelia, bless her dearly departed soul, was surprisingly organized. She had a new blog post every few days, and they were all dated and titled nicely. She must have been the girl everyone wanted to borrow notes from when they were sick.

There was an entry about four months back, with a picture of the sky at the top, titled "hittin' the road!"

howdy, y'all! i be heading eastwards as i be making my ways across 'dem wide open spaces in dis fine country we have heres. startin' in l.a. and ending in new york, i plan to wrangle up some... some...

okay, i don't know how to speak cowboy. sorry. i cringed at least twelve times typing this. anyway, i'm taking a road trip. i'll keep you guys posted. pray that i don't have a flat, because we all know i'll be royally screwed if i do.

xoxo, you favorite cowgirl, amelia

Jo hated to admit it, but judging by the hundred words she had just read, she thought she would have liked this girl.

This wasn't how the Amelia she had met had been like. That girl was all about smiting her rich parents and crying over her ex. Honestly, Jo had wanted to strangle her a few times, not laugh along at her attempts at being witty.

Jo suddenly felt uncomfortable typing on a dead girl's laptop, reading her memoirs. It felt like an invasion of privacy: Jo was pulling a serious Peeping Tom and watching Amelia's life through her laptop screen instead of her bedroom window. But it wasn't as if she had a better plan. Wasn't the creepiness justifiable if staring into a girl's window was the only way to find out the truth?

Jo figured Amelia would probably agree with her, and it wasn't like she had much of a case anyway, considering she was the one posting her every move on the internet anyway. She had given up privacy a long time ago.

Amelia's last entry was from Washington, D.C. Jo skipped the ones in the middle because she always read the last page of the book before bothering with the beginning—she didn't like surprises, and she could never wait to find out how the story ended. If she read the ending first, she didn't rush the entire story trying to get to the last part.

She guessed this was another example of her lack of patience, but she didn't really care.

This entry was entitled "the nation's capitol, yo!"

alright, guys. if you've got a message for anyone in the white house, this is your time to speak up. i'm currently chilling in farragut square, just my blackberry, this really horrible coffee, and i—me? with no car and no ride, life isn't looking too good.

*we'll see how things turn out though. hakuna matata, right?
i'm closing in on new york, which is the primary goal. i can't
help but feel like i should be collecting souvenirs for the folks
back home, even though i don't think i really* want *to go home. i
like being on the run. i feel like a fugitive with good hair.*

*mmkay, so some guy just walked up to me and asked me where
d.c. was. people always talk about loonies running crazy in big
cities. poor guy. anywho, if anyone wants a postcard, drop me
a comment. i'm not opposed to showing some love to my blog
roll! i think i'm going to hit up some museums before i begin
stalking mister president. it might have been a bad idea to wear
heels today, but i figure my calves will be* way *toned by the end
of this trip.*

ciao! -amelia

EDIT: *oh, karma, you are a delicious thing. guess who has a
ride? yup, that's right. gave some pocket change to a guy on
the street, and then a hottie bumped into me from behind. bow
chicka bow wow! his name is gregory, not greg. isn't that cute?
he's a peach. he says he's from cali, which i guess is ideal, if
not a little saddening. maybe elle woods was right to get away
from the sun and valet? i'm all mixed up inside, friends!
anyway, gregory the hottie and i are going to stay in d.c. for a
few days and then head toward new york. hooray! progress!
cute boy! victory all around!*

and you guys totally thought i was done for. oh ye of little faith!

Jo should have liked Amelia: that was the biggest hang up for her right now. Why wasn't the Amelia she had known briefly anything like this girl? This girl seemed like someone Jo could've easily gotten along with, even regret not having around. She seemed like someone that all the boys, including Jess, *would* fall for, because who wouldn't? She was absolutely charming, and the fact that she wasn't a complete dingbat was a relief to Jo. She didn't want to think Jess' type was a stupid, tall blond. Then again, she didn't really know why she cared what Jess' type was.

Ugh.

It was likely that Amelia was beat up by someone in D.C. No one ever said big cities were friendly. Everyone minded their own business in cities, kept their heads down and their mouths shut. The unsettling thing was that Amelia wasn't found in D.C. She was found in an ice box in Oklahoma.

The facts didn't add up. The last puzzle piece was shaped like a square, while the puzzle was missing a triangle. It made Jo frustrated enough to want to ruin it, to throw it across the room and to send the tiny pieces flying in different directions.

D.C. to Oklahoma, D.C. to Oklahoma—the two places weren't exactly close in proximity. There had to be something fishy about the guy she met: Gregory. People in big cities don't just walk up to a person and offer them a ride to another state. It was like a five hour drive to New York. What kind of a person just agreed to do that for a stranger?

With the exception of herself, who she knew was an anomaly, no one did that.

He probably dragged her to Oklahoma and strangled her, or something equally awful. Jo rested her head on her left hand, yawning quietly. It was too bad there weren't any entries after that. Searching for a mystery man with nothing more than a first name was going to be a little bit difficult. Plus she could only imagine how Jess would react to it. At least before, they had a full name, even though it was fake, and a place. She was still bothered by that; she wasn't easily duped, and Scott had seemed pretty serious when he whispered conspiratorially through the bars of his jail cell. Maybe he was stupid enough to be tricked himself. She wouldn't have been surprised. No one ever looked their intelligence anymore.

She let out another yawn, and decided she should rest her eyes, just for a minute. That computer screen wasn't good for her eyes, after all.

Jess

Jess woke up with a pounding headache and a pressing need to vomit. He somehow managed to untangle himself from the sheets on the bed and stumble toward the bathroom, but stopped dead in his tracks before he made it all the way there.

Why was Jo sleeping at a ninety degree angle? Her head was down on the table, her arms resting on the keyboard of Amelia's laptop.

Wait. Amelia's laptop?

He peered over her shoulder to try to look at the screen, but it had clicked off and gone to the screensaver, black with the time shooting around the screen.

Resisting the urge to wrench the laptop away from her and scream that it was *his,* he tried to calmly survey the situation. The first step was to extricate Jo from her sleeping position, so he padded across the hotel carpet toward her, lightly moving her arms away from the computer. Her fingers twitched in her sleep, but that was it.

He stared at her face, the sharp cheekbones, the pale, slightly freckled skin, the parted lips.

It would be so easy.

So, so easy.

They were close enough as it was. All he would have to do was lean in, just a few more inches. It would be *so easy.*

Except for the fact that he wasn't sure if she would push him away or kiss back. He had faced rejection before in his life, and he wasn't a big fan of it. He could clearly see her with her hands against his chest, giving him a huge shove backwards that sent him to the floor in shock. She would say something clever and witty that he couldn't even come up with in his own dreams, and then she would turn on her heel and head toward the bathroom, demanding a shower.

But would it mess everything up? Would she stop speaking to him, or demand that he got out of her car at the next diner? He wasn't so sure. He could see things being awkward for a while, see Jo tense every time he got close to her, like she used to in the beginning, but he couldn't see her putting an end to their camaraderie.

Jo mumbled something in her sleep that he can't make out, and he smiled to himself.

"Alright, Jo," he said softly. He carefully pushed her chair back from the table, and then slipped an arm under her legs and another behind her back. Jo was surprisingly light for the amount of sarcasm she was carrying around. He glanced down at her face for a second, and immediately wished that he didn't. She was curled into him, her face tucked into his shoulder. He felt her breath hot against his neck, coming out in short, small puffs.

He was going to throw up.

If he had any doubt that he was going to before, he was definitely going to now, with a brilliant girl in his arms. His heart was going into overdrive, beating so fast that he couldn't understand how Jo could possibly be sleeping through the loud *thump thump thump thump* of his heart rate going a million miles an hour down a highway with the cops in pursuit.

He carefully set her down on her bed before he could drop her, or worse, puke on her. With Jo safely out of the way, he felt less nauseated. His head was still pounding, this low, dull, yet still *enormous* pain, but he could deal with it if it meant he wasn't going to vomit all over Jo.

He aimlessly traveled back over to Amelia's laptop and sat down at the table. The screen came back to life the second he touched the mousepad, and he stared at the gray and blue webpage like he was dreaming.

"What are you doing?" he asked. It was always the same old tune. He never knew what was going through her head.

"Nothing," she said over her shoulder as she tucked a curl behind her ear. He caught a glimpse of gray and blue before she shut the lid on the laptop, walking back over to him and plopping down on the bed. "So what are we studying first?"

The memories hit him like a Mac truck. She was always updating that thing when she thought no one was looking. His eyes roamed over the page, and he recognized the name of the blog immediately. It was typical of Amelia to pull lyrics from her favorite song, and besides, it fit her. She was always larger than life, more than any one person could handle.

He was starting to feel sick all over again, but whether it was the hangover or the nostalgia, he wasn't sure.

He wondered briefly how Jo found this blog, but he quickly realized it wasn't important. Jo was incredibly determined; if she hadn't have found a direct link to the girl she was unraveling the mystery of, she would have found a way to make one.

The entry was from only a few months ago, entitled "nowheresville, louisiana where crap hits the fan and i hit cows."

BURNOUT STARS

Now that was a title. Amelia had always been enticing. If he had to assign one word to her, that was the one he would pick. Everything looked better while she was doing it. It didn't matter what she was doing—dissections in biology or frolicking through the woods saving wildlife—she always made him want to join in too. She just made everything seem so much more *fun*.

She even made dying look pretty good.

He looked back at the computer screen, took a deep breath, and started reading.

okay, before you all start to freak out, know that i'm okay. didn't even chip a nail. we're doing a++ on the amelia's health part.

however, we might have some failing marks in the car department.   yeah, so your worst fears have been acknowledged. whatever. blah blah blah told you so amelia you're so irresponsible your dad is going to kill you when he finds out you crashed your mercedes. whatever. get it all out of your systems now, i'll wait.

...
you done now? alright. i'll tell what happened. so all is fine and well in amelia land, not like rainbows and puppies and OPI's fall collection, but still pretty good. so i'm cruising along, la di da, when all of the sudden, i hit a cow.

... do you need another moment for that to sink in, dear blog readers? i understand if you do. i'm still processing it myself.

*yes, a cow. in front of my car. i don't know either. i guess i zoned out for a second and didn't notice the fact that it was **in the street**. until it was too late, that is.*

*so yeah. i hit a cow. cool story bro. my car is completely trashed. i dragged my sorry self to a diner up the road that had these fabric cushion booths that looked like someone had puked all over them. and the barstools just looked fishy. like you know how when it's really hot out and you're in a skirt or shorts and you sit down on a plastic chair, then when you get up it feels like your skin was ripped off, but the only thing left on the chair is some gross butt sweat that you hope no one notices because really, it's **butt sweat?** these stools totally had butt sweat. i could tell. i'm quite skilled in noticing these things, you guys. for real. so i didn't really want to sit down at all, but like, what else was i going to do? so i reluctantly sat down on a stool, next to this girl who looked at me like i had killed her favorite puppy, or something. our first conversation basically went down like this:*

girl who obviously wants me dead: *so what's your story?*
poor innocent me: *i hit a cow.*
girl who obviously thinks i'm stupid: *[snorts into coffee]*
poor stupid me: *yup.*
girl who obviously assumes i failed driver's ed: *do you... you know... look out the windshield while you're driving?*

yeah. harsh right? like i just had the most traumatizing experience of my life, woman. stop shooting me with daggers from your eyes. so anyway, i ordered an omelet that didn't really taste like it was made with eggs, and this evil chick just kept glaring at me. i didn't know what her problem was, and i'm trying to come up with rational excuses to justify her lack of manners, like maybe she's on her period or maybe she got a ticket this morning, so she's not in the best spirits.

okay, so i eat my nasty omelet and try to come up with a game plan here, because come on, i'm me, and i basically come up with: 1) hitch hike to new york or 2) develop super powers and fix car myself. now while that second option was mighty tempting, i wasn't sure i really had the time to locate some radioactive elements to help me out, so i decided to opt for number one. then evil girl speaks again.

evil girl: *where were you heading to, princess? i mean, before this whole cow incident.*
good little me: *new york.*
mysterious evil girl: *[raises an eyebrow all cool and mysterious and takes another sip of coffee] why?*
hopeless me: *i was taking a road trip. i started in l.a. and was heading to new york. then... cow. i guess it will moo no more.*
confusing evil girl: *[cracks a smile]*
slightly less hopeless me: *what about you? where are you going?*
vague girl: *everywhere. [cue sly smirk]*
hopeFUL me: *...does new york count?*

yup, that's right guys. i caught a ride with a girl i met in a diner. not gonna lie, i feel really cool because of this. like i feel so spontaneous and very un-amelia marie chambers. i just feel like amelia, some chick who is going to go see new york and try to find something worth finding.

BURNOUT STARS

it feels really good, guys. you should try this. go to the first shady diner you see that looks like it probably has drug deals going on in the back room and sit on some butt sweat and ask the person next to you if you can catch a ride with them. i was so smooth about it too. you have no idea. i wish i had a camera for these incidents.

anyway, not so evil girl (whose name is jo, by the way. isn't that cool? jo. one syllable.) is driving way faster than the limit right now, and led zepplin is playing, and i feel pretty fabulous about this whole situation. i don't think jo really likes me though; she seems a little annoyed by my existence, but then again, maybe she's just on her period. it happens. monthly.

oh god. i did the unthinkable though. i asked her about a shower, and she almost veered off the road. she really showed me. i didn't think she'd ever stop talking. anyway, i guess i'll just keep my mouth shut for a while. we'll see how well i do!

keep ya posted
(sounds like this should have a lot of wink wink nudge nudge's following it, idk),
amelia

He sat back in the chair and stared, unblinking and unthinking. He just stared.
Then he realized he was *really* going to vomit.

* * *

When people were upset, they always found a way to keep themselves busy. He could still remember going over to Amelia's late at night and finding her room turned upside down, Amelia in the corner with a bottle of Windex, looking like she came straight out of the pre-ball scenes of Cinderella. She always did that when she was upset. Her entire world would be falling apart, and she would be reorganizing her vocabulary cards in the middle of the hallway at school. He had always tried to convince her to move, but there wasn't much of a point. No one would ever dare step on Amelia Chamber's things, especially not when she had that look on her face, the look that said "my life stinks more than you can possibly comprehend with that little mind of yours, and if you do anything to make it worse, I will end you."

He wasn't much of a cleaner, or a talker, not really. When things fell apart for him, he buried himself in other people's problems, and tried to make things better for them.

That morning, after he finished retching the contents of his stomach into the toilet bowl, which was basically all drinks and free salted nuts, he sat back on the cracked tiled floor of the bathroom, and tried to decide who needed saving.

He finally decided on everyone. First on the docket was Jo, so he jotted a note down on the half-used hotel notepad and headed out the door.

There was a restaurant downstairs, adjacent to the casino. He ordered some food at the counter, two orders of waffles with sides of bacon. He looked around the room while he waited, trying to keep himself from thinking too much. He watched a woman with a purse toss her bag across the booth to her friend and a couple whisper to each other in the corner.

Why did he feel so bad about this?

He let out a sigh as he rubbed a hand across his face. He didn't know why he felt so *bothered*, really. He had already known that Jo had met Amelia, and it wasn't a shocker that Jo was a jerk to her, because that was just how Jo was. It was her defense mechanism, not anything personal. He wasn't bothered by the proof of them meeting, or by Amelia's distrust of diners, or really by Amelia hitting a cow—she had hit a fire hydrant back in high school, which wasn't even *moving*. He had little faith in her driving capabilities.

It was her blog. That was the whole problem. Jo was right; some part of him deep, deep down, had known that she was gone before the body was found. He had given up hope. He never thought he would hear from her again, never hear her thoughts or hear her voice in the way she wrote. His wounds had finally healed up, clotted, and scabbed over. But now?

They were ripped back open again, and the blood was flowing out, fresh and hurting just as much as before.

"Here you go," said the waitress, setting a bag of food down in front of him. He paid and left quickly, but once he was by the elevators, he realized he didn't really know where he was going. He didn't really want to go back up there, not yet. He needed to clear his head. He didn't want to explode all over Jo.

He decided just to walk around outside for awhile. Smoke was heavy in the air around the hotel from the people standing outside the doors, never acknowledging anyone's presence. Jess thought it was sad that in a city of so many people, no one wanted anything to do with anyone else.

He passed hotel after hotel, saw a little girl crying as her mom dragged her down the street, watched in shock as a man in his Sunday best dropped his iPhone on the concrete, and walked past a woman who was singing on the street. She wasn't very good, and the lack of attention she was getting was just, but he still handed her a five dollar bill as he passed. She smiled at him, and her song picked up, like her spirits had been lifted, and her music was too. Jess didn't know what was so hard about that. He just made a girl's day, and it only cost him five dollars. He would've spent it on junk anyway. He didn't understand why everyone in this city was so rude, so self absorbed. Everywhere he looked he saw people that were in a hurry, and not one of them was smiling. Why was it in such a big city, everyone always seemed so lonely?

* * *

When he opened the door, the first thing he saw was Jo siting back at the table.

"Oh, hey," she said when he walked in. Her eyes locked on his for a split second, and he thought he saw something there, something new.

"I got breakfast," he said, raising the bag up to show her.

"Thank God." She peered into the bag and said, "What, no eggs?"

The thought of eating an omelet made him want to puke all over again. He must had shown his distaste on his face because she lifted an eyebrow and mumbled, "Okay then. Save the unborn chicks. Whatever."

They ate breakfast in silence, which obviously bothered Jo to no end. After a few minutes of nothing but the muffled sounds of cheers and slot machines, Jo threw down her fork, crossed her arms, and stared straight at him.

"Okay, I'm feeling some tension in the air, so let me take a guess."

She tapped a finger on the table for a few seconds, shadows growing across her face. Finally, she groaned, pulling her hands into her lap.

She looked so much smaller all of the sudden. When she looked up at him, eyes wide and bottom lip between her teeth, all he could see was vulnerability, raw and naked across her face.

"Look," she said softly, and he was torn between fascination for this softer part of her and hatred for himself for putting that look on her face. "Sorry I didn't ask before using it. I just...didn't want to let you down."

Wait, what?

"What?"

"You know..." She shifted in her seat, looking so uncomfortable that it seemed like it was taking everything in her power not to bolt from the room. "My plan really didn't work, just like you expected, and I just..." Her eyes traveled around the room as she trailed off, trying to find the right words.

"I just didn't want you to freak out," she said finally.

"So you started snooping?"

"Investigating!" she protested, and he smiled to himself, because even when she tried to tell the truth, flashes of herself shone through. "Besides, it's not like she has a say in anything anymore."

She immediately winced and mumbled, "Sorry, my insensitivity kicked in again."

He laughed, and seeing the relief on her face made the tension in the room ease. The air between them became easier to breath. He relaxed into his chair.

"You're not that bad, Jo," he said, smiling at her. She looked half-embarrassed, half-flattered, and completely adorable.

"Gee," she said, with as much sarcasm as she could muster.

"Besides," he said. "I'm not bothered by it."

Her eyebrows raised, all traces of the creature he had just seen vanished.

"And you couldn't have said anything about this before I went all Disney channel on you?"

"I tried to stop you!"

"Don't lie to me!"

"Fine, fine," he said with a laugh that came out more like a huff.

"Next time try harder," she said, crossing her arms. "… so what was it that brought about this outpouring of emotional crap?"

"Just…" he hesitated.

"Come on, spit it out," she said with a groan. "If I talked about my feelings, you have to, too."

"Is that a rule?"

"Yes," she said. "*The Tao of Jo*, chapter six. 'If the great and almighty Jo utters the truth, all others must too, or they hath to suffer-eth."

"Suffer-eth, huh?"

"Yes," she said, nodding her head in complete seriousness. "Now speak."

He took a deep breath.

"Reading that blog was like talking to her again. It just freaked me out a little, I guess."

She nodded slowly, mulling over his words in that calm, analytical way of hers.

"It's sort of like communicating with the dead," she said.

"Exactly." He said quietly, "You were right, you know, about knowing that she was dead even before *knowing* she was dead."

She said, "I didn't want to be right," and he believed her.

"You were though. I'm okay, or rather, I will be."

"Yeah?" she asked, uncertainty ringing clear in her expression.

"Yeah." He added, "It just needs time to sink in. Again."

She nodded, and he could tell immediately the worst of the conversation was over, just as she could. She leaned forward in her seat toward him, and if she didn't hear the way his heart was beating in his chest, she had to be deaf.

"Well," she said, about as cheerfully as Jo could ever be. "Want to hear what I figured out?"

She didn't pause long enough to give him a chance to reply, just kept plowing forward, which he knew was just her way of doing things—no slowing down.

"One, sleeping at a right angle is awful." She cracked her neck. "Two, Amelia met some guy in D.C. and then disappeared from the internet."

"So," he said slowly, swallowing. He was starting to feel nauseated all over again. "He killed her."

"Not necessarily," she said immediately. "There's a lot of ground between D.C. and Oklahoma. Who knows what happened."

"We'll never find out, will we?"

"Maybe not," she said with a shrug. "but we can at least retrace her steps."

"That's your plan?" he asked. The way it came out sounded wrong, but he wasn't really sure it mattered; Jo seemed pretty serious about it, and it wasn't like he could change her mind.

"Don't sound so underwhelmed," she said flatly. She got up to go take a shower, and squeezed his shoulder as she passed.

* * *

Vegas wasn't mentioned on Amelia's blog, but the Grand Canyon was.

Jo was the quickest packer in the history of the suitcase: she shoved her clothes into her duffel in two minutes, and spent the rest of the time leaning against the door, tapping her foot and humming what he thought was "Holiday Road."

"Come *on,*" she whined every few seconds. "I thought you were a guy!"

It wasn't his fault that apparently drunken nights meant clothes strewn across the room. He found a tennis shoe under the bed, and briefly wondered how that happened before he decided just to shove it in his bag—he probably didn't want to know, anyway.

"Jess, what in—"

"Don't even think about finishing that sentence," he said, jumping to his feet, bag in hand. He had Amelia's laptop wrapped in four shirts in there, which he hoped was enough to protect it from any damage it could encounter if Jo ran off the road in the middle of the night. It was surprisingly unsettling when your entire well being rested on one electronic device.

Weren't computers bursting into flames a few years back?

"Are you ready, princess?" she asked, one hand on the doorknob.

"Oh wait, no," he said, and he was sure for a second she was going to punch him. "I lost my crown."

"Har har har," she said sarcastically, throwing open the door.

"Goodbye, Golden Nugget!" he called over his shoulder once they were out on the street.

"Who names a hotel that, anyway?" She frowned and said, "It makes me think of corny poop."

"Okay, mental image not necessary," he said immediately, and if his hands were free, they would have been raised in mock defeat.

"Just saying," she mumbled, tossing her bag in the backseat of her car.

The West made him feel like he was in a Hollywood movie with cars driving dangerously down rocky roads as they tried to evade the LAPD. He stared out the window at the mountains, wondering where the cop cars were.

"Do you ever fly anywhere?" he asked.

"I do not possess wings," she replied automatically, like a robot. She was a little freaky sometimes.

"You know what I meant."

She shrugged.

"Jo—" he said warningly, and she groaned in frustration, cranking up the music. He had absolutely no idea what was playing or what the singer was saying or even if it was English, but Jo seemed to like it.

"Haven't we had enough *Confessions of a Teenage Drama Queen* moments for one day?"

"Nah," he said, and he beamed at her when she glared. She sighed wearily: he was getting good at wearing her down.

"I hate heights," she mumbled. And if he was a crueler person, like her, he would have screamed out, *"What? What did you say, Jo? Might have to say that one louder! My poor, weak ears didn't catch that!"*

But he was not. He was Jess, not Jo, so he said, "I'm afraid of needles."

"Really?" she asked, looking at him curiously for a second, trying to see if he was telling the truth or not; she had realized he had no poker face. "Huh."

"So is it just planes, or do you flip out if you're on a roller coaster?"

"Oh my god, you know those things that take you way up in the air, and then drop you out of the blue?" she asked. He nodded enthusiastically, egging her on. "I almost peed my pants the last time that happened to me."

He laughed because he really couldn't imagine Jo being scared of anything, especially not an amusement park ride.

"Why did you go on it in the first place?"

"I was twelve!" she said reflexively. "I thought my distrust of swing sets was because Dexter Mills knocked me off one when I was six. I didn't know there were underlying psychological problems going on."

"He was probably just angry because his name was Dexter," he said, and she laughed. Her laughter was always so loud—it filled up the space around them.

"Good to know it had nothing to do with me," she said. "It's been bothering me for the last seventeen years, seriously."

"Well, now you can finally get some sleep."

This was so simple—this carefree, easygoing banter they had going on between them. It was effortless. He didn't think he had ever been able to just talk with anyone like this, without worrying about what he was really saying. It was nice.

"Good news, bad news time?"

"Dexter ended up bald, fat, and working at Wal-Mart?" he offered.

"No idea; I don't use Facebook, remember?" she said. "Good news, we're almost to Arizona. Bad news is you have to pass through the Hoover Dam to get to Arizona."

"Not seeing the bad in that bad news, unless you see a bomb squad up ahead, or something."

"It's going to delay us," she attempted to explain, and he shrugged, putting his head back against the headrest. He propped his feet up on the dash, but she quickly slapped his leg. "Don't you dare get my baby dirty."

"Sorry," he said, even though he knew he didn't sound it.

"I hear that smug tone in your voice, young man," she said, and all he could think about was how she would have been a really awesome kindergarten teacher. No kid would have dared knock anyone off of a swing set with her around.

"Like I was saying before you went all stone-age-level etiquette on me," she said, and he fought back a laugh. He didn't really think he should feel like laughing all the time, but she just made him feel so easy that everything in his chest just felt light. "We can't go see it because we won't make it to the Grand Canyon by nightfall, so don't throw a hissy fit when I drive straight by it."

"Wait, why does it matter when we get there?" he asked, genuinely confused. It wasn't as if they had hotel reservations.

"Don't you want to hit all of Amelia's stops?"

"Well, yeah," he said, feeling confused. "But it doesn't really matter how long it takes us, does it? I mean, she's dead, and all. It's not like she's waiting on us."

He didn't know if that was the right answer or not, because Jo just fell silent, and he couldn't tell if that was a good or a bad sign. When he thought about it, neither option was that comforting, really.

They had to go through a security check, which seemed to be more unsettling for him than it was for her, because he didn't know if she was hiding cocaine under the seats or something—he wouldn't have been surprised if there was a dead raccoon back there, really. It looked like a Sam's Club exploded in the backseat.

* * *

It was so hot outside, hot and dry. He could hardly swallow his spit. He suddenly felt thankful for her car, because if he had to walk through this desert he was almost positive he would die.

What if it broke down again?

"Are we going to be dorky tourists today, or just slightly less dorky tourists?" she asked, staring up at a sign that listed tour prices.

"I say full blown dork-a-saurus. Get me a fanny pack and cardboard visor, and I'm all set."

She gave him a look, a cross between adoration and embarrassment, and he almost fell over. This was *Jo* he was dealing with here, and she was all about death glares and sentences cloaked in sarcasm, not sidelong glances and actual proof of emotion.

This was intriguing.

"I refuse to stand next to you if you go to that extreme," she said coldly.

There went that.

"Oh please," he said. "You wouldn't abandon me. You wouldn't know what to do with yourself without me around."

"I was doing just fine before you came along," she said smugly, and he grinned because she had walked right into his epic, sure to make her swoon line.

"But now you're even better," he said, and he could see the small smile on her face as she turned to walk toward the open ticket booth.

Ah, sweet victory.

Their tour group was made up of mostly over weight, middle-aged adults who looked absolutely *overjoyed* (no sarcasm intended) to be visiting the *real* Hoover Dam and teenagers who looked as if they would rather shoot themselves than deal with their horrible lives for one more second. There were also a lot of fanny packs.

"See?" he said, elbowing her. "I need a fanny pack. I want to fit in."

"No you don't," she said stubbornly, and went back to pretending to pay attention to their tour guide.

"I want to feel like I'm in a *Lampoon* movie," he whined. "We're already traveling across the country. All we really need is some fanny packs and a dead aunt. We've already got a dead girl, so I figure we're halfway there!"

"I'm not buying you a fanny pack," she said flatly.

"I'll buy it then!"

"I'll burn it."

"What do you have against fanny packs?" he said, crossing his arms. She smirked at him, looking from his arms to his face.

She raised an eyebrow and said, "Really? You're a sixteen year old girl now?"

"Tourist traps make you angry," he mumbled, dropping his arms. Their tour guide was droning on about electricity and how Vegas was killing the environment because of how much power it needed—or something. He was getting flashbacks to the night when Amelia invited him over to "study" and then conned him into watching *An Inconvenient Truth.* He had kept falling asleep throughout it because it was Friday night, and he couldn't really make it through a whole week of getting up early without crashing at nine o'clock on a Friday like the eighty year old he was at heart. Amelia had kept shaking him awake, screaming, "This is really important to the well being of Mother Earth!" in his ear until he was sure he had gone partially deaf.

"I'm so glad I am not this guy," Jo muttered under her breath. The guide started walking, followed by the group. He started blindly following, but Jo grabbed his arm, holding him back. He looked down at her hand, fingers curled around his bicep. He slowly turned his eyes up to her face, but she wasn't looking at him. She was watching the group of people intently. Once every person in their group passed them, she let go of his arm and started walking.

"Wha—" he started, but she cut him off with a pointed look.

"I can't mock everyone if we're in the front," she said quietly, and he couldn't help but notice how close she was leaning into him. He looked down at the sneaky smile on her face and noticed the spark in her eyes. It was such a contrast to the dull look he used to see.

"Don't mock the fanny packs."

"Oh, I'll mock the fanny packs."

Jo must have been on the tour before, because she didn't seem to have any interest in listening to anything. She spent the next hour and a half doodling pictures of their tour guide being attacked by fanny packs on the back of the info packet Jess picked up at the entrance. Whenever he would try to get her attention by saying something like, *"Wow, isn't that cool?"* or *"What do you think about that?"* she would always give an intelligent response, as if she had been listening the whole time.

Maybe she was just really good at multitasking.

"Wait, stop," she said suddenly, grabbing his arm again. He stopped dead in his tracks, watching the rest of their tour group keep moving away from them.

She turned around once, twice, and then grinned.

"Look familiar?" she asked, and he glanced around the tunnel they were in.

"Wait…" he said, looking at the wet walls. Something clicked in his brain, and he smiled. "*Lampoon.*"

She nodded excitedly before tugging on his arm.

"Come on!" she said. "Let's see where Clark scaled the walls of the dam!"

Jo convinced him to break away from the tour group later, because they "weren't going to see the right *Lampoon* monuments."

Jo

The Grand Canyon was two hundred and seventy miles from the Hoover Dam, which wouldn't have been a big deal if Jess didn't constantly have to pee.

"Why are you like this?!" she screamed as he squirmed in the seat. He was like a little kid who didn't understand what happened when he drank three water bottles in the course of ten minutes.

"I'm stupid?" he offered, and she groaned.

"I'm not stopping," she said firmly. He looked at her with those huge green eyes of his and pouted.

"Nope," she said, and made sure to keep her eyes on the road. She was too weak these days. He would turn those big eyes on her, and she would crumble. *You want me to talk about my feelings, honey? Okay! You want to go to the beach? Aw, let's go! You want to stop to pee?*

NO.

"You won't win this time," she said firmly.

He sighed and said, "What am I supposed to do then?"

"Hold it," she said simply, then frowned.

She didn't know what this guy was doing to her brain, but she actually felt *bad* about being mean to him. This never happened. She snuck a look at him when he was staring out the window. He didn't *look* hurt. He just looked like he had to pee.

He could hold it, she decided. He wasn't four. He could wait. Besides, she wasn't about to go all soft on him. She needed to remind him that she was made steel.

"Hey, you know what we haven't done yet?" he asked, rummaging through the bag on the floor. She didn't know why he insisted on keeping all of his crap crowding his side of the car like that, but as long as she didn't have to deal with it, she wasn't going to say anything.

"Taken corny pictures with our heads in cardboard cutouts?"

"Well, that, and we haven't read Amelia's entry from the Grand Canyon."

Honestly, she didn't know why she was doing this. It started as clearing her conscience, but now that she realized it was probably the girl's own stupidity that got her killed, she felt better about the whole situation. Jo hadn't told her to follow some weird guy around and get herself killed.

She attempted to take another sneaky look at Jess, who was still busy searching for Amelia's laptop. He must have realized she was staring at him, because he looked up at her, grinned, and then went back to digging.

"Read it out loud when you get it up, okay?"

He nodded in response and pulled out the laptop.

A few minutes later he said, "Okay, I feel like we should make popcorn."

"Ha ha," she said. "Read it."

"Pushy, pushy," he mumbled. "Okay, it's called, 'the grand canyon and the grand mistake.' Oh God. Do you think she hit another cow?"

"Wouldn't put it past her," she said, which she knew wasn't really *comforting*, but whatever.

"She always has cool titles," he said, and he sounded distant, like he was reliving some memory that was taking him far away from here, from Jo.

"I guess," she said with a shrug.

"Okay, ready?" he asked, taking a deep breath. "'Welcome to—'"

"You're not going to read this in a girly, high pitched voice, are you?" she asked.

"I wasn't planning on it."

"Oh, okay, good. Carry on then."

"'Welcome to the Grand Canyon, where the winds are strong and the dust is painful in your eyes! Yup, I learned that first hand after a life altering experience. So my day was already majorly sucking because there were no bathrooms around for like a hundred miles, and I started cramping sometime during the three hundred miles in between the Hoover Dam and the Grand Canyon—' I feel like I *really* shouldn't be reading this."

"Oh shut up," she said. "I just want to hear if she hit a cow or not."

"'And I got sunburnt through my windshield, which I didn't even know was possible,'" he continued. "'So after all of that, I was in a really bad mood. Then I got lost in the park because the wind blew away my map, and when I finally made it to the South Rim after creeping on some people and following them the whole way there, the wind was so strong that it blew away my sunglasses. My Coach sunglasses.'"

"I think I'm going to vomit," Jo screamed. "This is pain and agony. I would rather be subjected to water boarding."

"I'm not seeing anything about a cow," he said, scrolling down the page. "Sorry to disappoint you."

"What?" she cried. "This *is* a grand mistake."

"Want to hear more? Maybe she'll fall down or something, and you can revel in her pain."

"Fine," she groaned. "Bring on the torture. I'm such a masochist."

"'I watched in horror as they fell down down down (into the ring of fire)'"

"Thank God she threw in a song reference to keep me from impaling myself with my steering wheel," Jo said.

"'That pretty much was the end of my grand time at the Grand Canyon. I was pretty pissed after that, so I just left. My wise words of advice? Don't risk your favorite sunglasses on a sightseeing venture. Ta Ta! Amelia.'"

"Tatas as in boobs?"

"I think she meant more in the 'TTFN, Ta Ta for Now' sense."

"Had me fooled."

"Well," Jess said. "That was that. Don't wear your sunglasses, I guess."

"Sunglasses are for wimps."

* * *

Amelia was right about a couple of things: the park really was huge, and it was pretty windy, especially on the rim.

Jess was really into this whole sightseeing deal. She had hardly stopped the car before he was jumping out and running all over the place, like an overexcited kindergartner. She had managed to calm him down enough for them to walk, not run, to one of the viewpoints. There weren't too many people at the one they picked.

She hung back as he ran toward one of the ledges. She heard him gasp.

"This is *amazing*, Jo. You have to see this."

"No thanks," she said. "I'm sure if you lean far enough over the edge you'll see Amelia's sunglasses though."

He sat down on one of the ledges, and she almost had a heart attack. That couldn't be safe.

"You're going to fall and die," she said confidently. "Fifty-three people have died from falling. Another forty-eight jumped off because they were brain damaged, and twenty-three were murdered, which just sucks."

"Are you memorizing morbid wikipedia facts?" he asked.

She shrugged.

"Jo," he said, and she looked up at him. He patted the spot next to him on the ledge. Oh *heck* no. "Come here."

"No freaking way," she said. "I would rather walk through a burning building."

"Come on," he said. "There's little ledges below this. We won't fall, but even if we did, we would be fine."

"Yeah, I have no plans for falling," she said, still firmly rooted to her spot. He sighed, standing up. For a second, she thought they were leaving, which would have been totally okay with her, *really*.

But then he stopped in front of her, and gave her this weird look that she couldn't read. He grabbed her hand.

"I won't let you fall, okay?" he said, and she stared down at their hands in shock.

"I don't—"

"Jo, look at me," he said softly, and she reluctantly brought her eyes upwards. He looked so earnest; she wanted to believe him.

"I promise."

She bit her lip, looking at the rim again. It was such a huge drop. If she slipped, even just once—

"Don't over think it," he warned her, and she looked back at his face. "Just... trust me. I won't let you fall."

She nodded, still biting her lip. He smiled at her and started to slowly tug her towards the ledge, and *oh my god oh my god oh my god they were so high up oh my god*—

"Hey, hey, hey," he said quickly, grabbing her shoulders. She looked at him, her eyes wide in shock.

"Just breathe," he said softly. Her heart was beating so fast she could hear it in her ears.

"You're fine," he said, in that same calming, quiet tone of voice. She nodded slowly. He carefully took a couple more steps toward the ledge, tightly gripping her shoulders.

"You're fine," he repeated.

They slowly sat down on the ledge, and even after he let go of her shoulders, she kept the death grip she had on his arms. She looked out over the rocks reluctantly. Sure, it was a pretty view, but she wasn't sure it was worth dying for.

"Isn't it pretty?" he said quietly.

She looked out over the horizon, the sun casting shadows over the rocks, twisting and changing the shapes. It was pretty in the same way that a fire was, beautiful and dangerous, strong and capable of destruction.

"In an eerie way," she said.

She saw him nod out of her peripheral vision. He was gazing out at the canyon, his eyes glossy. She knew that look, the feeling of being somewhere between reality and the depths of his memory.

"Jess?" she mumbled. She would have bumped shoulders with him if she wouldn't have fallen to her death.

"Huh?" He looked over at her, suddenly back in the present.

"Thanks."

He smiled, averting his eyes, and said, "I owed you one."

"For what?"

"A lot," he admitted. The sun slipped below the rocks, and he gave her shoulder a squeeze. "Ready to get out of here?"

* * *

It was a little bit creepy to look down at a spot on the ground and think, huh, a dead girl stood here.

She was standing by the sign at the entrance of the park, exactly where Amelia stood for a picture she posted on her blog. Jess had run off to the gift shop to buy overpriced junk he would never do anything with, but she didn't bother stopping him—she had done it once, the whole tourist thing.

Tracing the letters on the sign of the gift shop, she thought about stars. Amelia must have been a bright star to burn out so quickly. Jo sighed.

"What happened to you?" she mumbled. She looked down at her hands. Amelia hadn't been that stupid: as hard as it was for Jo to understand it, she just wanted what Jo had.

She shivered despite the heat. She could have been Amelia. *You still could be.*

A hand fell on her shoulder and she jumped, whirling around. Murder statistics ran through her head. *Twenty-three people, twenty-three people, twenty-three people—*

"Woah," Jess said, dropping his arms, his eyes wide. "I come in peace."

"Sorry," she said, feeling embarrassed. Who did she think was grabbing her? Gregory?

"It's okay," he said, and she could read the concern all over his face. "Are you alright?"

She shrugged. "What'd you get?" she asked, gesturing to his bag.

"Some fabulous overpriced items," he replied. "But no changing the subject."

"I don't know what you want me to say," she said, frustration growing. "It's not been an easy day in Joland, okay?"

"Okay," he said, and she had a feeling he would back off now. She was sick of him constantly pressing. She didn't want to talk, didn't want to feel. She just wanted to sleep off all of these emotions that were surging through her.

"Want some prickly pear taffy?" he asked, pulling it out of the bag.

"Dang," she said, probably more to herself than to him. "You always know what to say."

* * *

Amelia had chosen a town in New Mexico as basically a place to sleep in between Arizona and Texas. She ended up liking it more than she thought she would; *"the people were as sweet as pumpkin pie,"* she gushed in the blog entry.

"Was Amelia a Southern belle?" Jo asked, the disgust clear in her voice. She didn't *mean* to sound so hateful: it just happened. She had always been a bad liar when it came to things that didn't matter.

The sun was beating down through the windshield, and the air conditioning in her car was on the fritz. She liked the smell of the dusty air that filled the car, but she also liked the smell of Expo Markers and gas, so she guessed her nose was just strange.

"Why?" he asked.

"She writes like someone out of a television sitcom taking place in Tennessee."

He laughed a little and said, "You know what? I think she thought she was straight out of a TV show."

"Fair enough," she said, sounding less than amused. "You hungry?

"Nah, not really." His stomach growled. She raised an eyebrow.

"Not really?"

"Okay, fine," he said. "I just wanted to feel cool. Cool kids are never hungry."

She snorted.

"Watch a movie!" he exclaimed. "The hipster characters never eat. They just sit in the corner and listen to indie bands no one has ever heard of on their discmans and read Shakespeare."

"Do you want to feel like a hipster?" she asked, trying her best to sound serious. "I have a library in my trunk."

"Why do you have so many books, anyway? I never see you reading."

She pursed her lips as she thought. She used to pick up all sorts of knickknacks when she first started traveling: t-shirts she thought her sisters would like, books for her brother, scraps of paper with notes that belonged to other people, brochures from the towns she stopped in…

"I guess I…" She frowned and shifted in the seat a little. "I used to pick up things for other people, because it made me feel like I hadn't left them behind."

"But you wanted to leave them."

"I know, but wanting to didn't make me feel any less guilty."

"Fair enough," he said, mimicking her tone from earlier. "Can we get some food before I pass out? I think being a hipster is probably overrated anyway."

She pulled into the parking lot of Drella's Delicious Diner, rolling her eyes so hard at the sign she was sure she strained something. She hated alliteration. It was far too cutesy.

Jess, on the other hand, seemed overjoyed by their surroundings, jumping out of the car and running over to the left side of the parking lot.

"Cactuses! Cactuses! Cactuses!" Jess screamed cheerfully, running up to one, and if she didn't know any better, she would have *sworn* he was no older than seven.

"The plural is 'cacti.'"

He frowned as he tilted his head back, calculating, his eyes glossy. "Amelia hated my grammar," he said finally. "She was always correcting me."

"Someone has to," Jo said. He rolled his eyes, but was smiling. He turned his back to her to study the giant cactus, and something struck her. "Hey, Jess? Have you ever gone out of Kansas before?"

"I went to Oklahoma once," he said.

"Great," she said. "Did you get lost or something?"

"Yeah, actually," he said, frowning again. "How did you know?"

"I was joking," she said sadly.

"Oh, well…" his voice trailed off.

"So you've never traveled anywhere before?" she asked.

"I swear we've talked about this."

"I know," she said. "But I had assumed you had at least gone camping, or something."

"Nah," he said. "My mom was always working, and I didn't want to just go off on my own, at least, not back then."

"What about your dad?"

"He left when I was little."

Oh. Well. Crap.

She always got herself into these awkward social situations. It was probably one of the reasons why she didn't like people. They were too hard to understand. She always ended up making conversations impossible to navigate. The last time she tried to have a heart-to-heart with someone other than Jess, she ended up insulting some poor guy's midget mother. She just lacked people skills.

"It's not a big deal," he said immediately, and she examined his face. He didn't *look* like he was bothered, so he must have been telling the truth. She was still surprised that people like Jess didn't lie compulsively.

Man, she had some serious trust issues.

"I never really knew him."

"He was probably a retard," she said. She doesn't really know if there was a written etiquette for conversations that revolved around deadbeat dads, but if there was, she was pretty sure she was violating it.

He let out a genuine laugh, and she relaxed a little.

"Probably," he said. "My mom is awesome though. You would like her."

"Oh yeah? Is she incredibly sarcastic?"

"No," he said. "Just... unique. You two would get along. She kind of thinks like you, in that idealistic, out there kind of way that's great because it's so different."

"Gee, should I be feeling flattered right now?"

"Yeah," he said. "Like... you know that thing you said —about the stars?"

"I say a lot of things about stars," she said, tilting her head to the side. "They're kind of a long running obsession."

"The 'dying just to live' part," he said. "My mom would think that was brilliant. It's morbid in a beautiful way, you know?"

"Did you tell her you were leaving?" she asked, because she really needed to divert the attention from herself before she felt those girly feelings bubbling up inside of her again

She got her answer when he looked away from her face, back over her shoulder.

"*Oh.*"

"I just..." He sighed. "What was I supposed to say? 'Hey, sorry Mom, but I'm going to leave and run away with some girl I just met. Send you a card at Christmas!'"

The way he said it made it sound incredibly romantic, but she tried not to think about it.

"Whatever works, I guess," she said with a shrug.

"I left a note that said I'd be back soon." He said, "I didn't know what else to say. She knew what was going on with me, how awful everything was after Amelia disappeared. She would probably just be glad to know that I'm not hungover right now."

"You should call her sometime," she said. She really wasn't the person who should be giving advice on how to keep a healthy relationship with one's family, but the words felt right on her tongue, so she went with it. "She would probably be happy to hear from you."

He nodded slowly, thinking that over.

"What about you?" he asked, and *that* was the very question she had hoped would never come up during his many Q & A sessions.

"You don't want to know."

"No," he said slowly, pretending to be thinking about it. "Pretty sure I do."

She groaned. "Jess, why you gotta be like this?"

"Be like what?" he asked with a laugh. "Curious? My bad."

"It did kill the cat, you know," she said, her eyes narrowing.

"Yeah, but satisfaction brought it back." He winked at her.

"That doesn't even make sense," she argued. "If a cat is dead, it's dead. There's no Jesus scene. I don't think it's a zombie cat, so—"

"Oh, Jo," he said with an exasperated sigh. "You really love avoiding things."

Well, yeah, *duh*. She should have gotten a trophy for running by now. She was good enough at it.

"You really love prying."

"Touché," he said. "Look, I know you don't like to talk about these things, but if you ever feel like it, I'd really like to know."

He shrugged, signaling the end to the conversation, or rather, what he thought was the end. For her, the words kept spinning around in her head, making her feel dizzy.

Jess

The thing about diners was that they always seemed to have more character than charm. A person rarely walked into one and thought, *'gee, this sure does feel like home!'* On the contrary, most people usually walked in, decided they didn't feel like getting food poisoning that day, and promptly walked back out. He didn't really understand why Jo felt so comfortable in them, but then again, Jess didn't really understand a lot about Jo, other than the fact that she never ate ketchup and looked really pretty in green.

This diner's air was thick with the smell of fast food and day old coffee. The plastic booths looked like they had never been cleaned before, and the fry cook, who looked like he had spent the better years of his life on an isolated mountain top, appeared every few minutes to yell at the waitresses. They looked like they hated their lives about as much as they hated their uniforms, short skirts and too tight shirts that had obviously been designed in defiance to the woman's suffrage movement.

He ordered a salad, and she got chili fries. She looked out the window at the dusty roads, empty and rarely traveled. He couldn't understand why it would be a good business idea to put these diners in the middle of nowhere, but if enough people were like Jo in the world, they must be doing well.

"I think I've got you figured out," he said out of the blue, partly because he wanted to break the silence and partly because the idea had been gnawing at him all day.

"Oh?" she said, eyebrows raised.

"Yeah," he said. "I think I know why you travel constantly. You're searching for something great, something to make you feel alive."

She looked at him curiously, tilting her head to the side and narrowing her eyes. Her mouth twisted and her brow wrinkled, and he knew he got it. Whether she had figured it out for herself was a different story.

She looked like she didn't really know what to say, so when the food came, they both let out sighs of relief. It was unsettling to endure an uncomfortable silence from Jo, and he was pretty sure it was no picnic on her end of the table either.

"You're really strange, you know that?"

He looked up at her and saw her picking at her fries, pulling off cheese to keep her hands busy. Her hair was in her face, acting as the best possible shield she could get at the moment.

"I am?" he said with a fake sniffle. "You don't have to be so mean about it!"

She smirked and said, "You are though. No one else thinks of these things. You can just... figure things out. Figure *people* out. It's weird. I don't know anyone else like that."

"You've spent your life in your car and weird diners," he said. "You can't have that many people in your phone book."

"I used to know people," she said, and he bit his lip; he had already pried enough for one day. He didn't want to annoy her, even if he did feel the insatiable urge to bombard her with questions left and right. "Back when I lived in SoCal."

Must not ask questions. Must not ask questions. Must not ask—

"You're dying, aren't you?" she said with a smirk. "You're crazy. You should be an interviewer and have your own talk show."

"I'm like one of those balloons you fill with too much helium, and you're just waiting for it to pop."

"Oh, Jess," she said. She shook her head, but the smile was impossible to miss. "You're pretty cute, you know that?"

Oh my god oh my god oh my god oh my god—

"Where do I even start?" she wondered aloud, looking up at the ceiling.

He turned his head to watch the cook yell at a short blond, because he needed to do something, *anything*, to distract himself from the pounding of his heart and the dull hope rising in his chest.

"Okay, so, serious time," she said slowly, and it looked like she was really just psyching herself up for this, as if it was game time and she needed to be in the right state of mind. She let out a breath of air and said, "You know what? Never mind. I don't know if I can talk about this."

"Oh, *come on!*"

She shifted nervously, pulling her hands into her lap and staring at them. For a brief second, he thought about how vulnerable she really was, even though she tried her best to hide it. Maybe he should stop pushing her. If he shoved her too hard, she might break.

"Sorry," he said, and she looked up at him, confused. "You don't have to talk about it. I shouldn't keep prying."

That *really* seemed to bother her. She frowned, pursing her lips, before standing up and reaching across the table. The back of her hand fell to his forehead. She tilted her head as she said, "Well, you don't *feel* warm."

"Jooooo!" he whined, looking up to meet her eyes. Wow. They were close. She wasn't more then a few inches from his face. All he would have to do was move just a little bit, hardly at all. It would be so easy. He could just—

She sat back down, crushing his hopes and dreams in one, swift movement.

"You not prying is like the Earth not spinning," she said flatly, and he wasn't sure if he should take that as a compliment or an insult.

"I'm just trying to be supportive!" he protested. "No matter what I do I make you mad."

"That's not true in the slightest!" she exclaimed. Now she really looked angry. Her palms were pressed flat against the table top, fingers flexing, and she was halfway between sitting and standing. Mouth set in a straight line and eyes wild, she said firmly, "You're the one person who doesn't make me mad."

"Oh," he said. That was news to him. He always seemed to annoy her, because everything annoyed Jo. She was the exact opposite of Amelia, who was apparently only upset by sunburn and the loss of her favorite sunglasses. He could hardly remember Amelia ever being annoyed by anything. Even when she had four papers to write on two hours of sleep, she was still as cheery as ever.

Maybe that was why he found it so strange that he liked Jo—*liked* Jo, in the like-like way. She was so different from Amelia, practically the polar opposite, and he didn't really understand how he could care about both of them as much as he did.

"Don't act so surprised," she said quietly, bringing him back out of his thoughts. She lowered herself back down to her seat and brought her hands back beneath the table. "If I didn't like you, you would know."

She looked back out the window at her car and said, "People usually get the message pretty early on."

"Hey," he said, something dawning on him. She looked back at him. "Do you believe me now?"

"With what?" she asked immediately, and then, "Oh. *That.* Yeah."

"Yeah?" he repeated, the corners of his mouth turning up. Finally, she realized he wasn't going to leave. It was about time.

"Yeah."

She looked a little embarrassed by this, and if the situation was reversed, she would be teasing him about blushing. He half-expected her to implode and explode at once if he drew attention to the fact that her cheeks were *definitely* reddening right now. He didn't know if he had the heart to see her die of embarrassment, but he didn't think she would let herself. Jo would claw her way away from death. Countdown to topic change in three, two—

"So, uh, like I was saying, I'm from SoCal…"

One.

"I still can't believe that. In fact, I think I'm dying. I'm going into shock. Someone call the—"

He made gurgling sounds. She reached over and hit him on the arm, which kind of hurt—really hurt—but he did his best to not let it show on his face. It must have shown through

—oh, how he wished he had a poker face, p-p-poker face—despite his best efforts.

"Where was I?" she asked. "You keep distracting me. Okay. So, I guess typical 'woe as me, poor little rich girl' story. Parents never around. Didn't get along with my siblings. The life didn't suit me."

She shrugged. She looked incredibly uncomfortable at the moment; she had all but abandoned her food, choosing instead to pick at her cuticles and stare down at the floor. He vowed to someday get through a heart-to-heart with her looking at his eyes.

"You said Amelia was a poor little rich girl," he pointed out, and she smiled down at the ground.

"You know how they say Hitler was short, dark-haired, and possibly Jewish and homosexual? How he hated the things that he was?" She still wasn't looking at him, but he didn't need her to. He could feel the insecurity radiating off of her small form, hitting him like a tidal wave. She really had been looking for something to change her forever. He just hoped she had found it.

She tucked a strand of hair behind her ear and said, "Yeah. That's pretty much my story, I guess. It's not that I hated Amelia—even though she thought otherwise—it's just that I could see shards of myself in her, and I hated *that*."

"Why, though?" he asked, because he was really struggling here. "You're amazing. How could you hate yourself?"

She looked up at him finally, met his eye, examined his features. He didn't know what she was expecting to see. A sarcastic smirk? An eye roll? He wasn't her: he was horrible at hiding anything, and he never really cared enough to practice doing so. He had always been an open book. It was easier that way. Cleaner. More honest.

Whatever she saw apparently wasn't what she was counting on. She tilted her head, closing her eyes, and relaxed, slouching forward.

"*Wow,*" she breathed out. There was a change in the space between them, something new and electric. It raced back and forth between them, stinging his lungs when he inhaled and flying straight into her when he breathed out. He didn't know if it was good or bad, but he knew he didn't want to mess it up.

* * *

Motel water pressure was something to be desired. The shower was better than the sink, which only produced a thin trickle of water from the rusted tap, but not by much. Plus he swore the source of all foot fungus was in the tiles of the shower, brown and cracked from use and misuse. The whole room could really use a Magic Clean Eraser—or a magical bathroom fairy—but he wasn't prepared to turn into Jess, The Sparkling Bleach Fairy™ around Jo. He let it go for now.

When he emerged from the bathroom fully clothed, he spotted Jo sprawled out on top of her bed on her stomach, clicking furiously at Amelia's keyboard. She seemed tense, Jess noted, as she cracked her neck to the side and practically *growled* at the poor piece of technology.

"Why aren't you working?!" Something changed in her face all of the sudden as she slowly raised her head to look at him. Once she met his eyes, she quickly looked to the left and then dipped her head to look back at the screen.

Okay then.

"What's up?" he asked slowly, easing closer to the bed.

"God, I hate when people say that," she groaned. "It's so idiotic. Everyone always chimes in with 'nothing much' which is total crap, because we're freaking humans, for crying out loud! I want someone to respond with, 'A lot, actually. My aunt's in the hospital, my cat died, and I can't afford to pay my electricity bill. Oh, and by the way, I also failed out of med school and gained six pounds after an ice cream binge accompanied by Clark Kent's bare chest on last night's 'Smallville.' I've come to the realization that real men are not as perfect as fictional alien farm boys, and subsequently dumped the guy I was dating for the past three years. He's ticked off and threatened to bust the windows out my car, so I called up one of my gay friends and he's got some people watching him. All in all, life *rocks!*'"

He blinked once, slowly, processing.

"...are you feeling alright?" he asked. He wanted to see someone respond to a rant like that rationally. He hadn't been this confused since he was in his first car wreck.

"Peachy," she said.

"....was that your life story?"

"No," she snorted. "Just felt like spinning an elaborate tale or two. Really do hate the 'what's up' trend, though."

"I see," he said. "Then, uh, what are you doing?"

He peered over her shoulder at the AOL homepage. Maybe she had a hankering to catch up on celebrity gossip. He heard Kate Gosselin was dating some DJ these days, but that might have just been a joke.

"Trying to log into Amelia's email. I expected her password would be something like 'Justin Timberlake Forever' or 'I love soccer!' Apparently not though."

"She hated soccer. Running wasn't her thing." He laid down next to her and pulled the laptop over so it was between them. He typed in her password, and then clicked the 'log in' button.

"You've got mail!" the computer chimed.

Jo looked like she was going to faint, her mouth in a perfect 'o' and her eyes wide. "You... it... but I... how—what?" she stuttered.

He laughed and squeezed her shoulder.

"I told you about this already! I always saw her sign into her email."

"What was it though?"

He leaned in and whispered, "It's a secret."

Then she smacked his arm. He rubbed his arm, trying not to wince.

"Cacophony," he said, and she raised her eyebrows.

"Excuse you?" she said.

"Yeah," he said. "It was her favorite word."

"Interesting..." she said, pursing her lips. "She sounds a lot cooler when you talk about her. She was so annoying when we were together."

And yeah, that was definitely bothering him. Maybe Amelia had a twin sister that he never knew about, and she was the one that Jo met that had been murdered. That was pretty ridiculous though, even for him, and he *loved* denial.

"There must have been something else going on," he said finally. It was the only reasonable explanation. Jo hmm-ed beside him and stared at Amelia's inbox. He saw a lot of junk mail, emails from websites about special offers and discount sales. There was an email from a Marcy, with a subject line of, "ncase ur in town sat," which Jess figured would send Jo into another rant over proper internet grammar.

She kept scrolling through, eyes moving back and fourth across the page as she read the names and subjects. There was an email from Scott without a subject, and Jo clicked on it without a moment's hesitation.

Ams, I dn't know where you are but **please** *respond to this. Were freaking out. i need to no that youre ok.*

He probably should have gotten some sick satisfaction out of seeing the guy he absolutely hated during four long years of his life reduced to a pile of emotional constipation, but instead, he just felt bad for the guy. Jess hated his desperate desire to see everyone happy: it was incredibly exhausting and not very rewarding.

Jo hmm-ed again, clicking the back button. None of the emails had been read, and they were marked as far back as a month ago. The last email that *was* read was from Gregory.

hey, babe. can't wait to see you. farragut square, 8 pm?
Amelia hadn't replied.

He felt Jo take a sharp, deep breath beside him, and he looked over at her in time to catch a glimpse of the strange expression she had on her face.

"What is it?" he asked, and she frowned, staring at the email.

"Nothing, I just… His IP address looks really familiar. It's stupid though, I mean, IP addresses change. Just, never mind…"

"Wait, do you recognize it?" he asked. She bit her lip.
"Sort of? Kind of? Not really?"

"I have no idea what you're saying," he said slowly, carefully, enunciating the words. She laughed, rolling over onto her back. She brought her hands up over her face to press her palms into her eyes.

"Me neither, half of the time," she admitted.

"I thought you weren't tech savvy."

"Just because I think Facebook is pointless doesn't mean I'm a caveman," she said sharply, so he decided to drop it.

"So it just looks kind of familiar?" he asked. He was really lost. He felt like he really only understood Jo thirty percent of the time, and most of that time was when she was sleeping.

"Yeah, it looks familiar, but I don't know why. I don't think it's a reason to call home about. I mean, IPs change all the time. You go to Starbucks and connect to their wireless, wah-lah! New IP. It doesn't mean much."

He looked back to the screen and mumbled, "This Gregory guy gives me a bad feeling."

"Yeah, same," she said quietly. "I'm not sure it's really a bad feeling though. It's just a weird one."

"You're really not making sense at this time of night," he said, and she laughed. Then she laughed again. And again. And pretty soon she couldn't stop. She was curled into a ball on her side, laughing so hard that the bed was shaking.

"What? What is it?"

"I can't believe her password was 'cacophony!'" She snorted. "All she talked about when she was with me was how much she hated Scott and how excited she was for the Disney villains makeup line."

"Yeah, she was… complicated," he said. He still didn't understand why Jo thought this was so funny, but he really liked the sound of her laughter. He wasn't complaining. He flipped over onto his back and thought about how he could get used to this.

"Oh, man," she said, wiping her eyes. "This is the greatest. It only would have been better if her password was 'brouhaha.'"

"Why 'brouhaha?'" he asked.

"Brouhahas are *funny*," she said, like it was the most obvious thing in the world.

"My bad, I didn't realize."

She made a tsking noise before yawning. Then he yawned. Then she yawned again.

"Stop it," she said, elbowing his ribs.

"You stop it!" he said, yawning again. "You started it."

"No—" She yawned again. "You keep doing it though. Your fault. Not mine. Innocent."

"I don't think so," he said, and maybe it was just his imagination, but he was pretty sure her head was against his shoulder a few seconds ago.

"Let's agree to disagree," she said. "Because I'm really tired all of the sudden."

"Sounds good," he said softly.

* * *

He woke up in the middle of the night cold. When he sat up on the bed, he wasn't surprised why. For one, he was lying upside down on the bed. The comforter hadn't even been touched. Plus Jo had cranked the AC up again, so it was like the Arctic Tundra in their room. No wonder he was freezing.

Jo.

He looked down at the space next to him to find it empty. Her bed was empty too. Okay, this was suspicious. She wasn't in the bathroom, or anywhere else in their small room. He had no idea why at four in the morning he felt the compelling need to find her, but soon enough he found himself walking across the parking lot to her car.

She was leaning against the hood, staring up at the sky. He didn't know where else he really expected her to be.

"Hey," he said softly as he approached so as not to scare her. She acknowledged his presence by scooting over, giving him enough room to ease up next to her.

"So…" he said awkwardly. "How's the star gazing going?"

"Confusing," she said, her voice hoarse. "I don't know what that star is."

She sounded a lot more bothered than Jess thought was necessary, but it *was* four in the morning—any strange behavior was totally acceptable at four in the morning. One could dance down the street naked at four in the morning, and no one would even bat an eye. Mainly because hardly anyone would see him, but whatever, not the point.

"Maybe it's a new one?" he offered, yawning. He wondered absentmindedly if his hair was sticking up in weird places. He didn't know why that issue was pressing at the moment, but it suddenly really was. He ran a hand through it.

"I don't know," she said. "I just don't know."

"Well, I'm sure it's not a sign of Armageddon, or anything." He looked over at her and said, "So, why are you awake?"

"I could ask the same of you," she pointed out, and he held back the sigh. It was *way* too early for him to play this game. "Woke up. Then couldn't fall back asleep."

"Nightmare?" he half-joked—only half because he couldn't muster up the brain power to decide if he was being serious or not at this hour.

"Just a lot on my mind," she said.

"Really?" he asked incredulously. It seemed like her only concern would be when she'd have to hustle pool again. "What's wrong? Amelia?"

"Her, and some other things, too." Her brow furrowed as she stared at that stupid star.

"Is it the IP address?" he guessed.

"In part," she said. "I can't get past it. Isn't that weird? I know rationally it's no big deal. It's got to be nothing. Still, I feel like it's important. Then I still have that weird feeling, and I've got other feelings too, and I just… What is *that?* It can't be a planet, but it's so bright..."

"Maybe you just need to go back to sleep," he offered. Mmm, a warm bed with soft pillows and—

Wait, what did she say?

"Other feelings?" he repeated, and she flinched. His brain had gone from sluggishly processing his surroundings to screaming at him, *"Oh my god this is your chance! This is your chance, Jess! Are you alive? Hello? Hello? Is this thing on?!"*

She nodded, biting her lip, and he swallowed around the lump in his throat.

"Yeah, I've got some of those too," he said.

"Yeah?" she asked, and she finally looked at him. He couldn't make out that look to save his life, but he knew the sudden hope rising in his chest had to be a sign of something good.

"Yeah," he said.

It would be so easy.

He leaned in, just a little bit, just to try it out. She didn't back away.

Oh my god oh my god oh my god.

He touched the bridge of his nose to hers experimentally, and he breathed. It wasn't very quiet in this city. He could hear a police siren blocks away, a dog barking distantly, and the steady roar of cicadas in the trees around him. The most prominent was his heart, beating so loudly that it threatened to drown everything else out.

'*This is it,*' he thought in disbelief. This was how it was all going to happen, at four in the freaking morning in a motel parking lot. He didn't know how he had pictured it, probably on a beach or something equally as stupidly romantic, but this would do.

His head tipped toward hers—his brain screamed out *so easy*—but then she pulled back, her hands on his chest and her eyes downcast.

"Can't," she said hoarsely. She shook her head, more as a message to herself than to him, and confusion fell over him.

But it was going to be so easy.

"Why?" he asked, feeling stupid.

"It'll screw everything up," she said softly, and he got it. Relief washed over him in waves. At least it wasn't him.

"Only if you let it," he said. She was biting her lip and breathing too quickly. He slowly moved his hand from her arm to her hand, still planted firmly against his chest.

"I don't want to ruin anything," she said, but subconsciously, her face was moving closer to his.

"You don't have to," he said.

And with that, he leaned in. The first press of their lips wasn't what we expected—there was no flash of light or wedding bells or overwhelming instrumental piece swelling in the background, but there was something incredibly intense about the way Jo's breath hitched in her throat before she started kissing him back. She pulled him closer, and he suddenly realized that his brain had completely shut down. He had gone from carefully noting every change in Jo's movements to fruitlessly trying to connect his incoherent thoughts, which had dissolved into things like, "*oh my god this is really happening. This is* really *happening.*" and "*I really hope my hair looks okay.*"

She pulled away and quickly blurted out, "This is going to—"

"Shush."

When it finally ended, she buried her face in his neck, and he briefly thought that it probably *shouldn't* be this easy, that he probably *should* be worried.

Then he turned his head to kiss the top of her head, and the doubts left his mind.

Jo

This was bad. This was very, *very* bad. Monumentally bad. Catastrophically bad.

The worst part was it seemed like she was the only one freaking out. Jess was completely unmoved by the fact that, *hello*, he kissed her last night and she sort of kissed back. He sat across the table from her desperately trying to stab his eggs with his fork, looking as good as he usually did, and—and she was *so* not admitting that she found him attractive, not first thing in the morning, and not ever.

Maybe.

She stared at his face, creased with concentration, and smiled to herself. Jess was all about the little things, like seeing a cactus in person and getting to gamble for the first time. Little things excited him, and little things upset him. She was the exact opposite, only shaken by the big, massive, asteroid-that-killed-the-dinosaur-sized pitfalls in her life. It was weird, because they weren't alike at all, not beyond the "we both eat, breathe, sleep, and mock movies from time to time" shared facts of life. Still, she… he…

She couldn't wrap her mind around it. Heaven help her if she ever had to say it out loud. She couldn't even think about it without wanting to run around in a circle to let off some stress.

And yet, he was perfectly unmoved by this huge, life-changing event that took place only a few hours ago. He went on about his life as if nothing had happened, while she freaked out for *hours*. She still couldn't believe he had managed to sleep after that.

He had pulled back from the kiss as if nothing had happened, squeezed her shoulder, and said he was going to go back to bed. Then she paced the parking lot for hours before sleeping in her car—did they need to get separate rooms now? She was out of her element. Maybe it was easier traveling with girls after all.

She guessed the reason he was okay was because only the small things affected him. She had no doubt if it had been raining today, or if he had gotten a paper cut that morning, he would have been acting strange right now. Instead, the sun was shining, blood wasn't gushing, and she was the one sitting paralyzed in a diner thinking too deeply about a boy she hadn't planed to ever think deeply about.

This was too much. Her head was going to explode. Her brains were going to go all over the wall, and the waitresses wouldn't even bat an eye. She hoped her car wouldn't be impounded after her death, because that would just be unfair. Maybe Jess could—

Why did everything come back to Jess?

"Jo, you okay?"

She realized she must have been making an absolutely *atrocious* face throughout her whole thought process, because she was already trying not to scream out in frustration, and now Jess was looking at her like she had to be constipated, or something.

"Fine," she said slowly as she tried to relax the muscles in her face.

"This is really driving me crazy," he said, and for a second, she thought he meant her. It wouldn't be the first time she annoyed someone, but she was still stuck on the way Jess had looked at her last night, like she was the axis the entire world spun around, like she could never screw up.

She watched as he viciously tried to stab the eggs, never breaking concentration.

"What did they make these out of?" he mumbled.

Oh, right. The eggs were annoying him.

"They probably are eggs, but they cooked them too long," she said.

He looked up at her, clearly surprised.

"What?" she asked uncertainly.

"No sarcastic remark about them being made out of human parts?"

"Oh, please," she said, and forced an eye roll. It wasn't her fault he went and messed up her brain. Something probably wasn't rewired correctly—that's why she was acting so weird.

"Whatever," he said, opting to shovel the eggs onto his fork. "Now you're all going to die, little eggs. I bet you wish you wouldn't have been such jerks now, huh?"

"They're already dead," she pointed out.

"Okay, you are definitely off this morning," he said.

If she could have any super power, she would totally want the ability to melt into a pile of goo on the spot. She guessed she could also pick invisibility, but she would still be *there.* At least this way she'd be a brainless pile of goo that couldn't process anything happening around her.

She shrugged, because it was the best reaction she could think of.

Jess frowned and grew silent. He shoveled the rest of his eggs onto his fork quietly, once in awhile rubbing his neck absentmindedly. Jo didn't know if she was great at reading Jess by now or if he was just incredibly easy to read, but she could tell right away that his silence was plagued with regret.

Surprisingly, thinking about him regretting the kiss made her heart ache. She wasn't sure what she was doing anymore, and she didn't know how they were ever going to be normal again. Still, she didn't think if the situation was presented again she would do anything differently.

And that was a scary thought.

"I'll be fine," she said firmly, and he looked up at her, green eyes shining dimly with something that she thought might be hope, then smiled. She returned it.

They ate the rest of their breakfast in comfortable silence, which was strange for Jo, who had never seen silence as anything but ominous and foreboding. He joked every so often about the food, and she mocked the guy sitting two tables to their left. It was familiar. Maybe things didn't have to change after all.

"Hey, Jo?" he said when they were getting up to leave. She took one look at him, decided this was probably going to be a conversation she would rather not have standing up, and quickly sat back down in her chair.

"Yeah?" she said, mentally wincing already.

He looked to his left, not meeting her eyes for the longest time. It was enough to send panic racing through her veins. He regretted it. He must have. It was the only reasonable explanation as to why he was staring a hole into the floorboards of the diner.

"You don't regret it, do you?" he said slowly, finally looking up at her. His eyes were searching her face, looking for any obvious glimpses of emotion that could manage to get past her defenses.

"No," she said. Then, quietly, "Do you?"

"No!" he said immediately, without a second wasted, and she felt the relief rush through her.

"Okay," she said. "Good."

"Yeah," he said. "Good."

* * *

The thing about following in Amelia's footsteps was that it was one part conscience-clearing and two parts really freaking creepy. They stayed in the same motels as her, usually in the exact same room, ate in the same diners, and stopped at the same tourist attractions.

She should have probably been more sympathetic toward Jess and the ghost of Amelia, but honestly, thinking about how she was sleeping in the same bed as a dead chick was leading her to sleep in the backseat of her car every night.

As creepy as it was for her, which was *really really freaking creepy,* it had to be a million times worse for Jess— she would catch him staring off into space when he was standing in certain spots. It started under a motel sign displaying "Red Indian" in bright red lights, and it had kept happening after that. One day, she emerged from the bathroom and found him standing at the foot of the bed with his eyes glazed over, not responding to anything she said.

It was bizarre. She guessed he was either having extreme cases of Amelia-induced déjà vu or was possessed. And as horrible as it was, she kind of wanted it to be the latter.

"Hey, Jess," she said softly, snapping in front of his face. He was staring blankly at an old, ancient chair that had been carefully preserved in the front of the antique store. Jo honestly had no idea why they were in there, other than the fact that Amelia had gone in and bought an overpriced doorknob once upon a time. Amelia had "a love for unloved things." Gag. Gag. Gag. Jo wanted to claw her eyes out every time she read another blog post by Amelia Darling, who was straight out of a Jane Austen novel.

Antique stores were dusty, and they reeked of mothballs and canned spray. Jo had no idea why anyone would want to own a mattress that some guy died on fifty years ago. She wasn't superstitious, and she firmly believed that monsters were not going to come out from underneath her bed one night. Still, she couldn't help but think buying a dead dude's bed would lead to some kind of Casper, the *un*friendly ghost scenario.

She would be mad if someone sold the bed she died on to an antique store. She would totally haunt their butts in the afterlife.

Jess had to be seeing ghosts—ghosts of the past—judging by what she saw in his dull eyes. She was all for some good old-fashioned moping, especially since she was fairly positive he never grieved, but the whole *I'm a living zombie!* thing was starting to freak her out.

"Come on, Jess," she said, shaking his shoulder roughly. He blinked a few times and then looked down at her questioningly. "You keep zoning out."

"Sorry," he said, sounding embarrassed. She rolled her eyes: he had been doing this for days. They were both used to the staring routine by now.

"It's just uncomfortable, I guess," he said quietly. He looked down at the ground and then back up to her face, his eyes wide. "I mean—not *this*." He gestured back and forth between the two of them. "*This* isn't uncomfortable, you and me… it's just… Everywhere we go I can see her, and it's freaking me out."

"We can go somewhere else," she said. "No one said we have to follow some dead girl's blog around the country. We can go wherever we want." She bit her lip and then added, "Minus overseas. You'd have to knock me out with anesthesia to get me on a plane. I will bite and kick if we ever come within five miles of an airport."

Jess' smile was small, barely there, but it went to his eyes, and something in her chest let go, just a little bit.

"No, I—" he hesitated, searching for the right words. Finally, he said, "I think I need to do this. I know I'll never know what happened, but I need to know that she at least… didn't give everything up for nothing."

It was a reasonable enough request, and even if it wasn't, Jo didn't think she could have said no if she tried.

* * *

Jess always boasted that he was built to pull all nighters and run on negative hours of sleep, but if that was true, he probably wouldn't have given up on college.

He passed out every night at midnight, and sometimes even sooner. She really hated when he fell asleep before then, because they were usually still out and about, and she could only carry him so far. These days he seemed to be at least trying to stay awake until they got back to their room, but Jo got the feeling he was one of those people who always *tried* to get an A on the test, but just couldn't.

Once he was asleep, she got her best work done. She didn't really know what she was trying to find, but she felt like every night she needed to search a little bit more. Maybe one night she would figure it all out.

Amelia's laptop was incredibly organized. Everything was in a folder, which had a million subfolders, which had subfolders of their own. Every song in her iTunes had the correct album, genre, and track number. Her internet bookmarks had color-coded folders. Jo had a feeling her email must have been impeccable before Amelia found herself in a situation that left her unable to check it, because the emails from back when Amelia was alive were sorted into folders based on subject—friends, school, blog comments, junk, downloads, and etc.—with proper first and last names of the senders.

Staring at the mess it was now, Jo couldn't help but feel a little bad.

She didn't know why she was so insistent on figuring out what happened to Amelia, a girl she didn't want anything to do with a few months ago. She was fairly certain there was no real trail for her to follow. Still, she kept looking, wasting hours she could have spent sleeping.

She didn't think Jess was the reason why she cared so much about a dead body, though. Yeah, Jess was great, but she felt like she couldn't let this go. She re-read Amelia's entries hundreds of times, staring at the tiny pictures of her in front of landmarks and paying special attention to the mentions of people she met. There was a crazy guy in Farragut Square, a homeless man in New Orleans, and a sobbing hooker on the streets of Memphis.

There were hundreds of emails from Scott. If Amelia had been still alive and kicking, she probably would have sorted them into three folders: pre-breakup, awkward I-don't-know-what-we-are stage, and post-breakup. The ones before their breakup were stupidly cute: Scott sent her math related riddles when she was having a bad day. Still, as grossly cute as Scott was while he was dating Amelia, his emails after their breakup were mostly capslocked messes of obscenities, enough to raise Jo's suspicions.

There were about twelve unread emails from Jess, which Jo hesitated to read. It was one thing to read a dead girl's diary and another to read a living guy's probably panic-fueled confessions of true love.

There were a couple more emails from Gregory that Amelia had replied to, but they stopped after May 28.

Jo frowned, tilting her head. That date sounded familiar. She opened a new window and went to Amelia's blog, clicking back to May.

Jo's eyebrows shot up almost immediately. Amelia's last post was from May 28.

She dragged a few emails about viagra over to the "junk" folder and called it a night.

* * *

"I have a theory," she announced the next morning over breakfast. She wasn't feeling hungry for whatever reason, contentedly sipping a milkshake while Jess devoured a huge stack of pancakes.

"That it's a demon?"

"Bunnies," she corrected. "No, really though. *Buffy* references aside."

He set down his fork, folded his hands, and stared at her.

"Why did you do that?" she asked, gesturing at his plate. "You have food."

"This feels like a serious moment, and I don't want to choke."

She rolled her eyes. "Okay, fine, whatever. I have a theory—" she paused for a second, waiting for the song lyrics. Jess kept his mouth shut, so she continued, "about this Gregory guy."

He looked down at his food and then back to her. "I'm glad I stopped eating for this one."

"Gregory's last email to her was from May 28, telling her to meet him in Farragut Square. Amelia's last blog post was from May 28."

Jess took a deep breath, and Jo thought he looked like he was trying not to hyperventilate. She bit her lip watching him. Poor guy. Maybe she shouldn't have said anything.

"So," he said finally, pushing his plate away. "How do we find this guy?"

* * *

The problem was she really didn't know how to find him, considering they had practically nothing to go off of. They spent the next two days in New Mexico in a motel room that had seen better days, scouring blog posts and internet databases. Jo searched Amelia's computer for any mention of Gregory while Jess zealously read through text messages. Initial hesitance toward complete violation of Amelia's privacy faded away, and Jess became a detective extraordinaire.

"You're like one of the Olsen twins in their mystery book series," she remarked, watching him jot down incriminating phone numbers on the motel's half-used notepad.

"I hope I'm the cuter one," he said without missing a beat. They had gotten really good at bantering. They fell into it all the time now, without even thinking about it. It came naturally to the both of them.

"There was no cuter one," she said. "They were twins."

"No, one was totally cuter than the other. There was a whole song about it when they were kids."

"I'm appalled that you spend your time on these things," she said flatly. He sat down next to her on the bed and attempted to swat her hands away from the laptop.

"Move over. I'm searching Facebook."

"Oh, of course," she said, sliding over. "Check the almighty farming website."

She looked down at the numbers written down on the paper.

"Who are these people?" she asked.

"I dunno."

Of course not.

"Well, let's find out." She held her hand out. "Phone."

"Block the number before you call, *please*," he said. He took his cell phone out of his pocket and pressed it into the palm of her hand.

"Okay, Mother."

The telephone numbers didn't *look* like they belonged to murderers. They weren't like, 666-6666 or 1-800-REDRUM. She dialed 1-3-1-0—oh my God.

"Oh my God."

Jess was immediately in front of her, practically knocking the laptop off the bed in an attempt to get to her faster. His eyes were darting around the room, and she couldn't help but wonder what he thought could be possibly wrong.

"What? What? What is it?"

He reached for the phone and frowned, confused, when he saw the screen.

"Area code?"

"Yeah, it's uh." She looked back at the screen, feeling stupid. Just because she recognized it didn't mean she knew anything else. "It's the area code from my area. It's nothing."

His eyebrows went up. "Sounds like something."

"Yeah, well…" Awkward. "I don't know…"

"Where are you from?" he asked carefully. "I know SoCal, but other than that…"

She visibly cringed. She hated that question. Jess was smart to phrase it how he had; it wasn't really her *home.* Back there she never felt like she was where she needed to be. Now, even though she didn't have four walls and a roof, she at least had something of her own. Even if it was just a beat up car.

Maybe she could change the subject.

She looked up at Jess' hopeful expression and thought, *nope, definitely can't do that.* It was insane how badly she wanted to keep him from frowning. She wasn't a talker; she didn't like confessions or heart-to-hearts. Still, Jess managed to get a lot out of her these days, simply because she was desperate to keep him happy. And she trusted him.

Now that was a *really* scary thought for her. Trusting someone? Her? *Really?* She didn't *do* trust. People came into her life, got inside her heart and her head, and then they left. And what was left behind? Destruction.

Yeah, she had sworn off trust a long time ago.

But even though she had sworn off trust, he had managed to get past her defenses. It was worse than that. She didn't just trust him: she cared about him.

Wow. Scary.

"This ridiculously rich city called Rolling Hills."

"So," he said. He leaned toward her and whispered conspiratorially, "Are you a 90210 girl?"

"No!" she said with a laugh.

"The O.C.?"

"No!"

"Did you at least live in a mansion?" he asked, and she didn't deem that question with an answer.

Her silence and awkward eye shifting must have told him all he needed to hear.

"Oh my God!" he laughed, loud and pure, and she would tell him all he ever wanted to hear if he just kept laughing like that. "You were the rich girl behind the red door, weren't you?"

"Stop alluding to teen dramas," she grumbled. "It's losing you cool points."

"I have cool points?" he asked with what she *thought* was fake enthusiasm, but she wasn't entirely sure.

"Acknowledging your own cool points automatically sets you back to zero," she said flatly.

"You're pretty cool yourself," he said earnestly.

She ignored the change in her heartbeat and said, "You can't fool me that easily."

"Darn," he muttered.

She resumed dialing the number. Jess leaned in a little too close when she pressed the phone to her ear, but she tried not to focus on it: in this strange sort-of-together-sort-of-not thing they were doing, she tried her best not to question these things.

"90274," she said out of the blue. Jess immediately grinned.

"So close," he said. She rolled her eyes.

The phone didn't even ring; instead, a cold, mechanical robot voice started talking.

"This party's phone has been disconnected by—pause—*Howard Dowle. If you are*—pause—*Howard Dowle, and wish to reactive this phone, please call the provider."*

The message ended with a loud *click.*

All Jo could say was "uhhhh" as she stared at the blank phone screen.

"Are you sure you dialed it right?" he asked, prying the phone out of her fingers. He looked at the recent calls, confusion etching his features. She was pretty sure she was wearing the same look herself.

"Maybe it wasn't anyone?" she offered, even though the feeling she had in her gut was telling her otherwise. She didn't want to throw another person into this equation. Gregory, Amelia, and now Howard? Too many people. She liked it better when they were going to Mexico to interrogate Scott.

"No, look," he said, grabbing Amelia's cell phone off the bed. He held it up in front of her. The screen read, "Gregory

Fallon," and listed a number. She took his cell phone back and looked from the recent calls to Amelia's screen. The numbers were the same.

"So," she said. "Either Gregory's phone was deactivated by a guy named Howard, or he had an alter-ego."

"It gets weirder," he said, and the look on his face was nothing short of someone-killed-my-cat serious.

"Can it really?" she asked.

He nodded slowly and said, "Fallon is *my* last name."

Jess

"Maybe you're related!" she said excitedly.

"I really doubt it," he said, prying his eyes off of her to look out the window. The town they were in was filled with tiny, family-run businesses. It would have been charming if he didn't see Amelia everywhere he looked. "My family is pretty small."

"Really?" she asked. Her tone of voice had changed. He looked back to her and saw her smile was missing.

"Yeah," he said slowly. "Just my mom, sister, and me. My grandparents are gone. Neither of my parents had siblings."

"Maybe your dad had another kid?" she offered. He could tell by the change in pitch of her voice that she was trying not to sound heartless. He liked that she cared enough to try.

"I don't think so," he said. "Maybe it's more common than we think. I'm not related to Jimmy Fallon."

"Or so you think!" she quipped.

* * *

Amelia had gone to a ranch while she was in New Mexico, where she had ridden a horse and had a long talk with a rancher about the many uses for honey. Because her blog had become their map, they were now headed there too.

The gravel crunched under the wheels of Jo's car as she pulled onto the ranch's road. The ranch was in the middle of nowhere, which was expected—just a huge field surrounded by a rotting wooden fence.

He looked over at Jo, and knew they were thinking the same thing: perfect place for stargazing. He decided if they ever came back to New Mexico he would take her here at night, just so he could see the look on her face when she looked up at the sparks of light.

The ranch had a little store they wandered into on their way back to the horses. It was hot and smelled of wood; the doors were propped open to try to let air in, just like back in Mexico. Flies flew in, landing on the plate of fudge sitting on the countertop.

The whole scene probably should have been repulsive —he could see Amelia's nose crinkling in disgust in his mind —but he found it charming in a strange sort of way. The racks stopped below his shoulders and were stocked with products that were probably made on the ranch, like honey, jam, and oddly shaped soaps.

When they made it to the horses, he could tell something was wrong with Jo. She was in her usual uncomfortable stance, biting her lip and shifting her weight from foot to foot anxiously.

"Okay," he said finally, stopping in his tracks and spinning around to face her. She looked at him strangely, as if he was the one visibly freaking out. "What is it?"

She shrugged instinctively.

"No," he chastised. "What's wrong?"

"I'm not big on animals," she blurted out. "They don't like me much either. We have a mutual distaste for each other, okay?"

He grinned, filing that away for later. Jo hated heights, silence, and animals. Got it.

"We don't have to ride them," he said, and he could see the relief washing over her.

"Are you sure?"

"I'm not a huge animal fan either," he said. She didn't look convinced, raising an eyebrow and crossing her arms.

"Oh, really?"

"Really," he said with a nod.

"No dog?"

"No dog."

"No cat?"

"I hate cats."

"Fish?"

"I had a goldfish that I won from the country fair," he said. He could tell she was about to scream "AHA!" in his face, so he added, "When I was six. It died after three days. Poor Swimmy."

"Sorry for your loss," she said flatly. He started walking again, with her at his side. "Hamster?"

"No!" he said with a laugh. "Amelia had a hamster when she was ten. It was nice until one day in July. That's when it turned. All of the sudden it started biting people and crapping all over the place. She gave it away at a lemonade sale she had."

"Fascinating."

They didn't ride the horses. Jo seemed a lot more relaxed once she knew she wasn't going to get forced onto a hairy beast anytime soon, and they chatted quietly from the safety of the fence while watching the horses run.

"You folks wanna ride 'em?" asked a gruff voice. Jo immediately frowned.

"No thanks," Jess said. "We just wanted to see them."

"Alright," the man said, looking at them suspiciously. He looked back and forth between the two of them, and Jess wondered fleetingly what he expected to find. "You two wanna pet 'em?"

"We're good," Jo said quickly. Jess glanced over at her and saw her eyes, wide and alert, and wondered why she was afraid of animals. Maybe a pony flung her off at a birthday party when she was little. He could see it now: a little Jo eagerly jumping on its back, it flinging her off into the dirt, and Jo putting her colorful vocabulary to use, thus horrifying all of the parents.

He wished they could have been neighbors growing up. She could have lived on the other side of him. He would have convinced Amelia to let Jo into her treehouse.

"If yer sure," the man said, scratching his beard. He started to walk away, but stopped, turning back toward them. Jo shot Jess a look that clearly said *what the heck is going on.* He shot one back that he hoped read as *no idea but first sign of crazy and I'm running for the car.* She smirked and turned back to face the guy.

"What are you here fer?" he asked. "Folks don't come all the way out here to just look at horses."

"Our friend came here once," Jo said carefully. "She told us about it."

"Oh yeah?" the guy said, sauntering back over to them. "What's her name? I never forget a face."

"Amelia," Jo said.

"Curly red hair, green eyes, talked about honey while she was here," Jess said, and the rancher's eyes lit up. He felt Jo tense in excitement. He could practically hear her brain screaming "recent development!"

"I remember her!" the rancher said. "Cute little thing. Loved one of the ponies. Thought she was going to take the darned thing with 'er!"

"Did she, uh—" he stopped, because he really didn't know what he wanted to ask. Amelia came here, rode a horse, petted a pony, talked about honey, and then left. It wasn't a day that held much weight in the death of Amelia Chambers.

"Was she with anyone?" Jo asked.

"Good question," he mumbled under his breath.

"No," the rancher said, scratching his beard again. "Just her."

"Did she say anything about where she was going?" she asked.

"Well, I asked 'er!" the guy said. "She said she was on a road trip across the South, but that's all she said." He gave them an odd look and then said, "Say, did somethin' happen to 'er? You two are sure askin' a lot of questions."

"We just haven't seen her in awhile," Jo said with a perfectly believable smile. If Jess didn't know her so well, he would have believed it to be genuine.

"Oh, well," the rancher look up at the blue sky, completely void of clouds. "She was here. She had a little red car. Looked expensive! She rode Apollo. I asked 'er if she had horses back home, but she said her parents wouldn't let 'er. Sad, because she was good with 'em.

"She was a polite young lady. Said she liked the ranch. Asked me about stuff. She talked about products for awhile, and how they're reusable. Then she bought some beef jerky and left."

He shrugged. "I dunno much else."

Jo nodded, smiled again, and said, "Thanks for your time."

"Sure," the guy said. "Have a safe trip home, you two."

He walked off toward a barn. They stood there for a while in silence, staring out at the gravel road. He was still trying to piece together a story in his mind, starting from the last time he saw Amelia and ending with her body shoved in an ice machine. Everywhere they went, everything they did, he added another chapter in his mind to the story of Amelia. He figured Jo was trying to do the same, only differently. He wasn't concerned about the details: he just wanted to know where she was, what she did, and that was it. He could fill in the surroundings and what she was wearing on his own. Jo, on the other hand, needed everything. Maybe that was because she hadn't known her, and now she was desperately trying to get to know her through her past.

They bought some of the homemade beef jerky on their way out.

* * *

Their next stop was Marfa, Texas, at a little hotel with white plaster walls. The parking lot was packed when they pulled up, a strange change from the usually desolate lots that accompanied the motels they stopped at.

The lobby was bustling with activity. Jess hadn't seen this much action in one building since they were in Vegas. The sounds resembled the Golden Nugget, lots of muffled cheering, whooping, and yelling.

The girl working the counter was entirely too friendly. She beamed at the two of them the second they stepped in the door.

"Good evening!" she said. "Room for two?"

Jess was surprised there even was a room, considering how many people he kept seeing. Two guys stumbled through the lobby into another room, each carrying an arm full of Lone Star beers. There was a group of girls in the corner whispering fervently to each other and giggling every so often. Three people rolled their suitcases over to the elevators. Jess wondered if they had accidentally driven all the way to Austin, judging by the activity.

Their room was actually really nice. The carpet looked new, and the wallpaper wasn't peeling. There was a couch in the corner next to the bed, along with a shiny coffee table and a large television. The best part was it smelled like laundry detergent.

And there were no mystery stains on the ceiling.

"I think we hit the jackpot," he said seriously. She nodded in agreement, and then plopped down on the bed.

"You should go get food," she suggested.

"Why can't you?" he asked, but he knew he was fighting a losing argument. Like he would refuse to do something for her. Come on.

"I'm sleepy," she whined. "Too many scary horses. I'm coming down off an adrenaline rush."

"You're crazy," he said, grabbing their room key and slipping it in his pocket.

"You're lovely," he heard her say as he walked out the door.

* * *

"Hey, guess what?" she said, the second he walked into the room. She was lying on her stomach on the bed with the laptop.

"What?" he said as he put the food on the table. He sat down next to her on the mattress.

"You have a family crest!" she said, tilting the laptop toward him. Sure enough, there it was: a red shield with a white dog/horse/monkey/demon thing holding a yellow... thing.

"...what is it?" he asked. He tried tilting his head to the side like her, hoping it would make the image make more sense. It didn't.

"No idea," she replied cheerfully. "You're Irish though. Congratulations."

"Thanks?" He asked, "Did you find out anything else?"

"Famous Fallons include—wait a second." She clicked the keypad a few times and then continued, "Our best friend Jimmy; Admiral William Joseph Fallon who is a current commander; Ed Fallon, a politician from Iowa; Jack Fallon, a jazz musician; Kieren Francis Fallon, a jockey; and Michael Cathal Fallon, a British Conservative politician. What a big happy family."

"Any Howards or Gregorys?"

"Not yet," she said with a frown. "But I will keep looking."

"There's karaoke going on downstairs," he said, and she gave him a weird look.

"You want to go?" she asked. He couldn't tell if she was mocking him or being serious.

"I was wondering if you wanted to." he said, and she smiled.

"Are you asking me on a date?"

Was he? He might as well have been. Then again...

"This is kind of like being on a date 24/7."

"Hmm. I see your point," she said. "Either way, I'm game. Food, then bad song covers?"

He grinned.

"Deal."

* * *

Jo had won four games of pool and a game of poker since they left their room. She was good enough that she could win the fair and honest way, rather than just by hustling. When he mentioned this to her, Jo said he needed to ditch his morals, and quickly.

"I think I'm in love with this place," Jo said, spinning on her heel. "It's Heaven with less clouds."

With ridiculously cheap beer, gullible locals, and a jukebox playing nothing but Elvis, it probably was Jo's version of Heaven.

"Needs more ocean," he said. She laughed and grabbed his arm, pulling him over to one of the booths. She looked over his shoulder at the small stage sitting at the front of the room and snorted. There was a scruffy, burly guy wearing plaid belting out lyrics to "Don't Stop Believing" on the stage.

Badly belting.

Really badly belting.

"Look at these people!" she said, laughter in her voice. "This restores my faith in humanity. I love the universe."

"Boom de Yada?"

She rolled her eyes.

He looked from her to the stage, grinning as an evil plan formulated in his mind. "Truth or dare?" he asked.

She looked at him like he was insane. "How old are we, twelve? I'm not at a slumber party, thank you."

"Truth," he said, leaning a little too far into her personal space. "Or dare?"

"Conditions?" she asked, chewing on her lip.

"Conditions?" he repeated.

"I need something to help me make my decision," she said slowly, deliberately. "I'm not saying truth unless I know it's not something ugly."

"That's the whole point of Truth or Dare," he said. "You can't know."

He could tell she was getting frustrated now; her eyebrows were knitted together, and her hand was twitching. Her glare seemed unmovable. He experimentally grinned at her; she kept on glaring. He had definitely hit a chord with her.

"So what's it going to be?" he asked.

"Dare," she said, planting her hands on her hips. He smiled again. Just what he had expected.

He pointed to the stage and said, "There's your dare. Go sing a song."

She raised an eyebrow. "That's it?" she asked. "That's your best dare?"

His face must have shown his disappointment, because Jo laughed, squeezing his arm.

"You're really cute," she said over her shoulder as she walked toward the stage.

He stared at her back for a few seconds, just blinking, trying to figure out what he had done that was so adorable to her. He had thought he was being absolutely cunning. It wasn't fair: his plans always fell apart.

Jo worked the stage as if it belonged to her. If he hadn't known better, he would have thought she was a full time performer, just judging by how comfortable she looked in front of the crowd. Her voice was off key, and she lost her place in the song halfway through. But it didn't matter. She laughed it off, kept pushing through, and in return, everyone in the room gave her their full attention. They were completely enthralled with her, and they had the right to be.

It reminded Jess of the first time he saw her, how all of the light in the bar seemed to bend towards her, making it seem like she was the only thing that mattered.

The thing was, even when the light wasn't bending in, Jess still felt like it was.

She jumped off the stage once she was done and headed straight for the bar. He followed her through the throngs of people, mostly drunk, and came up next to her at the counter.

"You were amazing," he said, and she smirked. "Really amazing."

"Should have picked a harder dare," she said. "That was nothing."

"Here," he said, taking her beer from her. His fingers brushed the back of her hand, and he smiled at the warmth. "Let's go outside."

"Okay?" she said, sounding confused.

The sky wasn't as clear as he hoped it would be, but he could still see a few stars peaking out from behind clouds, trying to shine. She climbed up on the hood on her car, automatically throwing her head back to look at the sky. He wondered if she ever wanted to be an astronaut, or even an astronomer. She would have been good at it.

"I don't have a clue what I'm doing," she said abruptly. She looked bothered with her mouth twisted to the side and a hand buried in her hair. "I don't... I mean, I never. I— This is —"

"Jo," he said, catching her attention. She looked up at him reluctantly, brown eyes clouded with self-doubt. If he looked in a mirror, he was sure he'd see the same look. "I don't know what I'm doing either."

He climbed up onto the hood next to her.

"I don't know about this or Amelia or Gregory or why we're even doing this." He let out a deep breath and said, "I just know that I'm here and you're here, and that's enough."

She let out one shuddering breath. He saw her shut her eyes, breathe in deep, and let it out again.

"Are you scared?" she whispered.

That was a question he knew he could answer.

"Yes," he said. "I don't know if I want to know what happened. I know I need to know, though." He watched her breathe for another second and then asked, "And you?"

"I'm terrified."

He laughed softly, even if it was inappropriate; he felt like he had to, to remind himself that he was alive, to get drunk off the sensation.

"Truth or Dare?" she asked, shaking him out of his thoughts. He squinted his eyes as he looked at her. She looked different now, better. If a quick confession from him was all it took to change her demeanor, he'd tell her about the time when he was six and he stole a chocolate bar from the grocery store.

"Really?"

"Yes!" she said, as if it was the most obvious thing in the world. "You had your chance; now it's mine."

"Fine," he said with a sigh. "Truth."

She raised an eyebrow. "So you're one of *those* people," she said.

"One of what people?" He didn't even know what she was insulting him for, but he felt like he should be offended.

"You're afraid of taking a chance," she said. "You play it safe."

"That's stupid," he said immediately. "I already took the biggest chance I'll ever take."

"Oh really?" she said sarcastically. "And that was?"

"Leaving with you."

She immediately went into embarrassed Jo mode, fidgeting like crazy and focusing on anything but his face. He shook his head in amusement. He didn't know why she was so surprised. Not everyone would have done it.

"So," he said. "I pick truth."

"Fine," she said after clearing her throat. She looked down, and then back up at him slyly, through her lashes. "What was Amelia like?" she asked softly.

He leaned back on the hood, looking up at the vast emptiness of the night sky.

"She was… the most beautiful girl I had ever seen," he admitted, and saying it was like letting out a breath that he had been holding for too long. "Her eyes were always so bright. It was like they could see into your soul, and honestly, I wouldn't have put it past her if she could.

"I knew more about her than anyone else, but she still was a mystery. She had this crazy laugh that made *you* laugh, just from hearing it. She was fun. Just being around her was an adventure. She was always blurting out things that didn't make any sense and making spontaneous decisions to do things. She made people feel special."

He looked back down at the asphalt: cold, dry, boring, a lot like he used to be.

"She made me feel special." He frowned and then added, "But she was selfish, and she was self-centered. She was caught up in her own world that no one seemed to fit into besides herself. And that's why, I think, that even though we were close our whole lives—I mean, we grew up together—she always shut me out. Because in the end, Amelia was Amelia, and she couldn't fit anyone else into the equation."

"You loved her," Jo said.

"Yeah," he replied. "And I miss her. But I'm okay, because I think that even though I loved her, she wasn't a person who could love back, because it would have held her back."

Jo nodded, looking down again. He knew Jo must have understood that. She and Amelia weren't really that different. Jo wanted freedom. So did Amelia. The difference was that Jo hadn't let anything stand in her way of getting it; Amelia had spent years trying to bury her desires.

"Truth or Dare?" he heard himself ask, and Jo looked at him expectantly, waiting for the right moment where she knew she had his complete attention.

"Truth," she said. He could feel her eyes burning into his face: her gaze was so intense.

"What's your family like?"

It was hard to picture Jo with a life outside of her car, the stars, and a million crappy motel rooms with mysterious stains on the ceilings, but he knew at one point she didn't have any of that. The things she loved now had to have been preoccupied by other things, other people. He just wanted to know what.

"Horrible," she said immediately, looking back up at the stars. "My mom was having an affair with her personal trainer, and I'm pretty positive my dad's business trips are a really *special* type of business."

"Any siblings?" he asked.

"Oh God," she groaned, rolling her eyes. He guessed that was a yes. "So many. It was like I was living in an orphanage. Three sisters, one brother, some well-bred dogs. It was awful."

"It doesn't sound that bad," he said.

"Yeah, because you weren't there," she pointed out. "If you had been there, you would have seen. I still think I was adopted. I refuse to believe I share DNA with any of those people." She paused, tilted her head, pursed her lips. "Actually, if you would have been there, things might have been better."

Oh, *wow*. Jo was really in touch with her feelings tonight. It was mind blowing. He didn't think he'd ever hear this kind of stuff come out of her mouth.

"What about you?" she asked. "You have a sister, right?"

"Yeah."

"Older?"

"Younger." He added, "Cassie."

"Pretty name," she said. "How old is she?"

"Fourteen." He looked up at one of the clouds, moving a little too fast across the sky. A storm must be headed their way. "I miss her a little."

"At least she has your mom," she pointed out, and he nodded. That much was true.

"Do you think your family misses you?"

She snorted. "*Please.* They probably haven't even noticed I'm gone yet. It's not like we had dinner every night at seven, or family game night. I was lucky if I saw my parents together at Christmas."

"Sorry," he said, because he didn't know what else to say, not really.

"Don't be," she replied. "Family shouldn't be defined by what's running through your veins, anyway."

She leaned a little closer to him, just a little bit, and he noticed another star had come out in the sky.

Jo

"I don't understand what it is," he said.

She groaned. "You are so uncultured."

He cocked his head to the side as he studied the towering wooden mass rising out of the desert floor. It was faded and falling apart, showing no signs of its former glory.

"I don't get it," he said for the third time. "It's just a skeleton of a building. I don't get it."

"It's the Reata Ruins!"

The blank look he gave her confirmed the fact that he really truly didn't get it. Oh boy.

"It was the filming site for the movie *Giants*."

Still nothing. He kept staring at her with that dead, lifeless look. What kind of a childhood did this guy have, anyway?

"The one with James Dean, the last film he did..." she trailed off once she saw his face change from one hundred percent confusion to ninety-five percent.

It was progress.

"Oh," he said, turning back to the wood. "What did it used to be?"

"A huge Victorian mansion."

He frowned and said, "This is kind of sad then. It's like it withered away to nothing."

"Really?" she asked, tilting her head to the right. "I think the opposite. It has withstood fifty-five years. That's gotta have a lesson about endurance tucked away somewhere."

She saw him smile out of her peripheral vision.

"So you're one of *those* people," he said, and she frowned, because that was *her* line. "The glass is half full, huh?"

"Hardly," she said. She crossed her arms, and to her horror, he laughed. Her attitude used to instill fear in him. Now he thought it was cute. Her arms fell to her sides. Not fair.

"You think you can hide it, but you can't," he said with grin. "I can read you like a book. I aced Jo-101. I'm practically fluent in Jo-isms."

"Shut up," she said, but she was secretly fighting the smile and the laugh that was threatening to come up out of her throat. There was a feeling building in her chest, and it made her feel a little dizzy, like she couldn't see the ground.

"Not that I don't appreciate the wood here," he said, and he was totally lying. He was doing that weird Bambi thing again, where his eyes got incredibly big and his mouth fought to not turn up at the corners: Jess' lying face was a joke. "But I'm starving."

"Guess you won't want to see Little Reata, then."

"We can go see it," he said, and his face was back to normal. "I'll go if you want to."

She rolled her eyes, because she didn't know how to react to his cuteness sometimes. It made her feel warm, like someone was suffocating her with a hug.

"Nah," she said. "I'll spare you. Let's go get lunch."

The strange thing about this town was that everyone was *nice.* It was a little bit unnerving when strangers smiled at her from across the room without any noticeable intent. They were eating lunch when an old woman sat down at the table with them and asked them how they were enjoying the town.

It was bizarre.

She guessed in a city with a population of 2,000 everyone noticed when there was someone who shouldn't be there. They were nice about it though, as if they were genuinely happy to see a new face. Another woman asked them what their final destination was when they were looking around a gift shop. Rather than explaining the whole "we're traveling around the country through the South tracing some dead girl's steps in hopes of finding out what was the real cause of her death besides just being shoved in an ice machine" spiel, she said they were on a cross-country road trip before Jess had the chance to freeze up.

Leaving the little town was strange; she felt like everyone was watching them from the windows, waiting to see if they saw anything that could tell them if she had enjoyed the town or not.

"Let's get out of here," she mumbled, unlocking her car door. Her things hadn't been messed with, at least. She assumed this was one of those towns where you could leave your wallet out in the open all day and no one would touch it. Creepy.

"Amen," Jess replied. He wrenched open the door so quickly that she had to bite her tongue to stop herself from complaining about the hinges.

"So I'm not the only one creeped out then?" she asked as she climbed into the driver's seat.

"Heck no," he replied quickly. "I've been waiting for one of them to kidnap me since we walked into that cafe."

She snorted. "No, really," he continued. "They all had this crazy thing going on with their eyes."

"Oh come on!"

"No, I'm being serious!" he protested. "I was fearing for my life in there. I thought that one guy was going to invite us to stay at his place, and then cut off locks of hair while we were sleeping."

"Oookay," she said. "You've watched too many horror films. Calm down."

"This stuff happens!" he cried, and she could tell this rant was going to go on for awhile. She pulled out of the parking lot quickly, throwing a glance at the motel window. Yup, she definitely saw a face in it.

"It's always in small towns, too," he said. "You never hear about these kind of crazies in medium-sized cities, you know? *Never* in big cities, because they're so huge. People would rather report on bombs in subways than one crazy middle-aged dude who kidnapped some young couple and kept them in his basement for two days while he took pictures with them on his camera phone."

Couple. The one word stuck in her mind, and the rest of her thoughts about gas stations, highways, and Amelia's blog map vanished immediately. Couple. He said they were a couple.

Why was this so surprising to her? Were they not one? She didn't know what else they would be. They weren't really friends with benefits, considering the "benefits" didn't stretch beyond sanity. They weren't just friends, either. They were something more than that. But this thing they had stretched beyond the fact that now they were kissing in public places. Lately, she had had this growing feeling that she wouldn't be okay if he decided to leave. She didn't think he was going to, but she still worried about it when she woke up in the middle of the night and noticed the room was empty. He usually was in the bathroom, but it always still managed to send her into full-on panic mode.

As much as she hated to admit it, she needed him. She really, truly did. But she thought that he needed her too. Because as messed up as she was before she met him, he was just as bad. Yet when they were together, they weren't that bad. They weren't perfect, because they both still had enough emotional baggage to use as material for a fifteen season long soap opera, but they were much better than they were.

In a messed up way, they were fixing each other, even though they were both broken.

"Probably would post them all over his Myspace too, the creep. Even though no one even uses Myspace anymore."

Jess just kept ranting on the other side of the car, completely unaware of the epiphany she was having on her side. She smiled to herself, thinking about how oblivious he was.

"And, and—" Pause. "What are you so happy about?"

"Nothing," she said immediately, shrugging. She focused on the dirt road in front of her; she'd have to wash her stupid car once they got to Austin. She wondered if she'd see a gas station on the way there. It always felt like—

She could feel him just *staring* at her, watching for some clue as to what she was thinking about. She thought harder about car washes. The only problem with having broken windows was that she couldn't just run her car through an automated wash. But then again, they were always overpriced, and half the time they didn't even get the car completely clean.

Maybe she could find a high school fundraiser. That could work. Then again, the lazy kids usually took forever, and she really didn't want to bother standing around yelling at them to get their butts in gear—she would never just *leave* her *car* with a bunch of stupid teenagers. She sighed. There was only one option: she would have to wash it herself.

He was still watching her, as if he had nothing better to do with his time, which she figured probably was true—they had a seven hour drive to Austin, and it wasn't like she had TVs built into the back of the seats. But still, it was scaring her a little.

"Okay, fine," she said. "You called us a couple. Now stop staring at me."

She saw him frown, confused as usual. How was one person so lost all the time? She wondered how he even survived this long in the real world: he probably had to constantly stop and ask strangers how to do laundry and microwave his Easy Mac.

"I don't—"

"Get it, I know," she tried her best to say it sympathetically, but she was just really bad at that whole emotional empathy thing. Meanwhile, he kept staring. This was going to be a really long drive.

She sighed. "It's just… we hadn't classified it until now. That's all."

"Do you not want to classify it?" he asked, and she was kind of getting sick of this whole *whatever you want is fine by me* thing he was always trying to pull. She liked making her own choices, but having to choose for the both of them was weighed down by too much.

"No, I want you to stop wanting what I want," she said. "I don't *want* us to not be a couple, and I don't want to not call it what it is. I just want you to stop gaping at me because I'm still freaked out by Stalker City back there, and I don't understand why I can't be happy about something without you wanting to interrogate me."

She took in a huge breath of air. There. That should calm him down for awhile. Surely he would just get quiet now and mind his own business and—

"I just want to see you laugh more," he admitted, and she almost drove the car off the road. When did this become confession hour? She wasn't mentally prepared for these bombs.

"You have a pretty laugh," he said. He was just going to keep going, wasn't he? She had to endure seven hours stuck in a car with him while he went on about his secret love for her laugh and stared at her like a creep. She was going to suffocate.

* * *

austin, texas, baby!

everything is bigger in texas. ie: sandwiches. i'm dying. i feel my thighs growing. anyway, my wretched sunburn has faded to a nice golden brown. i'm spending the next few days chilling by the pool here. and by pool i mean the **fourth largest natural springs in the state.** *see? texans are obsessed with size. does fourth largest seem anything to brag about? no. i can tell you though i think my thighs have grown four times since i got here. now that's an accomplishment.*

anyway, i'm going to catch a concert while i'm here. there's a big music festival going on. sounds fabulous. worthy of a appearance by yours truly.

uh, so yeah. that's the austin plan. holiday inn (classy), jams, pool, and chicken sandwiches that make your butt too big for your jeans. awesome opossum. i feel like i should start teasing my hair while i'm here. fit in a little more.

It was a seven hour drive to Austin. When she stopped for gas, Jess ran inside and returned ten minutes later with two blueberry bagels.

"Breakfast!" he said in a sing-song voice, waving it front of her face.

She didn't have the heart to tell him that she really hated blueberries.

Instead, she took it with a probably far too cheesy smile and climbed back in the car.

"How long is it to Austin?" he asked after fifteen minutes.

"A really long time if you're already worried about it," she replied. She saw him cross his arms and— "Oh my god. You're totally pouting."

"Am not."

"Are too!"

"Fine," he said. "I'm pouting. You didn't like your bagel."

Ruh-roh. She thought she was good at faking, too.

"Sure I did," she lied. "I ate it, didn't I?"

"You choked it down."

"That's what she said."

"Jo."

"Mother."

"I thought you liked bagels!"

"It's way too early for this."

They fell silent, and she tried to focus on avoiding the potholes in the road.

"Why do you never drive on the highway, anyway?" he mumbled.

"Because," she said, already feeling exasperated. He was wearing his confused little baby deer look again, so she decided to take pity on him. "There's idiots and crazies, stupid teenagers and blind grandmas. Tons of people who shouldn't have their licenses because they don't look before changing lanes, stop abruptly, and don't tie down their freaking wooden cabinets in the backs of their trucks."

"Personal experience?"

She rolled her eyes. "Last time I was on a highway, a shelf flew out and came at my windshield. I'm still holding a grudge."

Ten minutes passed before she started to feel a little bad for being rude. She tried to get another look at him without driving off the road, but she could only see the back of his head looking out the window. She wondered if he was seriously sad that she didn't like breakfast. She had a boy who cared if she liked her breakfast or not. Even worse, he was sad when she didn't.

She never thought she'd stoop to this level.

"I appreciated the gesture," she said. He stirred out of the corner of her version. "Really."

He must have sensed she was dangerously teetering on the edge of discomfort, because he dropped it after that. She was glad they didn't have to go through the whole "I just want you to be happy and I want bagels to make you happy and I like it when you're happy because I like you" spiel again, because she wasn't sure she could have kept from crossing over the center line.

"Why are you anti-chick flick moments?" he asked.

"Stop reading my mind," she groaned. "This isn't cool."

"What?"

"Nothing," she said with a sigh. She drove past a billboard advertising Gerald's Cheese Barn. Some people were completely insane.

"So?" he asked, and she looked over at him.

"So?" she echoed.

"Why are you?" he asked, and she could tell he was getting some sick enjoyment out of this. He thought he was being clever again, with that hello-I'm-attempting-to-be-sly smile and that I-can't-raise-one-eyebrow-to-look-cool-like-you-so-I'll-just-raise-both thing his face was doing.

"You could probably guess," she said. Talking to him was like taking a lie detector test: good luck not telling the truth. It just poured out of her. It was pathetic, really. The worst part was she couldn't tell if she loved it or hated it. Congrats to him for being the only person to know anything but half-truths about her.

He was looking at her like he was watching a soap opera, halfway between pity and excitement.

She wondered how bad it would hurt if she threw herself out of her moving car.

"Oh, come on," she said. "Don't give me that 'oh please, Jo, please go on!' look of yours. I'm sure you can fill in the blanks. Didn't get along with family, didn't have a lot of people to profess my undying love for, etcetera etcetera."

He didn't say anything, which was completely out of character for him. She glanced over at him. He was smiling, looking down at his hands, but still smiling.

"What?" she asked, and he shook his head.

"You used to not talk to me," he said, and she could hear the smile in his voice.

"Don't get smug about it," she said, but he was pretty sure he could hear it in hers as well.

* * *

Austin passed in a blur of disappointment. There were no concerts going on. The pool was closed for cleaning. It felt like it rained for forty days and forty nights, and all that jazz. They spent two days sitting in their motel room, listening to the couple next door fight over who said what and if he really hated her cooking or not.

It would have been excruciating if Jess hadn't decided to rent movies on Pay-Per-View. It was funny: when they were lying on a smelly couch eating take out Chinese food and watching Sandra Bullock's latest flick, she forgot that they were following a dead girl's path through the South in hopes of finding out who killed her. Instead, she was struck with an overwhelming, panic-stricken sense of *normalcy.* Maybe this was what happened when two people were dating in the real world.

Amelia went straight from Austin to Baton Rouge, so like the dutiful blog readers they were, they followed suit.

"These drives are getting longer and longer," Jess mumbled as he emerged from the bathroom. He wiped the back of his palms on his pants.

"You know you can't wipe off the germs like that, right?" she asked.

"It just makes me feel better," he said, pushing past her and heading back toward the car. She raised an eyebrow as he stormed off. Someone was feeling angry today.

"What's your problem?" she asked, unlocking the door. She didn't like to admit it, because she really hated it when people were wimps about the heat, but it was hot—too hot. Times like these she wished she had better air conditioning in her car. Then again, her mileage was pretty amazing.

"Nothing," he mumbled, looking out the window.

Something was definitely wrong with him. Jess was mister emotional confessions. Her brain was firing up danger alerts, but would she listen?

"Oh, come on," she heard herself say, and no, apparently not. "*Something* is. I can tell."

She turned so her back was against the door. From this angle, she could see people walking across the parking lot, little kids skipping after their parents, overjoyed by the thought of french fries.

"I—" he started, and then stopped. He turned his head toward her for a second, probably trying to judge her expression, and she noticed the *hi-I'm-kind-of-sort-of-totally-obviously-hiding-something-from-you-ha-I-hope-you-don't-notice* look immediately. She rolled her eyes. She wondered why he even bothered trying to hide things from her anymore; he failed every time he tried.

"Spit it out."

"It'smysister'sbirthday," he said quickly. She stared at him for a few seconds, trying to process what he said.

When she finally did, she said, "Call her."

"What?" he asked, shocked.

What did he think this was? Prison? He was allowed phone calls.

"Call her," she repeated, shrugging. "Say hi. Sing a song. Whatever floats your boat."

"Oh-kay?"

He still looked surprised. She shook her head, looking back at the dash. She would never understand him. Ever.

Two minutes later, she glanced over at him and saw the phone pressed against his ear. He was cracking his knuckles. He had to be nervous. She wondered if she would be nervous if she called one of her sisters for their birthdays. She doubted they would even pick up.

"Hey, Cas," he said softly. He hardly had the second syllable out of his mouth before he was wrenching the phone away from his ear, cringing at the noise. She could hear a faint, high pitched screaming coming from the phone. "You know, I was hoping I would go deaf today," he said into the speaker.

Jo tried her best not to listen while he talked. It felt wrong, listening in on the conversation. It felt too private for her to intrude. She leaned her head against the headrest and thought about chicken sandwiches.

"I don't know," she heard him say. She lifted her head, and he was frowning. He had the Panic Eyes. This couldn't be good.

"I'll have to call you back," he said. Then, "No, really, I promise, Cas. I'll talk to you later."

He pulled the phone back from his ear, hit a button, and sighed.

"Sooo?" Jo said, hand already hovering over the key in ignition. He grabbed her hand, pulling it away from the keys.

"Wait," he said. "I need to ask you something. She wants me to visit her."

She felt her heart drop immediately. She was pretty sure it went straight through her stomach, all the way to her feet.

"Oh," she said, trying to figure out what to say. 'Nice knowing you!' 'Send me a postcard.' 'I never cared about you at all.'

"I know it's far off the trail," he said. "But I promise not to complain about peeing, if it's any consolation."

Wait, what?

"Wait, what?" She asked, "You want me to come with you?"

Cue Confused Bambi Face.

"Yeah?" he said weakly. "Do you not want to?"

"No, I do, I just—" she laughed nervously. "Never mind."

The engine made its familiar rumbling noise as it came to life.

"Where do you live again?"

"Kansas."

She groaned immediately. "Are you kidding me? You're going to be whining the whole time. That's like a 13 hour drive."

She pulled out of the parking lot before he could say anything.

Jess

"No."

"Joooo," he said, opening her car door. "Come on."

"No." She stubbornly held onto the steering wheel. Through a curtain of hair, she slyly looked over at him.

"I'm still here," he pointed out. She looked back to the road. Okay, this was insane.

"Come on," he said again. When she didn't move, he leaned forward and un-clicked her seatbelt. He grabbed her arms, yanking her out.

"No no no no no no."

"Yes!"

The house looked the same as it always did, small, white, two-story, ridiculous shrubs out front that blocked the kitchen window. He could see their trampoline peaking out from behind the back of the house, the same one he had broken his arm jumping on with Amelia when they were eleven. Cassie's bike was propped up against the side of the house, and the upstairs windows were open, which was probably a sign that the air conditioner was acting up again. The grass was mowed, but there were spots that had been missed, a sure sign that Cassie had taken over the lawn duty in his absence.

Next door, the blue house was dark. He wondered if Amelia's parents had moved.

With that obvious exception, it was like nothing had changed on the small street. He hadn't expected life to stop while he was gone, but he didn't picture it continuing as if nothing had happened. It was strange; if he stood with his back to Amelia's, everything looked exactly the same. It was as if the world had been spinning around their street for months now, keeping everything the same. The sidewalks were still lined with flowers, kids were still riding around on bikes, and the house to the right of his still looked abandoned—*haunted,* Amelia had insisted almost a decade ago, prompting their soon to be disastrous exhibition into the creepy, dark, wooden house. The pastel colored homes blended seamlessly together into the perfect color scheme, and he could only tell the differences between them if he leaned in close and squinted, taking note of the number of windows and where the fans were positioned on the porches. People were outside on the lawns, barbecuing and chatting about the latest town happenings, and Jo looked out of place amidst the Apple Pie setting.

"You should meet them," he said, releasing his death grip on her arm and reaching for her hand instead. When Jo was confident, she turned all the eyes in the room on her as easy as turning a dial. When Jo was insecure, she tried her best to shrink into the surroundings. As hard as she tried, her foreign aura stuck out, grabbing attention that was, for once, unwanted.

"I don't want to," she mumbled. "You should just go see them. I'll go get a burger. They want to see you, not me. In fact, I'm probably the last person they want to see, considering—"

"Quiet," he said, pulling her up the stairs onto the porch. The cushions on the wicker chairs looked slightly damp, and there was water on the white railings. He picked up the ceramic frog and shook it upside down. A silver key tumbled out onto the welcome mat.

"You guys hide your key in a frog?" she asked, peering over his shoulder. "That's so cute."

"What did you do?" he asked, and she let go of his hand to cross her arms. She looked off to the side. Jo's family must have really been lacking the "We Are Family" traits if every mention of them caused Jo to immediately relapse into her old, stolid self.

"We had our keys on us," she said. "The only time anyone lost them was when my brother got drunk and hit a stop sign. I woke up at three in the morning with him screaming at me to unlock the door. I didn't sleep with my window open after that."

"Geeze," he mumbled as he stuck the key in the lock. He didn't even have the chance to turn it before the door swung open, and he was knocked backwards.

"It's you! It's you! You're here! It's you!" A voice screamed in his ear. He laughed, wrapping his arms around her. His senses were overwhelmed with the smell he immediately identified as his sister.

"Suffocating," he choked out, and she gave him one last squeeze before pulling back. She was the same height as always, and her hair was still the same shade of blonde, grazing her chin. "Happy fifteenth."

She grinned bigger and jumped forward to hug him again.

"Missed you," she mumbled into his shirt.

"Same, Cas," he breathed, ruffling her hair. She immediately wrenched back from him to fix it, pursing her lips. *Girls.*

He looked over at Jo, who was trying to sneak back to the car again. Like he would let her get away.

"Cas," he said, grabbing her by the shoulders and turning her around. "This is Jo."

Jo immediately froze and whipped around to face them.

"Um," she said, tucking a strand of hair behind her ear. "Hi."

Cassie stared at her for a second and then said, "Sooooo… You two together?"

If Jo had been questioning running before, now she was planning on it. She kept looking off to the side, toward her car, and then glancing back at Cassie. Wash, rinse, repeat.

"Yeah," he said, earning a look from Cassie. He couldn't tell if it was of approval or disgust, or just general interest, but he knew Jo was about three seconds from bolting if he didn't do something. "But it's *your* birthday!"

That seemed to please Cassie enough, and she grabbed his arm, dragging him inside. He reached for Jo's hand with his free hand. She reluctantly took it. He guessed meeting the family wasn't something she did best. He almost laughed at the idea of it—she probably always showed up in her scuffed up boots and shortest skirt, makeup a mess and attitude even worse, and muttered cryptic answers to questions under her breath.

"Jess?" A petite brunette emerged from the kitchen.

"Mom." He grinned. The smile was immediately returned.

"Isn't this great?" Cassie gushed. "Best birthday present ever. Plus, look, Mom. It's a two for one deal!" She grabbed Jo by the shoulders, and Jess could practically hear her thoughts, panic-stricken exclamations written in all caps if they were put on paper. "This is Jess' girlfriend, Jo!"

"It's great to meet you," his mom said, immediately rushing forward to shake Jo's hand. Jo weakly shook it, looking over at him to send him a look he figured must have meant *help they're in my personal space and I don't know what to do about this help help help!*

"I don't have a gift," he said, trying to turn the attention away from Jo. Cassie rolled her eyes, and Jess had forgotten that Jo hadn't been the one to invent eye rolling. She wasn't even the first person he had seen roll her eyes. Cassie was the first girl who regularly did it around him.

"You are my gift, stupid," she said. She grabbed his arm again and pulled him toward the kitchen.

* * *

His mom's chocolate cake tasted the same as usual, and the chair at the head of the table was still wobbly. Jo seemed more caught up in the feeling of family than he was. It was like one of those Hamburger Helper commercials. Jo was completely enthralled in this life, listening closely to his mother talk and complimenting her cooking and decorating every few seconds. He had put together that Jo's family wasn't close, but he hadn't thought the concept of homemade birthday cake was that foreign to her.

"So where have you guys been?" his mom asked, gathering their plates and setting them in the sink.

"All over," Jo gushed. She really *was* enjoying this. And to think, she had wanted to stay in the car.

"We're sort of…" following a dead girl's blog around the South.

"Retracing Amelia's steps," Jo finished, and his mom's eyebrows shot up in surprise. Jo got a funny look on her face and looked over at him.

"We found her blog," he explained. "She had catalogued everywhere she went."

His mom sighed, sitting back down at the table. "Jess," she started, and he hadn't seen this look on her face since his pet fish died. "I don't know how to tell you this, but they found Amelia's body. She's—"

"I know," he said. "We know." He nodded at Jo. His mother's eyes widened in surprise. Jo smirked at him.

"How?" his mother asked, and Jess frowned. Now *this* was going to be a long story.

* * *

Cassie begged them to stay the night; they were both exhausted from being up for nearly twenty hours, and Jo was enjoying her trip into *The Brady Bunch* far too much for him to have the heart to rip her away from it. He had never seen her smile so much. His mother thought she was "intelligent and charismatic," and gushed every time Jo asked about another worthless knickknack they had lying around the house. Jo soaked up every ounce of the attention she got, leaving Jess to wonder just how bad her relationship with her parents must have been if she got this much joy out of hearing someone's mom talk at length about the time she was at a yard sale on the outskirts of town and found a monkey lamp at the bottom of a box.

He stared at his clean desk suspiciously. The small piece of organized sanity seemed entirely out of place in his bombshell of a room. Everything else was exactly as he left it, jeans discarded on the floor, books strewn across the nightstand, sheets ruffled. The closet door was thrown open, and clothes were lying at the bottom where they had fallen off their hangers. It was obvious he left in a hurry. He could still remember that night like it was yesterday, frantically running back and forth, shoving his favorite shirts into his suitcase and wishing he wouldn't have refused to ball up his socks last week when his mom dumped the clean clothes on his bed.

"Jess?"

He turned and saw Jo leaning against the doorway. "Hey."

"Hey," she said, glancing behind him at the stacks of books on his shelf. A second later she was crouched on the ground, pulling out paperbacks and smiling to herself.

"I don't get it," he said. She looked up at him, and he gestured between her and the books. They had reached the point now where they were good enough without words as they were with them. If it wasn't for Jo's hatred for silence, they might have given up speech all together.

"I don't really have time," she said simply.

"But you do like books," he said. "You said before you picked them up for other people."

She shoved *Great Expectations* back into its rightful spot on the shelf and pulled out his copy of *Inherit the Wind*.

"I used to read. Too much driving now. I love this play." she said, flipping it over to read the back. She grabbed another book, *The Odyssey* this time, and ran her fingers over the worn cover.

"It was my favorite," he said. "The adventures…"

"I was more of an—aha!—*Into the Wild* person." Half of his bookshelf was on the floor now, but Jo was beaming as she flipped through the book, so he didn't really care.

"Really? I thought it was boring at parts."

"Never." She glared at him. "This?" She waved it in front of his face. "This is *raw*. This is the best example of human nature I've ever seen."

"Of what?" he asked. "Of what happens when you get the idea in your head that you're invincible?"

"There's a quote in here by Leo Tolstoy," she started. He gave her a questioning look, and she sighed, handing the book to him. His fingers brushed hers as he reached out to take it. Even once he was holding it, she didn't let go.

"I wanted movement and not a calm course of existence. I wanted excitement and danger and the chance to sacrifice myself for my love." Her eyes were boring into his, and he was beginning to wonder if she was still quoting Tolstoy, or if she was speaking about herself.

"I felt in myself a superabundance of energy which found no outlet in our quiet life."

It hadn't resonated like this the first time he had read it. He couldn't even remember reading that quote, but now… He looked at Jo, really *looked* at *her,* and he got it. He finally got it. All of this time he had thought he was getting closer, thought that the taste of greasy diner food and feel of broken mattresses were finally starting to seem more charming than scary, thought the feel of the wind in his hair while they were driving down one of those long, empty roads was more fun than any day spent in Facebook chat, but now he understood all of it, even the gas station bathrooms.

She must have known it, because she immediately dropped her hand and started piling the books back onto the shelf.

"Everyone is trying to do something extraordinary, Jess," she said softly. "Some people die trying."

We're all just burning stars. Eventually, we burn out.

He moved to set the book back on the shelf, but at the last second, he laid it on his bed. Maybe it deserved a reread.

* * *

He hit the ground with a thud, slamming his head on the coffee table on his way down. Dazed, he stared up at the ceiling and tried to place his surroundings.

"You're going to get brain damage if you keep doing that."

Jo was sitting in the blue armchair, watching him with amusement. She was in a sweatshirt that he immediately recognized as his. She looked tired. The room was too dark for him to make out the time on the clock on the mantle, so he settled for oblivion.

"I told you you could have my bed," he reminded her as he climbed back onto the couch. He had always thought it was the most uncomfortable couch in the world growing up, but now, after months of motels, it felt like the best bed he could have ever imagined.

"I know," she said with a sigh. "But it was really quiet. Like eerie quiet. I kept imagining the sound of someone else's breathing. At least on the road when I can't sleep I can listen to your snoring."

"Gee, thanks," he said, reaching for the book on the ground. Maybe reading about some guy's lonely death wasn't the best idea before bed. He could make out Jo's shape in the darkness, perched on the edge of the armchair, sagging from exhaustion. "C'mere," he said, patting the cushion next to him. A second later she was sitting next to him. He had no idea how they were both going to sleep on the tiny loveseat, but he was too tired to problem solve and too awake to let her panic alone all night.

"So," she said quietly, leaning against his side. "Bad dream?"

"Don't wanna talk about," he mumbled. "I was there. Amelia was there. You were there."

"I better have been there, reeking havoc on your dreams."

He nodded against the side of her head, already falling back asleep. It was too inviting, nightmare or not.

"Hey, Jess?" she hummed against his shoulder. He grunted in reply. "I really like your family."

"I noticed."

She hesitated for a second and then said, "I never—I'm not used to—it's just nice. I wish my family would have been close."

"I think my mom will adopt you if you're willing," he said. "Even though it would make things a little weird between us legally. But whatever." He let out a long yawn. "I don't really care. You can be part of my family in you want."

She laughed softly and then said, "I'd like that."

He didn't dream of Chris or Amelia after that. He couldn't remember what he dreamed about exactly, but he was pretty sure it involved buying a puppy. He woke up to the smell of pancakes the next morning, and when he stumbled into the too bright kitchen, he found the rest of the house already at the table, Jo talking avidly about Vegas while his mom listened closely, chin resting in her hands. Cassie chimed in every now and then with useless trivia she had heard on TV while flipping through channels. He rested against the doorframe, watching his family.

"About time you woke up," Jo said suddenly. He sat down across from her and stole a bite of Cassie's pancakes.

"Jo was telling me about all the places you two have visited," his mother said, eyes practically gleaming. Someday he would show her New York, take Cassie, and have Jo drive. They would probably listen to Frank Sinatra on the way there, and Jo would drive down all the sketchy alleyways in New York just so she could avoid the mass majority of the cabs.

They spent breakfast talking about weird diners and failed attempts at gambling. Cassie left halfway through—after about a million suffocating hugs—for her soccer game, and Jo offered to help his mom with the dishes. It was weirdly domestic. He wondered for a moment if Jo would have felt differently about her quiet life if she had traded places with him growing up. He dismissed the idea after a few seconds though because Jo was Jo, and at the very foundation of what made her her, there was that innate desire for freedom. He could never change that, and he would never want to.

"I want to remind you two of one thing," his mother said later that morning, when they were all standing by the car. "Be careful. This is bigger than the two of you."

"I know, Mom," he said, and that was it. He hugged her, she hugged Jo, she told them to both come back soon, warned them to be careful once again, and begged Jo to follow the posted speed limits. He walked around to the passenger side of the car and stopped, staring at the street he grew up on. He suddenly realized most of the perfect houses' colors had faded. The flowers on the sides of the sidewalks were actually just weeds. The curbs were crumbing, and the cement was cracked. The kids who had been playing outside in the streets yesterday and every day before were gone today, and the streets were so empty that he wondered if they were ever really there at all.

Maybe some things had changed after all.

Jo started the car, and that's when he remembered something.

"Wait a second!" he exclaimed, and Jo rolled her eyes, tapping her wrist as if she had a watch there. He dashed around the front of the car back to where his mom was watching him curiously.

"I have a question," he said, and she nodded carefully, still not sure what he was up to. "Who cleaned my desk?"

She smiled sadly, put a hand on his shoulder, and said, "Amelia, honey."

"*No,*" he said. There was no way. His desk was a mess the night he left. He had knocked over his pencil jar trying to find his cell phone charger, and he had dumped out the contents of his suitcase on it when he was trying to pack. Camp brochures, dirty socks he had forgotten about, bits of crinkled up paper, it had all been lying on his desk. "It was dirty when I left that night."

She frowned and said, "I know. Amelia cleaned it a few days after that."

He couldn't breathe. The entire world was spinning five times faster than it should have been. There was no way she could have been there, not after years of *nothing*. Not after he was sure that she—

"Honey?" his mom was asking. "Are you alright?"

"F-fine," he choked out, stumbling backwards towards the car. "I'll—I'll call you."

When he opened up the car door, Jo had her lips pursed, and her head was at at forty-five degree angle. She didn't look up when he sat down, or when he slammed the door.

"Just drive," he begged, and she finally glanced over at him. She took one look at his face, nodded, and started the car.

* * *

After four hours, he started crying.

He didn't realize the sound was coming from him at first until it grew in volume, until the wrecked sobs escaping his throat were so loud that they had to be his. Jo nearly drove off the road in surprise. The gravel under the right wheels caused the car to shake, and the motion seemed to be enough to shake Jo back into alertness.

"What on Earth is wrong with you?" she shouted. Then she cringed, muttering, "Empathy, geeze," and eased the car over to the side of the road.

"Okay," she said, after putting the car in park and turning in her seat to face him. His vision was too blurry to make out the expression on her face, but he figured it was a cross between off-the-wall uncomfortable and I-really-do-care-but-I-don't-really-know-how sympathy.

"I don't really—I haven't ever—Crying people kind of —" She groaned and put a hand on his shoulder. He squeezed his eyes shut, willing the tears to stop, because he wasn't a teenage girl, for crying out loud, and he didn't want to freak Jo out anymore than he had to. He just needed to calm down. He tried to breathe through his mouth, inhale, exhale, try not to shake too much, try not to think about *her,* or her death, or her life, or the fact that she was alive a few short months ago and something had to have happened after he left that was the cause of her demise.

It just wasn't *fair.* He knew life wasn't meant to be, and he had heard the rumors his whole life about people who were left handed getting paid more, and about how white males were the least desired people during college application season, and how women engineers apparently still weren't taken seriously because of their sex, and none of that was fair. But this? This was beyond that. It wasn't fair to Amelia, or her parents, or Scott, or even him.

"She was a good person, Jo," he croaked out. "*Such* a good person. I just don't understand why this happened to her. W-why did she—"

"Shhh." He felt her squeeze his shoulder, and he wondered when their roles switched. It had always felt like he was the one trying to fix her. Now she was the one who had to put him back together. He hoped she was good at jigsaw puzzles.

"She was right there. Right. There. I missed her by two days." He punched the dash, and Jo flinched.

He hated himself. He really, truly did. He hated himself for leaving, and he hated himself for hating it. He was glad he left. He had to. He was burning out sitting around thinking about the past. A nonstop road trip was exactly what he needed, and Jo... Jo was...

He was glad he did it, all of it. He just wished he could have left later. Then he might have been able to stop her, to convince her just to stay home, and to avoid creepy motels at all costs.

"Jess," he heard Jo say. She sounded far away to him. "Jess, look at me."

He reluctantly opened his eyes. Despite how he thought she sounded, she was incredibly close.

"Answer one question," she said. She looked so serious. "Just one. Knowing that your answer won't change anything that's happened, with us, with Amelia, with anything."

He nodded weakly, and she took a deep breath, held it for as long as she could, and then exhaled slowly.

"Do you regret it?"

That stupid question was going to follow them around for the rest of their lives. It came up in almost every situation now.

"No," he said. "Because this—this has been the best thing to ever happen to me."

Jo's expression softened, and he swore he saw something in her eye that if he squinted, it might have been a confession on its own.

"There are some things you can't change," Jo said, tracing the stitching on the steering wheel. "At least, I think that. I think some things have to happen, like they're pre-set."

"You believe in destiny, don't you?"

"I don't know what I believe." Her head hit the headrest with a *thunk*. "I just know that I'm emotionally constipated, and that even if you had stayed, there is no guarantee that Amelia would have lived."

"Yeah," he said, then added, "about Amelia. I don't think you're emotionally constipated."

"Oh, please," she said, rolling her eyes. "I'm a mess."

"No, you're really not. I mean, you're no Doctor Phil, or anything, but you're better than you used to be."

She laughed, looked over at him, smiled. "Maybe you're just a good influence on me."

"Probably."

"Okay, so," she said, one hand on the gear shift. She raised an eyebrow as she said, "You okay?"

"Yeah," he said, wiping his face with the back of his hand. "Great."

Jo

After six hours, she stopped focusing on not focusing.

Jess was staring out the window like usual, but at least he wasn't crying anymore. Jo wasn't good at a lot of things. She wasn't good at doing what she was told, or being happy with what she had, or staying in one place for too long. But what she really was bad at was dealing with people who were upset. With anyone else, she would have told them to get over it and buck up, and she had, plenty of times. But this was different. She *wanted* to cheer Jess up; she just didn't know how.

"Hey," she said, nudging him with her elbow. "Want to play a road trip game?"

"You hate road trip games," he said flatly.

Ugh, stupid Jess needed to stop paying so much attention to her.

"I've had a change of heart."

"Yeah, right."

"Why do you have to be so difficult?" she groaned. "I'm *trying* to cheer you up over here."

He smiled looking down at his hands again.

"Do you even know any road trip games?" he asked, and oh, yeah, that could be a problem.

Her eloquent "uhhhhh" was enough to make him laugh. She guessed it was worth it.

"There's the license plate game," Jess said.

She looked out at the empty road, completely void of all signs of life besides her little beaten up hatchback rolling over the road. She raised an eyebrow at him.

"...or I Spy..."

There was a green field running alongside the road, and a telephone pole. If they were really lucky, they might see a bird.

"I guess road trip games don't really work out here," he said. He went back to looking out the window, and because she didn't know what else to do, she blurted out, "Did you know that you're made of stardust?"

He stared blankly at her for a few seconds before mumbling, "What?"

Why did she have to say these things? She felt like she was back in middle school, where all the other kids thought she was weird for being a walking astronomical encyclopedia.

"Nothing."

"No, I want to know!" he said. He straightened in his seat, eyes pinned on her, looking like the picture of alertness.

"Really?"

"Yes!"

Jess couldn't lie; she knew that much. He always got that weird look on his face where he was trying too hard to look natural, resulting in his eyes watering and his lips twitching. This wasn't one of those cases. Now he looked completely natural.

"You're made up of the same elements as stars: carbon, nitrogen, oxygen, iron, whatever. Essentially, we are all stardust."

"That's…"

Pointless, useless information that—

"Really cool."

"Yeah," she said, trying to keep her voice steady, even though her brain was a screaming mess of thoughts like *oh my god someone cares about my worthless star knowledge!* "Yeah, it really is. It gets cooler, too. Those elements? They're created by stars, in their nuclear furnaces. When a star explodes— burns up—the elements are released, and they're used to create new things. It's like the 'Circle of Life' without the babbling at the beginning that no one understands."

"How do you know all of this?"

She shrugged. "Hobby. I used to read all the astronomy books I could find. I ditched out on the real world before college, but if I hadn't, I totally would have found a way to major in astronomy and literature. I would have loved it."

"Why did you?"

Well, one thing was for sure: Jess was feeling better. His annoying intuitive nature was back.

She shrugged and said, "There was nothing for me there." She looked out at the road and added, "I didn't have a great relationship with my mom or a neighbor that I was madly in love with. I had a ridiculously expensive car and some designer shoes. So I traded my car with some stoner who probably thinks an angel swooped down from Heaven and blessed with him with a Mercedes, and I took off."

She paused for a second, and then smirked. "You pretty much know everything now, don't you?"

"You're like this really awesome book that's missing hundreds of pages," he said, and she wondered if he was hysterical. "I have the middle chapters and a few pages in between, but the beginning got torn out."

"You can always rewrite it," she pointed out.

"But it would change the ending."

"Probably for the better."

She smiled at him, and then turned her attention back to the road.

* * *

"So this is where it happened?"

The building didn't *look* significant, not with the white paneling and neon sign proclaiming it was open twenty four hours a day, but they both knew better. The parking lot was packed with cars covered in college bumper stickers, and she could hear music faintly playing from the inside.

"Yup."

She glanced over at Jess, who was looking impossibly awkward standing there in the middle of the parking lot, in a too big hoodie and a too blank face. The rest of the drive they had talked about movies they should rent the next time they get stranded somewhere, and Jess stared at her like a creeper when he thought she wasn't looking.

So basically, the usual happened.

"Well," he said, kicking at the gravel. "Let's go then."

He started walking toward the door before she could process what was happening. She hadn't thought they would actually *go in.* Part of her thought their grand road trip to honor Amelia's spirit or whatever was going to come to an end after Jess had the freak out of the year.

Admittedly though, she had kind of been waiting for it. It wasn't normal for someone not to mourn, not unless they were emotionally constipated like her, that was, and she was starting to worry that he was a robot, or something equally as insane.

"Wait," she said, grabbing his sleeve to stop him. He looked at her with Confused Bambi Eyes.

"Are you sure about this?" she asked. "You just finally grieved, you know? Maybe we should skip the trip down memory lane."

"No, I want to go in." She was planning their exit plan for when she had to drag him out hysterically crying when he added, "Besides, I'm hungry."

"Whatever," she said dismissively. "But it's your funeral. Don't say I didn't warn you."

The inside of the diner smelled sickly sweet, like too many baked pies. It looked the same as it did the last time she was here, black and white checkered floors and red vinyl barstools. The place was buzzing with people stuffing their faces in booths and laughing at each others' jokes. Jess, ever the small town boy, seemed lost in the crowd of people. She honestly wondered how he had survived this long in the real world without her.

"Come on," she said with a sigh, grabbing his arm.

She dragged him over the bar, where he continued to stare at the barstools like they were made of magic, or rather, Amelia's fear of butt sweat. With a sigh, she lightly pushed him down onto a seat.

"You're definitely not okay," she said, finally breaking him out of his thoughts. He looked over at her expectantly: he probably didn't hear her. She sighed.

It was usually at this point in the game where she would declare him a lost cause and move on with her life. Actually, she usually didn't last this long in the game. She usually quit after she realized there was no point running around in circles with the ball.

"I want a cheeseburger," he mumbled, reaching for the menu.

"I had a vegetarian omelet last time, because they're apparently known for it." She hesitated and then said, "I guess Amelia wasn't crazy about it though."

"Amelia was the pickiest eater in the history of humans," he said.

"Yeah?" she prompted. Some part of her, deep down, thought she should be jealous of Jess loving Amelia. It was the other parts that didn't really care, because it didn't really matter. He loved her too, after all.

Well, maybe.

She thought about his creeper stares. It was a definite maybe, at least.

"She was constantly trying to get the cafeteria ladies fired and bring in a real chef. She had a petition going and everything."

"You're kidding," she said, but Jess' little amused smile told her he definitely wasn't. She just liked hearing him talk, really. He *trusted* her, and the newness of the warm feeling she got from it hadn't worn off just yet.

"You know what's weird?" she asked. She didn't bother waiting for an answer; it probably would have been something like, 'fried chicken feet.' "We caught up with her."

"Huh?"

"We're caught up now, with her blog. We don't really need it anymore. I lived through this bit."

He looked at the counter top, tracing the swirls with the tip of his finger. "So all we don't know is the ending."

"Well…" Empathy, Jo. Empathy. "We know the *ending*, but we don't know the final chapters leading up to it." She rested her chin in her hand. "We should piece together what we do know."

"Hey!" he said suddenly, turning to look at her. "You don't know the beginning, do you?"

"I assumed it started with a hospital."

"No," he said with a laugh. "After that. How she left."

She racked her brain, trying to come up with the blog entry from when this craziness started. Wasn't there something about rounding up cowboys?

They ordered their food from a guy with a beer gut, and she tried to remember the face of the person who took her order the last time. She had seen so many people in her life that all of the faces were blurs. She could hardly remember what her brother looked like anymore, and it would have been scarier if she actually cared.

"I'm feeling story time coming on," she said excitedly, and he grinned at her, spinning in his barstool to face her.

"Okay, so it was like, March, and it was really cold outside—"

"Dark of night, rainstorm, blah blah blah," she said. "Get on with the exciting bit."

"You always interrupt me when I try to tell you these stories," he mumbled.

She smirked. "I like seeing your reaction."

"Okay, well." He couldn't stop *smiling*. She swore adorable was written all over him. "I had a test the next day, so I was in my dorm studying. Amelia knocked on my door, and when she came in, she was more excited than usual. I asked her what was up, and she said she was going away for awhile. She wanted to find herself."

His face started to change, and she could see the sadness setting in on him. It was never ending, wasn't it? She was about to ask him if he was okay, but it was pointless: he would have just said he was fine.

Fine, fine, fine, that stupid refrain, the chorus of their lives.

This was the first time she had been "fine" in the past five years, and even now, she felt like saying she was just "fine" was a bit of a cop-out. It was one of those vague adjectives you whipped out when someone crashed into you on the street. 'It's fine.' 'I'm fine.' 'We're fine.' It didn't really mean anything.

"I asked her why she couldn't find herself in college like the rest of the people our age, but she said it was something bigger than that. I don't know what happened after that. I was angry. She ignored me and left."

He shrugged, looking down at the counter again.

"Well," she said, eager to lighten up the conversation. Then again, they were talking about a dead girl, so. "We know she went from Los Angeles to the Grand Canyon. Were you going to college in Kansas?"

"Yup," he said with a smirk. "You know me, small town boy."

"She probably drove to L.A. to officially 'start' her trip there."

"She would have had to," he said. "So she drove from Kansas to California, Grand Canyon, New Mexico, Texas, and then she hit a cow."

"Wait wait wait. Slow down."

He raised both of his eyebrows. Hopefully one day she could teach him how to raise just one, because this look wasn't working for him.

"You're leaving out vital information," she continued. "Kansas. She went back there at some point to clean your desk."

"I'm still shocked by that," he said, sighing. "I don't understand. She had been gone forever."

"She must have felt guilty," she said. "Or she missed you. But when she showed up, you were gone."

"I left in July," he mumbled. "Early July…"

"She was in Austin in April, but I can't remember any other dates." Their food appeared, and she stole a fry off his plate. He made a face. "We can check later."

"Do you remember when you met her?" he asked.

To be perfectly honest, she only knew today was a day that ended in the letter "y."

"One of the twelve months?" she offered. "It wasn't Christmas because the annoying songs about reindeer weren't playing."

"Well, good," he said. "We only have eleven more potential months to go through. We can probably rule out November too, since the Christmas carols usually start then."

"See? Look at us!" she said, playfully punching him in the arm. "We're great detectives! We could put Scooby and Gang out of business."

"Right," he said flatly. He looked around the diner for a second, thinking, and then slowly asked, "What did you think of her? I know you didn't like her very much."

"I don't like a lot of people, remember?" she said with a smirk. It felt like he wanted her approval, which didn't make any sense at all, but she would entertain him. "I remember thinking that she was pretty. She was wearing shorts that were way too short—oh, hey, it must have been a summer month!"

"Down to four," he said. "Progress!"

"She seemed sad. And out of her league. I felt like she jumped into this headfirst without thinking about it twice. Then again, I guess that's the whole point." She stole another fry— she really should have ordered her own—and said, "She only annoyed me because she was always going on about Scott and how awful he was. It got really old after awhile. Like I'm all for conversation, but I really just wanted her to shut up."

"The timeline is screwy," he said with a frown. She reached for another fry, and he pushed the whole plate toward her. "I don't know why he would be on her mind if she'd been gone for a few months."

"Maybe he called her, or something. She had a ton of emails from him."

"Really?" he asked. "Did you—"

"Some of them, and I guess you must have been sleeping." She thought about it and then said, "Yeah, most definitely sleeping. You're comatose the second you get near a mattress. Did you know that?"

"Did you find emails from anyone else?" he asked, and he looked almost shy, looking up at her through his lashes. She added the look in the mental encyclopedia of Jess faces. She would call it Shy Face. Incredibly creative.

"I didn't read them," she said, and he let out a breath. "I figured they were dirty."

"No, they weren't!" he said, looking distressed. She laughed.

"I'm *joking,* Jess, geeze. You're too Apple Pie to write naughty emails."

"I don't even want to *try* to figure out your thought process," he said and she smirked at him.

"Whatever," she said, grabbing a handful of fries. "You ready to go, or should we take some pictures for posterity?"

He looked around the busy diner, complete with its barf-colored cushions and butt sweat covered barstools, and then down at his seat, probably mentally tracing the areas Amelia walked, touched, and breathed on. Finally, he looked up at her and smiled.

They stood up to leave.

* * *

New Orleans might have been her favorite city in the country, and even when Amelia was along, she had refused to let her ruin it for her. Amelia had been crying about Scott and her dad and her millions of other white girl problems, so Jo set her up at the first bar she saw. Alcohol was like instant medication for the pain in the butt that was Amelia, and Jo spent the rest of her night at the French Market, where she found a guy who had set up a telescope on the sidewalk. She talked about extraterrestrial intelligence and the Hubble telescope until she realized she had gotten a lovesick girl drunk and had left her alone in a bar in a strange city.

It was probably not the best idea she had ever had.

Amelia had been hungover through the next day and half—and didn't hesitate to let Jo know about it—and Jo ultimately regretted meeting her in the first place.

This time around, she still planned to spend hours looking through some guy's telescope and get her companion drunk, but ditching Jess wasn't part of the agenda.

"You know what's really awesome about this?" Jess asked, throwing their bags onto the bed. He could not stop smiling. Maybe she should have been suspicious about his complete 180 compared to yesterday, but she didn't really mind all that much.

"The fact that I can finally sleep?" she asked, kicking her duffel bag off the bed in an effort to get under the covers.

"The fact that I never ever thought I'd see New Orleans."

"Well, you know…" She yawned and said, "At some point you have to stop dreaming and start doing."

She drifted off to sleep listening to Jess talk about his mom and foreign movies. She dreamed of Paris.

* * *

"That doesn't make sense," she mumbled, grabbing a piece of paper labeled "Kansas" and pulling it out of the line. There was paper all over the floor, color coded to boot, adding more decoration to the boring motel room than the weird picture on the wall of a horse ever did.

"I don't know where else to put it!" he protested.

She stared at the white slips of paper with places labeled in red ink, red for Amelia. Jess called blue, and she took purple, her favorite.

The idea had sounded a lot more simple than it was proving to be. Label slips of paper? Okay. Line them up in order of date? Cool, cool. Fill in the blanks? Uhh…

The first paper was labeled "Amelia Leaves," which Jess claimed happened on the fifteenth of March.

"How can you possibly remember that?" she had asked.

He had grinned and said, "Ides of March. Come on, Jo!"

She had thought that if events were pre-set their meeting had to have been a huge one.

Jo's part of the timeline was filled with uncertainties; she hadn't paid attention to the date since she had been in high school, and even then, it didn't matter as long as time was passing. She couldn't remember when she was where, so they were constantly moving her pieces of paper around. Jess' memory was better than hers, but his timeline wasn't very impressive. All of his events lined up with hers or Amelia's, so there wasn't much use for his papers. He ended up adding a line of blue ink along the pieces that also applied to him— basically everything in the past three months of Jo's timeline, and Amelia's departure.

Amelia's blog proved to be a godsend for half of her timeline, but it could only get them so far. There was a gap of time between Austin and Baton Rouge, where Jo picked her up, and another huge one between the last day she updated her blog—a week after Jo's patience ran out and she lashed out at Amelia, causing her to leave the second she could get a taxi— and nearly two months later, when they found her body.

Then there was the time when she went back to Kansas. At first, they had thought it had happened during the first gap of time, because Jo knew she didn't drive to Kansas until months later. However, that was only a month and a half after Amelia left, and Jess hadn't left yet. So that didn't make sense.

"She must have gone back after she left me," Jo said, frowning. "But I don't know *how*. She must have hitched a serious ride."

"There's probably other vagabonds out there," Jess said. "I just wonder what happened."

"Yeah, well." Jo stood up from the floor and stretched, popping her back. "You, me, and everyone at the police station."

Jess

He woke up to the sound of someone puking. Opening his eyes slowly, he was relieved to see it wasn't him. At least he still had that claim to his name: never thrown up in his sleep. Once his eyes focused on the empty side of the bed next to him, he started to panic.

There weren't a lot of places to hide in the small motel rooms they stayed in, so he found Jo immediately, on her knees, retching in front of the toilet. Overall, not a pretty picture.

He wasn't one hundred prccent sure what to do in a situation like this, but he decided to wing it. Crouching down next to her, he pulled back her hair the best he could and waited.

After awhile, she pulled back, coughing weakly. She just sat there, looking down at the cracked tiles, seeming impossibly small. He reached up to flush the toilet, and then turned her around.

"You okay?" he asked, even though it felt like a stupid question.

"No," she spat back. She looked back down and mumbled, "But I think I'm done puking."

He pulled her to her feet and stood her in front of the sink. He was really hoping it was just the lighting in the bathroom, but she looked incredibly pale. Her hair was sticking to the sweat on the back of her neck, and he swore he could see her hand shaking.

"Okay, come on," he said when she was done brushing her teeth. He slipped an arm around her waist and guided her back to the bed.

"I'm fine," she mumbled, batting his hands away when he tried to pull the covers up over here.

"Oh, really?" he said flatly. She made a fake sobbing sound in response. "Tell me how you really feel then."

"I feel like butt," she groaned.

"How eloquent."

"Don't mock me!" she whined, rolling over onto her side. "Sick."

"Okay, okay." He sat down next to her on the mattress and pushed her hair out of her face.

"What are you doing?" she asked, her voice gravely.

"Uh, showing affection?" he offered.

"Creepy," she said, rolling over onto her other side.

"Fine," he said, standing up. "I'll go get you some water then."

"Whatever," she said. He heard her cough as he trudged back to the bathroom. Jo was impossibly difficult sometimes.

She fell asleep before he could make it back to her, so he busied himself rounding up sick people things. He found a bottle of aspirin in the backseat, and bought ginger-ale from a vending machine. There weren't any tissues in their room, so he stole some from the motel office—no one was there, so he wasn't too worried about getting caught. He dug around in her trunk looking for books that screamed Jo. He finally settled on his copy of *Into the Wild* and a book about astrology. He didn't know enough about the other books to tell if they were full of stardust or promises of freedom. These would have to do.

He piled everything up onto the nightstand and waited.

And waited.

And grew bored.

He wondered what Jo was sick with. She couldn't be hungover. Maybe she had the flu. He really hoped it was a twenty-four-hour bug if anything; he didn't know if he could spend too many days sitting around staring at the bed like this.

The sound of his phone ringing pierced through the silence in the room, and Jo mumbled something in her sleep. He quickly pulled it out of his pocket, took one look at the screen, and dashed toward the bathroom.

"Cas?" he said, shutting the door tightly behind him and backing as far away from it as he could.

"Hey, stranger. I was just calling for my brother *who said he would freaking call me."*

He winced. Oh yeah. It was too easy to forget about everything when he was on a permanent vacation. He felt like time had frozen, and nothing really mattered as long as Jo was playing obscure music and making him feel inferior.

"Sorry, Cas," he said quietly. "I've been busy."

"Why are you whispering?" she whispered.

"Why are you?" he whispered back.

"It's like mass hysteria. You panic; I panic. You whisper; I whisper." He smiled at that. Even hundreds of miles away, he could see her pacing around her room, gesturing wildly as she tried to explain her reasoning.

"So are you going to tell me how your life is, or what?"

"Life is life, I guess," he said, leaning his head back against the wall. "We're in New Orleans. Jo is sick though."

"Ew, were you guys swapping spit?"

He cringed. "Don't say it like that."

"Could have said something else."

"It's not like that, Cassie," he said, wondering when his kid sister became not so much of a kid.

"Whatever you say," she said with a laugh. *"So Mom said you were surprised to hear about Amelia."*

"Yeah, well, I... I didn't think she was still out there when I left."

"Me either."

"Neither," he corrected, and the second he said it, he remembered Amelia yelling at him about the difference between "affect" and "effect."

"Ugh, shut up," Cassie groaned. *"I was going to tell you about something I found, but since you're being mean..."*

"I'm just trying to make sure you don't fail out of school."

"I don't want advice from you on that subject."

"Okayyy," he said, sighing. "That's far enough. Tell me what you found."

"You're going to flip out," Cassie said, excitement seeping into her voice. *"She left something for you. A note."*

"What?!" he shouted, momentarily forgetting about Jo. He hoped she wasn't a light sleeper. "Are you sure it's from her?"

"Yes!" Cassie cried gleefully. *"It's her perfect hand writing. This is epic."*

"Do you have it?" he asked, and she snorted.

"No, Jess. I burned it. Of course I have it, idiot."

"Well *sorry*," he said. "You're killing me with anticipation."

"And anticipation makes you angry, apparently," she said. *"Here, I'll put you out of your pain and suffering and read it to you. Oh, wait. Where did I put it?"*

"Cas," he growled.

"Fine, fine. I can't have any fun anymore," she grumbled. *"'Jessie—* Sorry that I missed you. I just...' *She marked out the last bit. I* think *it said* 'missed you.' 'really needed to talk to you. Something bad happened. I don't know what to do. Will you call me when you get this? Thanks, Amelia' *Then there's something on the back, hang on."*

He heard a crash, but he hardly processed it. His heart was hammering against his chest so loudly he could hear the blood coursing through his veins. She was in trouble. She needed him. And he was gone.

"Sorry, dropped the phone," Cassie said with a laugh. *"Okay, uh...* 'You were right: I'm not headed toward anything. I'm just running away. But sometimes running away is all that you can do.' *Kind of depressing."*

He could remember the night like it was yesterday.

"I don't understand why," he had said, feeling hysterical the longer he looked at her and her stupid duffel bag.

"I need to find myself."

"Why can't you find yourself here?"

"It's not... I can't..." she groaned in frustration, throwing her hands up in the air. *"You don't get it. Cool. Whatever. I don't care. I just know I can't stay here. I need to*

be out there! *In the real world! I need to see things and do things and remind myself that something is worth living for."*

"Your whole life is here, Amelia. You can't just walk out on it."

"No, I can. I will."

"You're being selfish," he had growled. "Selfish and stupid."

She had smiled in that subtle way that showed more in her eyes than her mouth, and had said, "It's always the selfish people who end up with something to show for their lives."

She was gone the next morning.

"Yoo hoo, Jess? Oh brother of mine?"

He almost jumped at the sound of Cassie's voice. "Yeah, hi, I'm here," he said quickly.

"Good. Isn't this cool? It's like getting a message from the dead."

The bathroom door swung open, revealing a very pale Jo grabbing at the door frame in an attempt to hold herself up.

"Cas, I've gotta go," he said, and he heard a muffled *"Huh? Why?"* before he ended the call. He immediately grabbed Jo's shoulders to try to steady her.

"You okay?" he asked, and she shook her head.

"Dizzy," she mumbled, pressing her face into his chest. She sniffled. He hesitantly brought a hand up to the back of her head. Thankfully, she didn't say anything this time.

"You should be lying down," he said softly.

"I don't remember the last time I was sick," she said pitifully. "I must have been twelve."

"Well," he said, resting his chin atop her head. "First step is lying back down."

She sniffled again and pulled back, wiping her left eye. He looked at her curiously, earning a glare from her.

"M'not crying," she mumbled. "I don't cry. I'm sick."

He decided not to point out that he had seen her cry before, and instead led her back to the bed. She laid on top of the blankets, looking up at the ceiling.

"Cassie called me," he said. Jo looked far too surprised by that. "She found a note from Amelia."

"No way," Jo said, sitting back up again. He narrowed his eyes, and she fell back down. "What did it say?"

"She was looking for me…because she was in trouble." His mouth was dry all of the sudden. He swallowed, but it only made it worse. He felt a hand grab his. Looking down at their fingers clasped together, he thought about what Jo had said about pre-set events in time. He wasn't a huge destiny believer, but sometimes, it felt like he wasn't really the one in control.

"Your hands are freezing," he said, squeezing her hand.

"Yeah, well, I only feel like I'm dying," she said flatly and reached for a tissue. "Don't blame yourself, Jess. Please." She blew her nose. Her statements didn't pack as much strength when she was trying her hardest to enunciate her words correctly and still failing.

Two hours later, they were still in the same spot. He had started reading her astrology book, figuring he would rather dream about personality types than dying extremists.

"Hey, Jess?" she mumbled, and he glanced over at her. He raised his eyebrows questioningly, and she groaned, "I feel like crap."

* * *

Jo and Amelia had driven from New Orleans to Montgomery, Alabama, where Amelia spent an afternoon eating boiled peanuts in a park, and Jo wandered off to the Hank Williams museum so she didn't kill anyone.

It was actually funny how different their recounts of the event were. Amelia's blog said that she *"spent most of the day not thinking about anything in particular, and it was nice for a change."* Jo, on the other hand, described the experience something akin to "having wisdom teeth extracted sans anesthesia." Until she went off on her own, of course.

Jo was still sick, curled up in the passenger seat sniffling weakly, but she had told him if she had to spend one more second in that motel room she was going to kill someone. Since he was the only one around, he decided it would be best if he drove.

This time around though, she said to just keep driving until he hit Tennessee.

"I don't want to go to the same museum," she mumbled. She had her hair tied back into a tight ponytail, and an arm thrown over her face. "There's nothing I want to do there. Let's just keep going."

He couldn't say no to Jo when she was healthy, so there was no way he could say no to her when she was sick. After a google search or four, he had concluded she probably just had the flu. Jo wasn't comforted by his new found medical knowledge, however.

"Are you awake?" he said quietly.

Her muffled reply was, "Unfortunately."

"How many sisters did you say you had?" he asked, and she pulled her arm away from her face to look at him. She didn't tilt her head, since it was already pinned against the headrest, but she did narrow her eyes.

"Three," she said, sounding suspicious. "Why?"

"Just wondered," he said, shrugging. "I like knowing things about you."

"London, Elle, and Greenlee," she said, closing her eyes again.

"Wait, what?"

"Their names," she said. "You were just going to ask if I didn't tell you."

He smiled. She had a point.

"London, Elle, Greenlee, and *Jo*," he said, trying to figure out why her name sounded so wrong in the mix. "Don't be mad at me," he said, looking over at her quickly. He hoped she read the sheer panic in his expressions. "but your name doesn't really fit with the others."

Her laugh was cut off by her cough.

"Jo's a nickname, stupid."

"*What?*" he shouted. She gave him this why-are-you-so-stupid look, and he said, "But you went on and on when we first met about your name and how great it was!"

"Hmm, let's see," she said, tapping her chin with her index finger. "Would I rather go by Josephine or Jo? One plays with dolls, one plays with matchbox cars."

He fell silent, watching the other cars on the interstate—one perk of him driving was getting to use the interstate.

"Josephine's a pretty name," he said softly, and she snorted.

* * *

It was times like these when he really wished Jo was awake, because she probably would have known what the massive, black pyramid sitting in the center of the city was. It was the only thing he had noticed so far about the city, and he almost drove over the center line while he was staring at it. It was just so huge and out of place.

If his first problem was not knowing what it was, his second, probably more pressing problem was the fact that he had no idea where he was going. "Drive to Memphis" didn't really give him that much instruction. He finally decided to pull off at the first gas station he saw. He put the car in park and turned it off, closing his eyes to rest. Maybe he could get a quick nap in.

"You stopped driving."

He jumped, hitting his head on the roof of the car. He distantly heard Jo start laughing, and when he finally opened up his eyes, she was doubled over in the passenger seat.

"And *I'm* the creepy one?"

Her laughter died off, but the smile stayed on her face. "Yup."

"You woke up the *second* I turned off the car," he said.

"Sorry I don't fall into a coma every night like *someone*," she said pointedly. She looked a lot better than she had earlier. She still wasn't back to normal, but there was definitely some life in her eyes now.

"You just took a five hour nap," he said. "I think that qualifies as a coma."

"You were just quiet," she said dismissively, hand on the car door. "So… Can I take over now?"

Yeah, she was definitely feeling better.

"You know where we should go?" she asked as she walked around the front of the car. She stopped in front of his door, waiting for him to get out.

"Do I *want* to know?" he joked, and she rolled her eyes.

"Graceland!" She pulled out her jazz hands. Apparently a nap and aspirin was the miracle cure for flu. "Come on," she said with a fake smile. "Don't leave me jazz hand-ing."

"Yeah, fine, let's go."

"Yesssss," she said, fist pumping. She pouted and said, "Amelia didn't want to go with me."

"What did she do?" he asked, finally getting out of the car.

"No idea," Jo said. "Probably cried in a mall or something."

* * *

When her car rolled up into the parking lot of Graceland, his first thought was that Amelia would have hated it here. Everywhere he looked there were people sauntering around in sweatpants. Amelia would have cried from the horror of it.

"Welcome to the Motherland," Jo said, taking the keys out of the ignition.

"Is this a pilgrimage for you?" he asked as he climbed out.

She put her hands on her hips. "Is that even a question?"

"Sorry," he said, raising his hands in the air. She linked arms with him the second he walked over to her side of the car, and he had a growing suspicion she didn't find him as creepy as she claimed to.

He had a good feeling about this tourist trap the second he walked into the first, very purple building with a very strange carpet.

"I feel like I'm in an 80s music video," he said.

"Oh, you haven't seen anything yet, trust me."

The line for tickets was long, and the ticket prices were outrageous. The people behind them in line were particularly vocal about their feelings about it. He resisted the urge to tell them that Jo had to make her money hustling pool. He figured it would probably just cause more problems in the long run, so he kept quiet. Jo didn't seem bothered by any of it. She just stood there in line, her lips curved up into a smile. It was nice to see.

"How horrendous do I look on a scale of one to crap?" she asked when they were outside. He didn't really see why it mattered when everyone else looked like they hadn't showered once in their sorry lives.

"You never look bad," he said sincerely, and she smirked.

"You're totally smitten," she said with a laugh. He couldn't deny it, so he just put an arm around her shoulders. They waited in another line, took a dorky picture, and got on a cramped bus with a driver who probably hated his life.

"This house is really ugly," Jess said an hour later as he stared at a room with green shag carpet all over the floor and ceiling. There were scary monkey statues everywhere he looked.

"No, don't say that," she said, elbowing him in the side. "I like it. It has hidden beauty."

He wasn't sure he saw any beauty in any part of the tacky house, but if Jo saw it, it was good enough for him.

* * *

"You know," Jo said, lying on her back on the bed. "It was those fried peanut-butter-and-banana sandwiches that killed Elvis."

"That and a ton of drugs, most likely," he said. It felt like someone was stabbing him in the stomach over and over again. His mind kept replaying eating that stupid sandwich over and over again until he started to wonder if he could come up with plans for a time machine.

"I still feel like I'm going to die though," she whined. She rolled onto her stomach, but it must have proved to be a bad idea: she groaned in pain and quickly rolled back over. "Don't try that at home."

"Got it," he said, staring up at the ceiling.

"What's wrong?" she asked, and when he looked over at her, he really just wanted to hug away the look she had on her face. He wasn't used to seeing her look so...worried. Her empathy was improving.

"Nothing?" he tried,.

"Jess," she said, like she was warning a little kid to behave.

"I just..." he sighed. He really hated feeling this way, because he felt like it was unfair to Jo, more than anything. He didn't want her to feel like she was stuck in the shadow of Amelia's casket. At the same time, he just wanted to tell her everything, partially because he couldn't lie, but mostly because Jo was his best friend.

"I just wish I knew what happened to her," he finished, and she nodded.

"Sure. Getting shoved in an ice machine isn't exactly that peaceful resolution you imagine."

"She was scared of something," he whispered. He turned on his side to face her, and asked, "Do you think someone was after her?"

She looked to the side, thinking, and then looked back to his face. "I think Gregory was."

He shuddered involuntarily. Just when he thought he was at peace with Amelia's death, it started to bother him all over again.

"I just need to know," he said. "I need to let go of it, but I *can't*."

Jo studied him for a few minutes, just staring at the lines of his face, and then slowly said, "Let's go straight to D.C. Forget everywhere else."

"But what about—"

"Who cares?" she asked, propping herself up on her elbows. "If we go to D.C., maybe we can find a clue. Even if we don't, maybe seeing where she spent her final days will be enough for you."

He thought about it for a second, and then said, "Let's do it."

* * *

Jo had to be the only person on Earth who a) had a map in her head of all the back roads and highways in the country and b) could drive for days straight seemingly unaffected.

"This is going to sound pretty bad," he said, as they drove out of Nashville. "But you were made to be a truck driver."

She laughed and pushed a CD into the stereo.

That was how they spent the next few hours, just listening to music, staring out the windshield. The second they hit Knoxville, things got more difficult. They got trapped in a traffic jam the second they passed the sign, and Jo spent twenty minutes honking her horn and flipping off everyone around her.

"You're going to make that woman cry," he said, and Jo rolled her eyes.

"Like I care. I'm not going to see her again, anyway."

"That's a great philosophy," he said. "Like, 'who cares if I hit a dog? I'm sure I'll never see it again.'"

"You're so difficult," she said sadly, shaking her head.

They stopped in Pulaski, VA to go to the bathroom, in Roanoke to get food, and in Lexington to refuel. He fell asleep ten minutes before they drove through Harrisonburg, dreaming about the ocean. He was shaken awake after seeing a dolphin out by the horizon, and when he opened his eyes, he wondered why it was so dark. He had sworn they were on a sunny beach three seconds ago.

"Guess what?" Jo asked. His brain was sluggishly processing his surroundings, making out simple things like, "oh, it's dark," and "right, Jo's car," and "yay, she's smiling again."

"Hrnugh?" he choked out, and Jo laughed.

"We're in D.C.," she said, and he felt another gear turn in his brain. Right, D.C. That's where they were going. Huh.

"After all of this, can we go to the beach?" he said as he tried to rub the sleep out of his eyes.

"Of course," she said, and he liked the sound of that. "Okay, get your bag. I need to get a room so I can pass out."

He dragged his sad, sleepy body through the crowded parking lot and into the dimly lit lobby of the hotel. Jo was already getting them a room by the time he caught up with her. She looked confused.

"What do you mean there was another Halwood who stayed here?" she asked. She didn't acknowledge his presence, just kept staring at the boy behind the counter, who was beginning to look uncomfortable. "How long ago was this?"

"I'm sorry," he said weakly. "I can't say: customer confidentiality and—"

"*You* were the one who brought it up," she said sharply, and Jess swore he saw the poor guy flinch. They both watched in horror as Jo leaned over the counter until she was *far* too close to him. "When were they here?" she asked, her voice steady.

"A few months ago," the guy squeaked. He looked back and forth between Jo and his computer monitor, blindly clicking away on the keyboard. "Uh, it was, uh, May. May 25?"

"Thank you!" she said with a smile, finally pulling away from him. He let out a sigh of relief. "So…" she said, and the guy looked up at her nervously. "Our key?"

"Oh!" He reached below the counter, and Jess heard something fall. Jo was smirking, obviously getting some sick enjoyment out of watching the guy suffer. Good old Jo.

"Here," he said weakly. He pushed the key over the counter toward her. "H-have a nice stay, Ms. Halwood."

Jo took it, and for a fleeting second of terror, Jess thought she was going to say something else to the guy. She must have thought better of it, because she looked back at Jess and said, "Come on!"

He gave his best look of sympathy to the guy—Owen, according to his name tag—as he passed.

"Have a good weekend, man," he said, and Owen nodded, still looking a little dazed. He wouldn't be right for days, poor thing.

It wasn't until they were in the elevator that he realized he learned another bit of Jo trivia.

"Halwood, huh?" he said, and Jo crossed her arms, immediately looking uncomfortable. "Pretty."

"Shut up."

"Josephine Halwood," he said out loud, and she elbowed him in the ribs. Hard. "Ow," he said as he exhaled.

"I don't like it," she said as the doors opened. She stepped through them and turned back around to face him. "That's who I was. I'm Jo now."

"That's okay. I like Jo best anyway."

He was pretty sure he saw her blush, but she would deny it if he mentioned it. She pushed the door open to their room, and immediately shut it the second he was inside.

"You almost hit me with that," he said as she locked the door. She pressed her back against it and closed her eyes tightly. His Jo danger senses were tingling. "What is it?"

She shook her head, looking over his shoulder. "I don't get it. Do you think it was a different Halwood?"

"Most likely," he said, shrugging. "I guess our last names are popular...or maybe you're related!"

"Shut up," she said softly. "I have a really bad feeling."

"Well," he said, trying to find *something* comforting to say. "Do you think it was your parents?"

"I wish that idiot would have told me," she said under her breath.

"You already traumatized him for life," he pointed out, and she smirked. She looked up at the ceiling for a second, and then confusion flooded her features. She looked back at him, brow furrowed.

"May 25."

"What?" he said. Her train of thought was a mess most of the time, impossible to follow.

"May 25," she repeated. She moved around him, picking up her bag, and dumped the contents of it onto the bed. There was a stack of cards tied together with an elastic hairband, and she grabbed it immediately and began flipping through the cards. She kept mumbling, "May, May, May," as she searched through the cards until her hands finally stilled.

"Oh my God," she said softly. Then, louder, "Oh my God."

Jo looked like she was standing still until he got closer. Only then did he notice she was shaking.

"Hey, hey," he said softly, putting his hands on her arms. She shook her head, squeezing her eyes shut. He carefully took the cards from her hands. The one on the top read, "May 23 - DC" in red ink. It was the second to last card they had made.

"Come on, Jo," he said, squeezing her arm. "Look at me."

"I don't want to."

"Jo, we don't know anything for sure, okay? Coincidences happen, weird twists of fate. It could be nothing, okay? Just open your eyes."

She reluctantly did.

"Okay," he said, pushing her hair back behind her ear. "Just stay calm, okay? The guy's name was Gregory, remember?"

She nodded weakly and mumbled, "Can I use the laptop?"

"As long as you breathe," he said and passed the bag to her. She weakly smiled her thanks as she took it. Jo immediately set up her work station at the table, so he decided to have some quality TV time. Lying on top of the bed, he flipped through the channels, wondering how many there were.

Jo

Okay, so there was another Halwood staying there during the same time Amelia was. That didn't *mean* anything, right?

Right.

She just needed to calm down, like Jess said. She clicked on the yahoo homepage and read an article about Triceratops. She took a shower, watched the news with Jess, and ate an overpriced bag of peanuts from the hotel room. But as hard as she tried to take her mind off of it, she still had a sinking feeling in the pit of her stomach.

"Please try to calm down," he mumbled into his pillow. She thought he was asleep, leaving her to spend the night watching infomercials, but apparently not.

"I'm calm," she lied, and he opened one eye to look at her.

"You need to teach me how to do that," he said.

"Do what?"

"Lie," he said. "I'm not very good."

"Oh, really?" she said sarcastically. "I never noticed."

The next time she looked over at him, he was asleep. She sighed, turning off the TV. Sleep would take her mind off things at least. She crawled under the comforter and shut her eyes.

Five minutes later, it hit her.

She threw back the covers and scrambled over to the computer. She hadn't checked her email in three years, so she could only imagine the kinds of crap in her inbox. After logging in, she was greeted with a message reminding her about her six hundred emails, 98% percent of which was junk while 2% was band news. Surely there was some kind of—

Her eyes fell on the search button, and she grinned. She typed in the email address and hit enter, taping her fingers on the table as she waited for it to load. There was a message about thirteen emails down she had read before. She clicked on it three times because it wouldn't load fast enough. When it finally did, she caught sight of the time and date stamp: 3:46 AM, May 27, 2009.

She told herself it was no big deal. Thousands of people send emails during the month of May. It wasn't proof of anything.

Then she saw the IP address: 208.72.16.868.

"Oh God," she whispered. Her heart was beating so fast she was expecting it to burst out of her chest at any given moment. The room was spinning, and her head hurt. She couldn't *think;* this was just too much.

She brought up Amelia's email and clicked on the last email from Gregory.

208.72.1—

She slammed the lid of the laptop down before she could read the last few numbers. She didn't need to. She already knew.

* * *

Maybe it was just a fake. Anyone could fake his IP address. Maybe it was no big deal.

Denial really should have been her middle name.

She was sitting on a park bench in the middle of Farragut Square Park. People were eating lunch and jogging along the streets, walking dogs and talking loudly on their phones. It was the best thing about big cities, in her opinion: she was comfortably invisible amongst the crowds of people. No one stopped to talk, and no one made eye contact. They went about their day on their own, not taking the time to get involved with anyone else.

Jess was next to her, watching the people go on about their lives.

"Hey."

She looked up to see a man clutching a knit cap around his hair. She raised an eyebrow.

"Yes?"

"Do you know how to get to D.C. from here?" he asked urgently.

mmkay, so some guy just walked up to me and asked me where d.c. was. people always talk about loonies running crazy in big cities. poor guy.

She could hear Amelia's lazy accent speaking the words in her mind. Judging by the clouded look on Jess' face, she was pretty sure he could too.

"Hello?" the man asked. Jo thought he looked kind of crazed. "Do you know where D.C. is?"

Jess, ever the honest man, said, "You're in D.C."

The man twitched, and mumbled, "Of course I am. Of course I'm in DC."

He wandered off toward a bus stop, walking through a sea of dark colors and heels.

"It's like we're living in her blog," Jess said, voice full of awe.

"Yeah," she said flatly. "Maybe we'll run into Gregory next."

Jess visibly stiffened beside her, but didn't say anything. It probably wasn't the best thing she could have said.

* * *

A plain white ceiling with slowly spinning fan blades stared down at her. If she focused on it long enough, she could see the individual blades, as clear as the day. Jess was softly breathing next to her, but she could tell he must have been having a nightmare again, because every so often his breath hitched, and his back tensed. When things got particularly bad, he trembled a little. Every time, she considered trying to wake up, but eventually the shaking died down along with her concern.

Well, some of it, anyway.

Gregory... Gregory... Where would that name have come from, anyway? It was such a creepy name. She would expect to be murdered by a guy named Gregory too, right after Jason kidnapped her because she resembled his dead mother. Sighing, she closed her eyes, waiting for sleep.

* * *

Her door swung open.

"What if I had been naked?" she asked. The guy in the door ignored her in favor of walking over to her stereo and tossing her Madonna CD onto the floor.

"You have to listen to this girl," he said excitedly. He pushed his dark hair out of his eyes. She knew he hated the length, but he hated pleasing their parents even more. The more their mother begged him to cut it, the more inclined he was to walk around blind.

"If you step on my CD, I will kill you in your sleep."

"You're so thoughtful, Sis," he said. She smiled sweetly at him. The song started with a soft, gentle voice accompanied by an acoustic guitar.

"God, this is depressing," she groaned. She grabbed a pillow and pressed it over her face. She had just finished reading another dystopian novel, and her dad had been gone for twelve days now: basically, she had lost enough faith in humanity for one day.

"It's brilliant," he corrected, grabbing the pillow. She tried to snatch it back, but there was no point. Her stupid brother was like Sasquatch. She stared up at the ceiling, watching the fan turn too quickly for her to focus on the individual blades. They came together in one big blur of confusion.

The song finally ended before transitioning into another, and she mumbled, "Glad that's over."

"But you got it, didn't you?" he asked seriously.

"Do you think I'm stupid?" She sat up on the mattress and said, "People are selfish. They'll do whatever they have to to win. They'll knock down anyone who gets in their way. Boohoo, people suck."

"Well, at least you get it," he said. He looked a little disappointed. Shaking her head, she decided to humor him.

"Who was that, anyway?" she asked.

"A solo artist going by Gregory something. Found out about her through a music exchange." He grinned and said, "Isn't she great?"

"Sure," she said. "She's great."

She jerked off the bed in surprise, eyes wide and breathing dissolving into short gasps, just desperate attempts to get air into her lungs. Jess was still sleeping beside her, shaking again. Her head fell forward into her hands, and she was pretty sure she was shaking too.

* * *

The weather was dreary while they were in D.C., and for a fleeting second, Jo wondered if that was their doing. The sky was always overcast, and Jo just wished it would rain already. She was getting tired of waiting for something to happen.

They stumbled into a museum in the afternoon, where they both stared unenthusiastically at artifacts stuck behind plexiglass walls.

"Are you okay?" he asked her.

"I could ask the same to you after the way you slept last night," she said to divert the conversation. Jess' shoulders slumped, and he said, "I keep having these dreams where I'm running."

"Not feeling athletic?" she joked. She wondered if there was coffee in this place. She could really use some, especially after her refreshing ten minute sleep the night before.

"I'm running away from something," he said, running a hand through his hair. "But it's the worst feeling. I can't explain it."

"Hmm."

He paused and turned around to look at her, green eyes as bright as ever.

"Want to get out of here?" he asked. "This is kind of depressing me. We could go get cheeseburgers somewhere."

She nodded, feeling a little relieved. What she needed was a lot less Amelia and a heck of a whole lot less murderers.

The diner they went to was probably in the worst part of town they could have gone too. She was half-expecting someone to jump out from the shadows wielding a knife. The specials board was unreadable, just smudged white chalk, and she wasn't sure there was actually a cook in the kitchen. Regardless, they sat down in a booth by the window. Outside, she saw a man sitting on the steps of a building with a cardboard sign at his feet: "BUSH IS A TERRORIST" it read. She thought it was a little outdated, but if it made him happy, she wasn't going to say anything.

"You really do seem out of it," he said.

She wanted to tell him. She really did. It would be so easy to confide in him. It was harder to tell him that her brother was a potential murderer who had killed the love of Jess' life.

"It's weird, being here," she said, because it was the truth. "That's all."

He nodded. Tentatively, he reached across the table to touch her hand. She didn't pull away.

* * *

She didn't even bother trying to go to sleep the next night. Instead, she waited until Jess fell into hibernation, and then opened up Amelia's laptop.

Okay, so her brother was a murderer. Whatever. But why have two aliases? Wasn't one good enough?

She clicked on the comments for one of the entries, scrolling through the meaningless names and emoticons, until one name jumped out at her: Howard.

The next entry had comments from Hannah, Stefany, beautyblogz, fusion, and Howard.

The entry after that yielded similar results.

She shivered. He had been planning this for awhile. He had read her blog. He had read a girl's confessions and feelings, and knew everything about her. He had practically *stalked* her.

Jo had always thought he was creepy, what with his unwashed hair and habit of sneaking out in the middle of the night, but this was a whole new level.

She was blindly flipping back through entries when one caught her eye.

today i'd like to tell you, my dear blog readers, about my best friend.
his name is jess. jess fallon. like the famous guy.

Well, there she had it, Gregory Fallon.

"Nice job, big brother," she muttered, staring at the bright computer screen with disdain. What a way to get inside Amelia's head. And her heart.

She walked over to their timeline, which was spread out on the floor. Grabbing the May notecard and flipping it over, she wrote:

Gregory Fallon —> Music, Jess
Howard Dowle —>

She paused to stare at it for a second. There was an 'H,' and an 'A', and a—

"Oh, you bastard," she whispered.

She marked off each letter as she went along. After writing "Halwood" next to Dowle, she was left with four letters: 'W,' 'R,' 'D,' and 'E.'

Gregory Fallon —> Music, Jess
Howard Dowle —> Drew Halwood

Any hope she had left went out the window. There was no use in denying it.

She knew who killed Amelia.

* * *

Jess had been looking like a sad and dejected puppy all day. It was so pitiful even Jo felt bad for him.

"I think we should leave," she said. "We can go somewhere new. Make our own adventures. Forget."

He stared off at the distance, eyes cloudy and unfocused. She could feel the disappointment radiating off of him. She knew what he was thinking when they came here. He was expecting all of the clues to fall into places, to catch the bad guy, and to finally feel at peace. He was at a dead end, and she didn't feel that much better off.

She couldn't tell him. She just couldn't. When she thought of Jess' stories about Amelia, and his wobbly love-struck smile when he looked over at Jo from the passenger seat, she knew she would never say anything. Why did it matter? Amelia was dead and gone. No amount of confessions could change that. Was it really so bad to want things to stay the same between them? Was it really so bad to not want him to leave?

Was it really so bad to be scared? She was scared he would freak out. She was scared he would look at her differently. She was scared she had enough feelings for him to become dependent on his constant, unwavering presence. She was scared because she knew it was all true.

"Yeah, okay," he said, turning toward her. "Let's go."

They were walking back to the parking garage when she put her hand on his elbow, catching his attention and those green eyes, and said, "I'm sorry."

He smiled sadly and said, "Me too."

Jess

It had been roughly three weeks since they left D.C., and even though he felt better, he couldn't shake the feeling that something was wrong with Jo. They still bantered back and forth as usual, but something always seemed off nowadays.

He tried his best to ignore it, and tried even harder to justify it. He tried to tell himself it was probably the loss of purpose making Jo feel out of place: they had spent so many months dead set on retracing Amelia's steps and finding out what had happened to her, but now it was all over. They were back to motels and diners with some added tourist stops— because even though Jo had said she hated them months ago, they both knew it was a lie.

He was acutely aware of Jo breathing beside him, too fast to be sleeping.

"Can't sleep?" he asked, and she looked over at him shyly. "You haven't been sleeping much lately."

She attempted to shrug from where she was lying, and that was when he realized she had turned back into her old self: silent and moody, flighty and secretive. She had gone from telling him anything to only speaking to ask what he wanted on his burger, and he had no idea why.

The next day, they were driving along the Jersey Shore when he realized how much he hated this. Back then, he had told himself Jo would eventually come out of her shell once she realized he wasn't going to leave. Now, he didn't have much hope to cling to.

It was near sunset, and the only thing Jo had really said to him in the past hour was to stay out of the water because it was the time of the night when sharks came out, and she wasn't willing to ruin the upholstery with his bleeding carcass.

She had been silent since then, eyes focused on the way the waves lapped at the shore, hair whipping around her face in the wind. He supposed she might have looked peaceful, but he knew there was something wrong. He could feel it. It was driving him crazy.

"Jo," he said, reaching out for her shoulder. She looked down at his hand accusingly before slowly bringing her eyes up to his face. "What's wrong?"

She shook her head and looked back to the ocean. Desperately, he kissed her, hoping he could physically convey all of his worries. She kissed back just as urgently as him, and for a second, he fooled himself into thinking that this was a turning point for them.

That night, they were back on the road when Jo abruptly hit the brakes. He immediately started looking around for signs of disaster. Road kill? No. Car crash? No. Dead body?

He felt cold thinking about the last one.

"I can't do this anymore," she said, pulling the keys out of the ignition. He wanted to tell her it was probably a bad idea for them to just stop in the middle of a road, but he didn't want to risk Jo taking back her words.

"I'm done," she said, throwing the keys on the dashboard. She stared at them for a second, and then let out a sound that sounded suspiciously like a sob. Another followed it. And another. Soon enough, she was outright bawling, not even bothering to hide it. Her head fell forward onto the steering wheel, and she cried.

His hand fell to her shoulder, and she jumped at the touch.

"Stop," she said, throwing it off. "You don't want—you don't understand—you, you…" She let out another sob.

"Jo," he said softly, as if he was trying not to scare away a wild animal. "Jo, you're okay. We're okay. Everything is fine."

"No, no it's not," she said. She shook her head back and forth a few times before it fell back onto the headrest. He watched as she took careful, measured breaths, in and out, in and out, trying to calm herself down. Once the sobbing stopped, she turned in her seat to face him, and said slowly, "I know who killed her."

He felt the blood drain from his face, and he suddenly felt a little lightheaded.

"Who?" he asked. It sounded so stupid compared to a punch in the gut like her confession, yet it was just as important.

"My brother."

He stared at her for few seconds, trying to process what she had just said. Once the words finally sunk in, he was overwhelmed by emotions—confusion, betrayal, anger, concern. Why did Jo know? How long had she known? Was she certain? How could she keep this from him?

He watched her face, hoping to find answers to his questions. Jo was done talking now—there wasn't much left to say: in the end, his questions didn't really matter. Knowing the answers wouldn't change anything. She stared at him blankly, emotionlessly, and waited for his reaction, waited for the explosion.

"H-how long?" he asked. He swallowed, his mouth suddenly impossibly dry, and asked, "How long have you known?"

"I figured it out in D.C.," she said. "The other Halwood from the hotel... It was my brother. He had sent me an email while he was in D.C.—going to 'law school'—and the IP address matched the one from Gregory's email to Ameila."

"The—"

She ignored him, continuing, "Gregory and the Hawk was one of my brother's favorite singers. And Howard... If you unscramble Drew Halwood, you get Howard Dowle."

"Oh my God," he groaned, feeling sick. He was going to puke. This wasn't happening. This couldn't be happening.

He threw open the car door and puked onto the pavement. He threw up until it felt like everything he had ever eaten in his entire life was lying on the concrete. He swore he saw an Almond Joy from the Halloween when he was seven in the mess. When everything was purged from his stomach, he straightened back up and shut the door again.

"You've known for almost a month," he said, his voice gravely.

"I know, I—"

"A *month*, Jo," he said, and his voice sounded so angry that it was foreign to his ears.

"Jess, I—" she tried again, desperately trying to explain herself. He knew water was welling up in her stupidly gorgeous brown eyes again, but he couldn't see past the blurry outline of her figure.

"You didn't think you should tell me this?" he shouted. He wanted to dial it back so badly, but at the same time, he was filled with inexplicable *rage*. He just wanted to scream, scream until his voice was gone.

"I was afraid!" she shouted back.

"Not a good enough reason."

"It's every bit of a good reason!" she said hysterically. "You're all I *have,* Jess. I didn't want to risk losing you."

His head fell forward into his hands, and he tried to breathe. If only he could calm down, everything would make more sense. He needed to count to ten and run a mile and take a long, hot shower. Once his head was clear, he'd be able to sort all of this out.

"Jess?" Jo said softly, tentatively.

"It's okay, Jo," he lied, rubbing his eyes. "Just keep driving."

* * *

He dropped the shampoo bottle three times within the first five minutes of his shower because he was shaking too much. He eventually just left it on the floor of the shower and leaned back against the tiles. The water was more cold than hot, but he didn't really care.

Jo had known what happened. She had figured it out, and she hadn't even bothered to tell him. He had the right to be angry. He deserved to be raging mad.

But Jo had only kept it from him because she knew he would be. When he thought about how panicked she must have been the second she figured out the last puzzle piece, the moment she drew the line from Gregory to herself, he couldn't

330

help but feel a pang of guilt. Her concern was justified. She must have thought he would blame her for all of this.

He wondered if he should.

He knew deep down that it wasn't her fault: Jo had nothing to do with it. It wasn't her fault she had a serial killer brother. People can't pick their families. If they could, Jo probably would have picked—his.

It didn't matter. None of this mattered.

He shut off the water, smiling to himself. He didn't care if Jo kept it from him—he would have done the same thing. Yeah, it was pretty big news, but anyone would have jumped to the same conclusion as her. She assumed he would have blamed her. She assumed he would have left. As crazy as Jo was with her abandonment issues, it didn't make a difference.

He loved her. That was the truth.

He pulled his clothes on and threw open the bathroom door, half-falling into the motel room.

"Jo, I—"

He looked around the small space, his heart racing.

"Jo?"

Nothing. Distantly, he thought he heard a car driving away. He shut his eyes, taking in one shuddering breath after another. When he reopened them, his eyes fell on something sitting on the bedspread. He walked over the the bed slowly, feeling like the room was spinning.

It was a note, written on one of the extra notecards. Trembling, he grasped it between his fingers, and tried to make our her messy scrawl.

I'm sorry.
For what it's worth, I think I loved you.

He gave up trying to regulate his breathing, and it quickly dissolved into desperate sobs. He sat down on the mattress before he had the chance to fall to the floor. As he stared at the note, he swore he could hear Amelia's Southern drawl in his head, murmuring, *"But sometimes running away is all that you can do."*

Epilogue

She went back to her simple life, the one from before she started chasing after dead girls and falling for boys she had sworn off of long ago. Just the open road and empty diners, devoid of all emotion: she fell back into the grind easily.

"Where are you going?"

"Everywhere. Everywhere and anywhere."

She was not satisfied with simple answers anymore. Everything around her seemed meaningless. She drove down the long roads, heat causing the back of her thighs to stick to the plastic seats of her car, her left arm tan from the sun streaming in from the window. She stopped twice a day for food, always avoided the meat, and made sure to get a table in the very back corner. She checked into small motels on the sides of roads that had no other cars in the parking lots. She didn't get ice.

She used to love this kind of life, but now it felt empty. She couldn't see the point in any of it any longer.

She spent a day lying on a broken mattress in a Motel 6, staring up at the cracks in the ceiling. Memories flashed before her eyes like an endless movie reel as she tried to figure out what to do with herself.

She kept driving, kept eating, kept staying in motels.

Somewhere between Long Island and Seattle it occurred to her she had become a tourist. What disturbed her the most was the fact that she had always been one. She had never really lived anywhere for longer than a week and everywhere she'd been she'd only been visiting.

In the middle of the night, she started driving West. She didn't really have a plan, didn't *really* know what she was doing, but she knew she had to do something. So she drove.

When she pulled up on the street, a shiver ran down her spine. She got out of the car and walked up the long drive. It was all too familiar. Shards of memories from her childhood pieced themselves back together inside her brain, and she was struck with such a strong sense of nostalgia that it almost sent her sprawling to the ground, tears streaming down her face.

Her hand hung in midair over the door, and she suddenly realized she couldn't knock.

She left this life behind, and she no longer fit into the picture. She wrote herself out of this story long ago, making thick, heavy lines across the scenes she appeared in, scribbling out her name.

That was all she was to them now, a scribbled out name. It wasn't that the life couldn't fit her: it was that she couldn't fit into it.

She walked back to her car and left without saying goodbye.

She drove, because she didn't know what else to do.

In a diner in Chicago, she watched the people move in and out. The streets outside were packed with people who had better places to be than here.

She had never realized before that her life was without purpose. Every time someone came into it, that person became her main focus, finally something for her to channel her energy into, finally something for her to occupy her thoughts with.

Without anyone, she was stuck in an endless circle of roads, dirty diner utensils, and smelly motels.

Pushing through the crowds of people on the streets, she wondered how many of them really had a purpose. Did they honestly have a reason to be alive, or were they spending their time trying to find one? The woman to her left was carrying a recycled tote bag—she made herself a purpose when none was clear. She probably recycled her water bottles and ate organic fruit, read Rachel Carson and composted her banana peels. The man to her right was talking into his cell phone, walking as quickly as he could through the throngs of people. He probably buried himself in work to make himself feel needed and important, spending long nights at the office and turning down dinner invitations with work as his excuse. Eventually, the invites stop coming.

Jo thought she saw *him* when she was in Detroit, standing at a crosswalk and trying to see through the fog. She stood petrified to her spot on the sidewalk, trying to decide if she should run to him or away, toward the past or the future. When the guy turned around, the decision was made for her. She didn't try to hide the disappointment that etched her features as she walked down the sidewalk.

She thought she saw him again when she was in a book store in South Carolina. There was something about the way he was slouched over in the corner that made her feel hopeful. When she got closer, she saw what he was reading—*Into the Wild.* Her heart fluttered as she reached out to grab his shoulder. When he turned around, she tried her best to ignore the way her vision was blurring.

It was only another week before she saw another familiar looking back of a head in a gas station. She didn't bother going over to him. She was in Georgia now, and she was feeling suffocated. She climbed back in her car and drove.

She realized one night, near the border of Tennessee, that she had run out of places to run. He was everywhere she looked. She couldn't escape him.

She took an abrupt turn and started heading toward the interstate, ignoring the feeling in the pit of her stomach.

* * *

She stumbles off of the belt, nearly falling when her foot hits the end of the sidewalk—*caution: the moving walkway is ending. Caution: the moving walkway is ending. Caution: the moving—*

The departure board is too big for her to see or understand. She pushes past people who give her offended looks—so unlike the people she's used to—in an attempt to read the arrival times. She eventually gives up and asks the first uniformed person she sees where she's supposed to be. The boy is a few years younger than her, with dark hair and gray eyes, and he gives her a shy smile that brings back too many memories. She turns away from him the second she gets her answer—B7—and starts walking.

She doesn't know if this is what she needs or if this is what will finally break her. She stopped listening to music a month ago, and put ketchup on her burger yesterday. She knows it's probably stupid, torturing herself like this—*it won't make anything better, only worse*—but she doesn't like the other alternatives, denial or acceptance, and certainly not happiness. So this is what she decides on: torture.

She figures it works in movies.

She buys a book she's never heard of from a news store. She hasn't read anything besides blog posts in years, but if she doesn't take her mind off of her surroundings, she might just throw up. She gets settled in an uncomfortable blue chair with crumbs in the seat and reads.

The book isn't as bad as she thought it would be based on the cover—a clothesline with an ugly dress waving in the wind. It's easy to get lost in the comfort of prose, and she doesn't hear the boarding call. A woman is tapping her on the shoulder, looking concerned, repeating, "Ma'am?" over and over again.

When Jo looks up, the woman gestures toward the open door to the plane, and Jo nods her thanks.

Staring at the square opening, she feels her heart speed up. Jo read an article once about a test to cure claustrophobia. Basically, some cruel scientists shoved some claustrophobes in an elevator for a few hours and watched their reactions. She doesn't remember how many people were tested, but she knows a few of them had heart attacks. The ones that made it out alive felt like they were better because of the experiment: now that they had overcome their fear, they felt alive again.

She takes a deep breath, studying the door. There's a line of people waiting to show the girl in blue their boarding passes, most of them looking bored and impatient. If she would let herself, she could become one of them. She could take a nine-to-five job and buy a cell phone, wear high heels and a pencil skirt and take one week of vacation time whenever she got lucky. She could give up and submit to reality. It wasn't as if she had anything holding her to her old way of life anymore, just unspoken regrets and chronic nightmares.

She tilts her head as she watches the people walk onto the plane. They made it look easier than it felt.

"Are you going to do it?" she hears behind her. The breath catches in her throat, but she doesn't turn around. She's half-afraid of being wrong, and half-afraid of being right.

"I don't know," she says shakily. "I want to. I think."

"Where are you going?" the voice asks, and she swallows the lump in her throat.

"Paris," she replies. "I-I've seen everything here. I figured Europe was the next place to go."

The air behind her shifts; she can feel it in the way the goosebumps spread out over her skin. She would turn around if she had any strength at all. It's all gone now: any ounce that people saw was fake, but no one really seemed to notice.

"Hmm."

She hears footsteps behind her, and the next time she looks away from the door, she sees a familiar face in front of her. He looks the same as he had when she left—only he looks a little sadder and his hair looks a little longer. Everything else about him is the same, the way he walks and the way he looks at her through his lashes, as if he's trying not to scare her away.

"You cut your hair," he says softly, and for one fleeting second, she thinks he's going to run his fingers through it. His hand stops halfway between them, hanging in the air, as if he just remembered who they are in juxtaposition to what they were. She brings her eyes up from his hand to his face. She realizes suddenly that he doesn't look the same, not to her, someone who really knows him. There are bags under his eyes, and he looks a cross between panicked and shy. She supposes it's fitting, especially considering she's probably wearing the same look herself.

"Yeah," she says awkwardly. It barely hits her shoulders now. She cut it one night in a bathroom at a club, watching her reflection stare back at her with the same loathing she felt every time she woke up. She had wanted to feel like a new person, and it worked for a night. The next morning, when she woke up, she realized she was the same horrible person she was the night before.

"I like it."

Silence falls between them as they both struggle to find the words to phrase what needs to be said. Jess shoves his hands in the pockets of his sweatshirt and rocks back and forth on his heels. She would hum if she let herself. Instead, she stares at the carpet. Her black, scuffed boots look strange against it, like they don't belong.

"Don't go," he blurts out, and when she looks up at him, he looks more panicked than before. He has one hand in his hair and the other gesturing wildly as his words blend together. She picks out every third or so, and tries to connect "you" and "me" and "then" and "who cares" and "love" and "stupid Paris."

"I can't hold you responsible for anything someone else did!" he cries, and suddenly he looks angry. She subconsciously takes a step forward. She wants to feel his rage. She wants to feel sorry. She wants to hate herself a little bit more, just to feel something.

"I can!" she protests, dropping her stupid bag onto the floor. "Every time I see my own reflection I see him, and I see Amelia, and I see you. I can't handle this kind of guilt, Jess!"

"I don't see any of that!" he shouts. Half of the airport is watching them now, but Jess doesn't seem to notice. "All I see is *you*, Jo. The same stupidly brilliant girl I met in a bar in

Kansas too many months ago. The same stupidly emotionally constipated girl I fell head-over-heels in love with, and even when you tried to pretend you didn't care, I could always tell that you did. You cared about everyone and everything around you."

Jess presses the palms of his hands into his eyes, taking one shaky breath after another.

"That's why you left, I think," he says softly. "At least, that's what I like to think. I could be completely wrong."

"No," she murmurs. "You're right."

"Final boarding!" the woman at the door calls, and Jess looks defeated, finally breaking their connection and looking away, out toward the runway.

"I've spent my whole life watching people leave, Jess," she says quietly. That's when he looks back up at her, angrier than ever.

"*You* left, Jo. *You* did it. Now you're leaving again."

"I had to," she protests. "You would have if I didn't!"

"No," he says, his voice dropping again. "You're wrong, Jo."

She stands there for a few seconds, just staring at him. Finally, she asks, "What?"

"I never would have left," he mumbles. "I just needed time to process everything. I never would have done it: I wouldn't have been able to. I love you too much."

The woman is still screaming about boarding, and Jess looks like he's been kicked in the stomach. She doesn't know how she looks, but she can feel her mouth hanging open.

She had spent the past five months torturing herself for no real reason. She made herself miserable. She made herself hate herself. And Jess, oh God, Jess—

"I'm sorry," she whispers suddenly. "I thought—I—"

He shakes his head, shrugs, and gives her a small smile —how can he still smile at her after everything she's done?

"It doesn't matter," he says. He crosses the space until he's standing right in front of her, closer than anyone has been for months, and says, "Answer one question for me."

"Okay," she says weakly.

"Are you going to get on that plane?"

She looks up at the woman ripping off the ends of boarding passes. There's only three people in line now, and Jo could still make it if she got in line.

She looks back at Jess—awkward Jess who wears his emotions like his ratty sweatshirts, stupid Jess who messes up her tough girl façade and turns her into a fifteen-year-old girl from a badly written teen drama, perfect Jess who still loves her, despite everything—and says, "No."

He nods, grinning, and says, "Okay, good."

He picks up her bag from the floor and throws it over his shoulder. The stickers are still peeling off of the canvas, but she can still see the outline of where the Kansas sticker had been. Looking at Jess, she thinks there is something from Kansas she values after all.

He looks down at the floor for a few seconds and says shyly, "I was afraid you burned out."

"Almost," she admits quietly. "But I don't think I'm done living yet."

He smiles at her and takes her hand, and they start walking toward the door.

BURNOUT STARS

Thank You

My personal story is like any other: I'm a relatively normal girl. I'm the person who crashes into you in the grocery store and accidentally cuts you off in traffic on her way home from school. Back in May, I hadn't planned on publishing a book, let alone writing one.

To me, this book is a testament to what you can achieve when you put your mind to it. I look at this tiny little book that consumed my entire summer, and I remember long nights filled with salsa, obscure indie rock, and carpal tunnel. But I also look at it and can't believe I actually did it.

I'd really like to thank you for reading, and I hope you had fun riding along in Jo's backseat. I know I did. To the future authors out there: don't doubt yourselves. Sometimes fairy tales do come true; you just have to get the ball rolling.

BURNOUT STARS

Acknowledgements

The writing was the easy part. What came next was breakdown-inducing, and I never would have gotten through it if it wasn't for these people.

I would like to thank:

— **My mom, Jennifer Myers,** for editing and never complaining once, for the instant ego boosts, and for being so supportive. I should probably also thank you for, you know, giving life to me, and for being so perfect, and for adoring my friends, and for being the prettiest mom at school, and for being my best friend in the universe, but I'm trying to keep this book related.

— **My dad, John Myers,** for helping with everything, from ISBN numbers to marketing input to handholding, and for making me love stars. Sorry for using all of the computer paper. I'm still not sure you really noticed, but I've been feeling guilty about it. And I'm glad this was your first fiction. I hope it wasn't too terribly disappointing.

— **My best friend, Noora Aljabi,** for taking the cover shots, for editing twenty pages, for keeping this a secret, for the confidence boost, for the time when I had a complete breakdown in the rain in the parking lot (sorry), for not complaining when the creeps were out at the park that one night, for always being excited, for the eyebrow man doodle on the scene about Chin, and for the lawlz.

— **My other best friend, Sujin Kim,** for being on both covers, for being so gorgeous, for keeping this a secret, for freezing to death during the cover shoot, for not thinking I'm stupid, and for coming to America in the first place.

BURNOUT STARS

— **Anna Iovine** for designing the cover with practically no direction, and for being one of the most supportive, helpful friends throughout this whole ordeal. When you finish your book, I promise to repay the favor. I can't photoshop, but I can dance around and sell copies on the street, or something. I'm looking forward to the hipster-esque shots of this on tumblr, by the way.

— **My other other best friend, Stéfany Péloquin,** for pretty much being in charge of my marketing team and for singlehandedly saving the entire book. I honestly don't know if I can ever thank you enough for fixing the cover. Oh, and I'm curious to see which weird couple you'll ship. I'm putting my money on Scott/Jo.

— **Bill Christian** for also starring on the cover. You have the best back of head ever.

— **Andrew Wilkerson** for his car, which is featured on the cover, and for dealing with me that night. Sorry for making you think this was an elaborate prank when I showed up late. I still have major guilt because of that.

— **Everyone else who was there during the cover shoot: Nadia, Amira, and Mrs. Aljabi; my parents; and Jessica.** Mrs. Aljabi, I'm most sorry to you about the creep with the beer and possible gun. I swear, that park is a lot less sketchy during the day time.

— **Mr. Zimmerman** for making me love writing as much as I do. Your cookies are on the way.

— **Mrs. Bayles** for trying to point me in the right direction. It didn't pan out, but I still appreciated the effort.

— **My other other other best friend, Alexis Co,** for being you. (You were totally waiting to see your name, weren't you?)

— **You** for reading. (That was corny, sorry.)

BURNOUT STARS

BURNOUT STARS

About the Author

Ashlyn Myers is a seventeen-year-old high school senior from Indiana who loves Mickey Mouse, vanilla ice cream, fancy dresses, and math. This is her first novel, inspired by summer road trips and her dad's fascination with astronomy.

BURNOUT STARS

Made in the USA
Charleston, SC
10 May 2011